Circus Excite

'Take it off.' He nodded at her, locking his eyes on hers.

As if mesmerised, Julia reached for the top button of the shirt and worked it loose. She held Robert's gaze as she undid the buttons, feeling as though she were stripping for a teacher. Something told her it was wonderfully, dangerously wrong to be undressing for Robert alone. He sat relaxed in his chair, impassive, as he had during her audition. Julia pulled the shirt off and sat in her revealing wrap, now crumpled and ridden up. She had wiped off the panstick with cold cream, but traces of it remained in the folds of her skin, white rims of paint rubbed into her fingernails and between her toes. She knew that under the short fringe of the wrap, her pussy was still brushed with make-up, and she thought of her painted clit with a frisson of desire as she wondered what Robert would ask of her next.

'Close your eyes.'

Circus Excite
Nikki Magennis

BLACK LACE

Black Lace books contain sexual fantasies.
In real life, always practise safe sex.

First published in 2006 by
Black Lace
Thames Wharf Studios
Rainville Road
London W6 9HA

Typeset by SetSystems Limited, Saffron Walden, Essex
Printed and bound by Mackays of Chatham PLC

ISBN 0 352 34033 9
ISBN 9 780352 340337

1

'FREEEEEEEEEEEEEEEEDOM!'

A girl in a crumpled ball gown and stilettos stood at the top of the steps waving an empty champagne bottle in one hand. Her dishevelled hair and flushed cheeks gave her a wild look that was a far cry from her usual poised demeanour. Julia, watching from the street below, knew the girl from her classical dance class. She'd always thought her a stuck-up prima donna and was quietly delighted to see her sweaty and hysterical with mascara running down her cheeks.

Julia smiled. Tonight was the last time she'd be together with all her fellow students. She and her friend Karin were sitting on the wall outside the Union and downing an illicit half-bottle of fizz before they went in to the graduation ball. It was a balmy summer evening; the air was full of celebration buzz, and she felt a surge of anticipation that made her light-headed and jittery.

A funky up-tempo Stevie Wonder song was playing inside the hall, the music spilling out of the tall windows and into the street. Without thinking Julia started counting the beat, moving her shoulders along with the rhythm. She couldn't help herself – whenever she heard music she started keeping time, like one of Pavlov's dogs. She felt her hips twitching and the butterflies in her stomach start to jump. She elbowed Karin.

'Freedom indeed,' she said. 'Are we ready for it?'

'Ready? Are you crazy, girl? I'm gagging for it. No more 6 a.m. starts, no more Advanced Pilates ... Christ, Julia, we'll be able to join the real world again.'

Julia watched as a couple of guys climbed the steps, white shirts unbuttoned at the neck, hands in pockets. They moved with the natural grace of male dancers, muscles taut and spines straight. Julia eyed them wickedly.

'Yeah, but I'm going to miss Contact Improvisation.'

'Julia, when you're let loose from here you'll have the whole of London to practise your moves on. A world of men to fuck.'

'True. But you know, dancers do have the most phenomenal stamina.'

'And they're phenomenally over-sensitive. At least we won't have to deal with the jealous fits any more,' Karin reminded her.

'Oh, you're right there. Three years of sulking boys is more than enough.'

'Three years of juggling lovers would be enough to exhaust anyone. Specially with six hours of practice a day on top.'

Julia nodded.

'I guess the dance classes were supposed to be the important part.'

They watched as the boys entered the glass doors to the students' union, joining the throng in the entrance hall. As she looked at the crowd of glammed up, excitable new graduates, Julia saw it all play back in a whirl. Sweating bodies, aching muscles, the pounding of her heart as she relentlessly practised, practised, practised – and all along the steady beat pounding out an endless rhythm she couldn't resist.

'To the dance!' she said as she turned to Karin, holding up her glass.

'*Fuck* dance, darling, let's drink to escape.'

'And wild adventures.'

Behind them, the noise of the party spilled down the

steps. Julia drained her glass and jumped down from the wall.

'Let's get moving. Our last chance to seduce the undergraduates.' She smoothed her silk dress over her hips. The fabric was silver and shimmered like the skin of a fish, revealing her toned curves and the taut musculature of her thighs. 'The night is young.' With a wink at her friend, she sashayed up the steps and into the school's foyer.

Inside was a mess of balloons and streamers, girls in fancy dresses and men in tuxes, shirts unbuttoned at the neck and dishevelled. Drunken students clung to each other, slurring promises of undying friendship. Karin stepped lightly over an inert body lying passed out on the floor, heading towards the ballroom where the music and chatter built to a deafening roar. The corners were full of writhing bodies, couples kissing in a frantic last-minute surge of emotion. It could have been a scene from a French masquerade. Julia walked with a confident stride through the crowd. She turned heads as she did so, men eyeing her high, rounded ass and toned legs. Julia dressed in clothes as playful and vivid as her personality – calculated to tease. She knew everyone was staring at the outline of her tits under the dress, and smiled back at them as she walked into the dark cavernous ballroom.

In here, the music was loud enough to make her guts vibrate, and she felt herself break out in a sweat with the heat of a couple of hundred bodies rubbing up against each other. The dancefloor was packed, and the girls fought to get through the crowd. Julia grabbed Karin's waist and clung on tightly, feeling the temperature rise as they made their way towards the bar at the far end. It was easier to get through if you jigged yourself around, and Julia found herself crushed against the dancers, grinding her hips against other revellers and dancing onwards. Arms wrapped around her waist; a hand stroked her spine; she felt a warm pressure on her arm as a girl brushed her breasts against her. The atmosphere was jubilant, intoxicating. Bodies en masse writhed and bumped in time to the music. Julia felt herself melting in the heat, her heart beating strongly and her body pulsing with the bass drum. Karin grabbed her wrist and shouted to make herself heard.

'It's like Dante's inferno in here. I'm going upstairs. Get me a vodka, will you?'

She pushed a £10 note at Julia and disappeared into the throng, leaving Julia to bump, grind and fight her way to the bar. It was three deep, and piles of empty bottles and glasses were strewn over the counter, while the exhausted bar staff struggled to hand out more beer. Julia realised it would be a hopeless battle to get served

A dark-haired boy leaning against the pillar caught her eye. She squeezed into a tight space next to him.

'Rory!' She had to shout over the joyful sound of Donna Summer and a disco beat.

'Hey.' Rory smiled back at her. His hair was all mussed up and sweaty and he looked as sweet and sexy as ever with his impish face and high sharp cheekbones. Julia hugged him hard and leant in to his shoulder.

'Aren't you going to give me a dance?' she asked, knowing exactly what the answer would be. She found Rory particularly easy to manipulate.

'I guess getting a drink is looking unlikely,' he agreed, taking Julia's arm and swaying back towards the floor. With one arm looped round his neck, Julia started swinging her hips. She could feel the muscles under his suit, and the way he held himself perfectly tensed, ready to respond to every turn she made. They fitted together snugly, clicking into the groove and winding round each other with practised fluid movements. Julia grinned, knowing his body and how good he looked under his clothes. She pressed herself closer till her mouth brushed his neck and she inhaled the scent of his aftershave mixed with the tang of sweat. The familiar smell gave her a sudden rush of nostalgia, a rising feel of sweet affection for the life she was about to say goodbye to forever. She let her hip bump against him in time with the music, and sank into the familiar, delicious feel of moving with a man. Rory swung her round and folded her into his arms, pulling her against him so he could press her up against the length of his body.

'Nice moves, Jools,' he whispered into her ear, so close she could feel the tickle of his breath warm her neck. 'You always were the sexiest dancer in class.'

Rory had his arm round her waist, and he pulled her in tight, so she could feel the bulge of his cock rubbing against her ass. Julia knew he was telling the truth, not just flattering her. For a start, her body was far from the delicate fragile ideal of a classical dancer. Her breasts were full and heavy, her hips curved and sensuous. Though her muscles were rigorously toned, and she had the strength and graceful lines of a cat, there was a soft extravagance to her body that invited men to touch it. In the centre of the dancefloor she looked at the bodies surrounding them. Usually clad in sweaty T-shirts and leggings, tonight everyone was glammed up. In the throng surrounding them, bodies moved with abandon, forgetting the precise and measured movements of their schooling and enjoying the sheer pleasure of rhythm.

Across the floor, Julia recognised the girl chosen as principal dancer for the school's company. Around her was a circle of girls shaking their hips like divas. They wore ball gowns with plunging necklines that showed porcelain skin and modest little breasts pushed upwards with padded bras. Standing tall and willowy in spike heels, the girls seemed to be haloed with a special aura of preciousness, as though destined to be spot-lit and adored. They were flawlessly made-up, hair pinned in elaborate chignons, their lips painted hard dark shades of red. Although their movements were faultlessly executed, they didn't have the special dirty kind of moves that Julia had. She smiled inwardly, knowing that in this environment she was queen. In the rarefied strict atmosphere of the studio she had looked wildly out of place, her full extravagant figure and shimmering outfits a splash of vibrancy. While the girls in the circle danced with effortless control, turning exquisite poses and holding themselves gracefully, Julia had been too full of a desire to move wildly. She had struggled to maintain her poise. She was just too sensuous to be a dainty ballerina.

On nights like this, she was let loose and her body ached for it. As she felt Rory jam himself hard against her and reach down to stroke his hands along her thighs, Julia kept shimmying with the music, feeling the light jiggling of her tits, the rub of fabric against them as her nipples stiffened and stood out. In front of her, another man turned to see her, and moved irresistibly towards her, blatantly staring at her cleavage. She wasn't surprised – her dress had a low stiff bodice that held her breasts gently and threatened to let them spill over the top. She met his eyes and held his gaze. Still feeling Rory at her back, working his hands at the fabric of her dress, letting the hem ride up so that her stocking tops were exposed, Julia locked her eyes on the man in front of her and bit her lip. He was dancing closer to her, pulling his own dance partner round so that he was next to Julia. Now they danced side by side, the man still twirling the girl he was dancing with – girlfriend? Julia didn't care. She adored this illicit flirting with strangers and the thought of turning on another guy while he danced right next to his unsuspecting partner was enough to make her wet. Their shoulders rubbed together, and Julia smiled at him as Rory nuzzled his face into her back and bit gently on her neck. If he was aware of Julia's divided attention, it wouldn't shock him.

'You like that guy staring at your tits, babe?'

So he had noticed.

'Shut up and keep dancing, Rory.' Julia felt a surge of power as she was crushed between the two men, the focus of their rapt attention. Hidden by the darkness of the dancefloor and the confusion of flailing limbs, she reached for the man beside her, pushing one hand quickly up under his shirt so she could feel the lines of his muscular stomach. She worked her fingers under his waistband, slipping her hand over the brush of hair that led down into his boxer shorts. He stiffened under her hand, twisting round so that their antics were hidden from his dancing partner. Julia felt a little thrill of victory.

At the same time, Rory had managed to pull her skirt up so that her bare ass was rubbing against his trousers. She felt his thumb hook the elastic of her G-string and pull it aside. It was a delicious risk to take, him practically stripping her in the crowd. Julia felt herself getting dangerously turned on so it was becoming hard to keep dancing. The three of them were locked in a tangle, and any minute someone next to them might notice they weren't just pretending to dance sexily.

As she felt her knees start to weaken and strained her hand to reach inside the guy's trousers, Julia noticed Karin approach through the crowd. Even in the disorientating atmosphere of the packed and dark dancefloor raked with strobe lights, Karin grasped the situation in a split second. She raised her eyebrows at Julia as though questioning her. Ignoring the two men, she grabbed her friend by the shoulders and leant in to speak to her:

'You've got some fucking nerve, girlfriend.' Her tone was teasing. 'How many d'you think you can do at once?' Julia sensed a dare in her question.

'How about we put on a little show?' she retorted, feeling gleeful as she sensed the two of them were about to start their favourite game. Dancefloor power plays were a regular feature of their nights out. All it took was a little imagination.

'I'm game,' said Karin.

'Come here and give me some tongue, then, you dirty bitch!' Julia laughed, knowing how to play the game with Karin. Without pausing, she reached out with her free hand and pulled Karin towards her, making a pout and winking at her. It never failed. As soon as the girls started mock-kissing and dancing closely with one another, the whole dancefloor would be focused on their erotic routine. She looped her arms round Karin's body, now feeling herself the centre of a knot of three people working their bodies against hers. Getting worked up, Julia looked around to check who was watching. She saw with satisfaction that a couple of girls were stealing sideways looks at the curious rhythm of the group of bodies dancing next to them. She gave the tall blonde girl a teasing little smile and stuck out her ass further, loving the feel of displaying her body as though she were fucking in public. Beside her a guy materialised, broad and bulky with his face wearing a dazzling smile.

'You've just made my fucking night, girls! Don't stop, babe.' He shook his head at Julia, making a low whistle as he nodded and let his gaze sweep over her bared legs and the tangle of her limbs meshed with Karin's.

'I'd bend you over and fuck you right here if I could,' he roared at Julia's ear, and she felt Rory pinch her ass hard, playing jealous. 'Mind if I cut in?' The newcomer was worming his way between Julia and Karin, trying to push right up against Julia's tits. She could see the sweat running down his face and feel the bulk of him imposing on her as he pushed his leg between hers, letting her crotch rub up against his thigh. Julia now found herself caught in the middle of three guys, and saw Karin, pushed out of the circle, throw up her hands in surrender. Around her other heads were turning, but instead of feeling embarrassment she revelled in being centre stage. Her dress had been crushed, crumpled up and pulled aside: she was showing so much flesh she might as well have been wearing just her underwear. Rolling herself around, straining against the arms and thighs of the men moving with her so intimately, Julia knew this was how she was meant to dance. This display of her sex, voluptuous and sensual, was the desire that had driven her since she was a teenager. She needed this, needed to feel eyes and hands, mouths and skin on her body. She felt the gaze of every man around her running over her, wanting to touch, wanting to bump up against her and possess her.

What was dancing about if it wasn't sex? What was the pounding beat, the pulse of the bass, but an invitation to bang your body against someone else's? Julia felt herself dissolve in the rhythm, the crowd around her surging and rocking in time, the night melting into a charged electric buzz while the beat of the slinky electro kept urging the crowd on. Under the white strobe light, Julia saw flashes of the dancers: a bare back glistening with sweat; teeth flashing in a sharp smile; eyes turning towards her; smiles; hands reaching for her. She realised with a thrill she was now the apex of the crowd. There were no other women around her. Karin had slipped into the background and Julia was on her own, surrounded by men who fixed their gaze on her grinding hips, the sight of her stocking tops and braced thighs. She heard the music resonate through her feet and up her legs, and felt a shiver as she recognised the opening beats of one of her favourite songs. Pulsing through the hall now was a dark throbbing electro bass line that looped slower and slower as the sound of a woman mewing rose in pitch. Julia felt her own excitement rise as the intensity of the woman's cries melded with the steady thud of the drums, her voice growing louder till the whole hall reverberated to the sound of the singer groaning in ecstasy. A song to fuck to – or to dance to as though you were being fucked.

Julia slipped into the movement and felt every beat resonate through her body, knew just how far to throw her hips, thrust her tits and lean back, aware of every pair of hungry eyes following her movements, aware now of herself as part of the music, a lush sensuous fantasy made flesh. She felt Rory's dick pressing urgently against her ass, so hard now it was digging into her with urgency – as was the cock she could feel stiffening as she brushed it with the back of her hand, while the bulky third guy roved his hands roughly over the curves of her body. She watched as a the onlookers moved nearer, circling in towards her, dancing so close she could feel the heat from their bodies increase her own temperature, till she was at boiling point, melting, wanting to rub herself off in full view of the crowd.

The floor was slippery underfoot, awash with spilt drink, and Julia felt herself sliding, falling back against Rory so that his hard body supported her, leaving her front openly displayed to the other two men – and the crowd that surrounded them. Her long wild curls were now soaked with sweat, and the men's bodies rubbing against hers were damp from the heat and their own arousal. Julia struggled to keep track of whose hands were pulling at her tits, rubbing her nipples, and whose were pulling at her G-string, making the soaked fabric cut into her cleft and agitate her clit as she squirmed to feel more. She felt the shock of the onlookers staring at the spectacle, knowing her breasts were on the point of spilling out and she was virtually fucking three men in the middle of the dancefloor. It only made her writhe more sensually, wanting to feel that mixture of lust and outrage that she knew her pulsing, horny body would provoke. She'd always been a show-off, and now she knew just how to get the attention she so hungrily craved: sticking her tits out; offering her half-undressed body to the crowd; inviting them to look while daring them to touch her.

Then she closed her eyes and revelled in the sensations. She was surrounded by a group of men hungry to fuck her, feeling hands sliding all over her, a hard cock rubbing at her thigh, a stiff shirt collar brushing against her throat, a tongue flickering over her earlobe. She was bathed in sweat and the smell of it mixed with aftershave, the scents of the men around her pungent and exciting. The music soaked into her skin, pulsing at the same deep rate as her heartbeat, urging her to relinquish the last shreds of control. As she danced Julia let her body take over, loving the mix of her scandalous display and the snatched intimate groping of Rory and his competitors. She felt the bouncing and swaying of the crowd, the excitement of the night, the climax of the hours she'd spent sweating and grinding in the dance studios. The music built to a strident throbbing beat, so Julia could feel it vibrate in her chest and deafen her as she gave in to it, abandoned control and became nothing more than a body melded to others, fusing in the heat and the noise.

2

Two weeks later, and the memory of her riotous graduation ball had faded into history. Julia was sprawled on the sofa, wearing knickers and a T-shirt and combing the 'Situations Vacant' in the back of *The Stage*. The reality of life as a dance school graduate was turning out to be a bleak and precarious one. There were no more than a handful of adverts, most calling for experienced dancers. It was dry season in the world of theatre, most of them going 'dark' till autumn, and Julia was giving up hope. She flicked through the paper, grim desperation rising in her. The thought of working in an office made her want to curl up and die, but she had to find work soon.

She looked around at her tiny living room. Sharing with two other girls, Julia had got used to the noise and chaos of a student flat. The hall was as busy as King's Cross, with various visitors and lovers coming and going at all hours: Karin leaving for her bar job just as Julia got in from afternoon classes; phones ringing and the radio blaring. It was handy for college, and Camden Market was just down the road. Julia loved the buzz of the place, even if it was barely big enough to swing a cat. But now ... Julia looked at the brick-wall view out the window and the dead spider plant on the sill. Her gaze fell on the pile of dirty plates stacked up in the sink. Behind her the washing machine sputtered and gave out a weak moan as it broke down, again. Maybe it was time to move on.

It was then that the small advert, just two lines at the bottom of the page, caught her eye:

Dancer (f) wanted for
Circus Excite.

Circus? It wasn't exactly what Julia had in mind. She was a serious skilled dancer, not a cabaret performer. Dancing didn't usually involve nipple pasties and garters, in her opinion. But the idea of a circus tickled her. And it was the only advert left to try. Julia grabbed the phone and dialled the number. It rang twice before a recorded message cut in.

'Are you ready to excite?' a deep female voice asked, the line crackling. 'If you're looking for adventure and have an open mind, visit us on Friday 1st of May between 10 a.m. and 8 p.m. at ...' The voice gave an address in the centre of London. Then the message cut off, leaving Julia holding the receiver, puzzled. She had been expecting at least a little more information about the job, an idea of how to prepare for the audition. What to wear, what kind of routine to rehearse.

She sighed and threw the paper on the floor. She went to dress for the gym, still turning the message over in her mind. The woman had had a slight accent that Julia couldn't place – Eastern European, perhaps? As she walked down the street, she remembered the voice, and the tempting phrase:

'If you're looking for adventure ...'

In the gym Julia got on an exercise bike and started pedalling. She liked to build up a sweat before practice, get herself loosened up and start the adrenaline flowing. She pedalled harder, going at high speed until her pulse started racing. She felt the rush that she always did when her body was working hard. The pounding beat of MTV kept her in rhythm, and her mind wandered. The voice of the woman played again in her head. As she thought about the obscure message, Julia imagined herself onstage in a feather headdress. The idea was so ridiculous she almost laughed out loud. Would it be some kind of Moulin Rouge affair, high-kicking and spilling out of a diamante bikini? What kind of people watched cabaret anyway? Julia could picture a half-empty bar, with men in suits watching her dance. She could see the look on their faces; eyes glazed with desire as she wrapped herself suggestively round a pillar. Despite herself, she started to feel excited. She pressed her crotch against the pommel of the bike and racked up the gears, pushing harder as the resistance increased. Overhead, the TV screen showed a music video full of voluptuous women grinding to the beat. What was dancing about, if it wasn't exhibitionism?

By the time she stepped off the bike, Julia had made up her mind. She'd go to the audition, and see what happened. It sounded more fun than temping, at any rate. What did she have to lose?

On Friday morning Julia found herself wandering the near-deserted streets of Soho. The venue for the audition was proving hard to find. Eventually she stumbled across a narrow dark alley buried deep in Fitzrovia. Julia checked her scribbled note. This was it. She looked again at the street, cluttered with kitchen bins and drifting rubbish. She walked down the street uneasily, as though rats might emerge any minute from the shadows and attack her. Trying to walk on the balls of her feet, Julia pulled the denim jacket tightly across her chest. She had considered what she should wear for the role of 'cabaret dancer', and in the end decided on black. Black leggings, black T-shirt. The costume wasn't exactly showgirl material, but Julia reckoned it would cover just about any eventuality. After several failed ballet auditions and blunt comments from her dance instructors, she was also keen to disguise her ripe curves, and head-to-toe black gave her a sleeker silhouette.

Halfway down the alley a piece of card had been taped onto a door, reading 'Audition, top floor'. As she climbed the stairs, Julia was struck by the silence. Normally auditions were abuzz with the clatter of dancers running in and out, people doing warm-up vocal exercises, sometimes the twanging chords of a piano from inside the room. Today there was no noise at all, just the echo of her steps as she climbed and the sound of her breathing. Maybe she'd got the wrong date? That would be typical bad luck. As she reached the fourth floor, she was preparing herself for the disappointment of finding an empty room and the prospect of a wasted journey.

The door was a huge reinforced slab of steel. Padlocks hung open from the sliding bolts and another paper sign was taped up:

'Circus Excite. Knock and wait.'

Julia rapped on the door with her knuckles and heard the sound echo down the stairwell. She waited for what seemed five minutes, and was about to turn and leave when the door was abruptly pulled open.

She found herself being scrutinised by a tall dark-haired woman. Her eyes were underlined with thick lines of kohl, giving her a hard feline appearance. The woman's gaze travelled briskly from her head to her feet and swept back up again, blatantly sizing her up. Julia felt as though she was standing naked under this critical appraisal, and straightened her spine defensively. The woman gave her a withering look.

'No. Thank you for coming.'

The door was slammed back into place with a bang that reverberated in the hallway and down the staircase.

Stunned, Julia stared at the solid steel in front of her. Swearing, she shook her head in disbelief. Gritting her teeth, she banged on the door with her fist. They could damn well watch her dance before telling her she wasn't good enough. She banged harder, pounding at the metal till her knuckles were stinging.

She nearly fell forward into the room when the woman opened it again. This time, she was wearing a sardonic smile, and stood aside to let Julia enter.

'Okay, better,' she declared, motioning Julia forward. 'Much better.'

Inside was a vast, chilly space, empty but for a table and chair in the centre of the room. The floor was dusty concrete, the walls were unpainted plaster. Julia's steps echoed as she entered. Obviously, this was not a particularly successful company. There were no posters on the wall, no sign of any schedules or activity. Nothing, in fact, but flat grey stone. Light crept in from cracks in the shutters, which had been pulled shut over the high windows. Julia stood uncertainly in the room, feeling a shiver dance down her spine. Now she was the other side of the armoured door she was having second thoughts about whether she wanted to be locked in here. The woman was walking round a corner into a darkened passageway, leaving Julia alone in the silent room.

'The ringmaster will be with you shortly.' She tossed the remark over her shoulder as she disappeared. Julia recognised the voice – deep, scratchy and tinged with an accent. It was the same voice that had purred *If you're looking for adventure . . .* ' on the answer phone message. It added a hint of exoticism to the words, the woman's accent rolling the *r* of ringmaster, putting the emphasis on the word 'master' as though he was some kind of sadistic Svengali, whipping the circus into shape with a mixture of cruelty and indulgence.

Julia was looking forward to meeting him.

* * *

When she first saw Robert, she was taken aback. The first thing that struck her was how young he was. She'd expected a kind of father figure, fifty or sixty, imposing, silver-haired. Possibly wearing a top hat. Robert was mid-thirties, tall, laconic and handsome in an intense unsettling way. Dressed in a crumpled white shirt and jeans, he could have passed for a slightly jaded rock star. He introduced himself with a handshake, smiling lazily and meeting Julia's gaze with intensely dark eyes. His hair was tousled and he was unshaven – in general he had the air of someone who'd recently risen from bed. He moved with an easy confidence, walking slowly to the chair and pulling it round backwards to straddle it. He sat with his arms crossed loosely over the back and scratched his stubble.

'So let me see what you can do,' he said lazily, fixing Julia with a curious heavy-lidded stare. Nonplussed by his languorous attitude, but determined not to show it, Julia dropped her bag on the floor and took off her jacket.

'It's great so far. I like you undressing.' Robert's voice was calm, with a teasing lilt in it. 'Keep going.'

Julia was thrown off balance. Was this a joke? She wasn't shy about her body, but she hadn't anticipated her interviewer asking her to strip. She wasn't quite that desperate for money.

Nevertheless, something in Robert's voice had challenged her, and Julia loved a challenge. Standing straight-backed and proud, she met his gaze and answered steadily: 'Are you looking for a professional dancer, or a stripper?'

Robert laughed, a low sexy laugh that Julia felt tickle her inside. He shrugged.

'It's up to you, babe. If you want to join us, you'd better not have any false modesty. We work as a very close team.'

'You mean you want me to forget about the professional dance angle?'

'Not at all, not at all. Circus Excite is unconventional, sure. But we're totally professional. Our show is designed very precisely, even though it looks kind of unpredictable to the audience.' Julia raised an eyebrow. She was intrigued by the sound of this, although something made her wary. Robert continued, standing up and approaching Julia as he talked. 'We try to open the minds of the audience, more than merely "entertain" them.' His voice had turned as smooth as honey, and he leant close to her as though he were telling Julia an intimate secret. She had to steady herself not to back away from him. He reached out a hand to her hair, as though to brush a strand from her eyes. 'Sometimes the most effective way to entrance people is . . .' He pulled a feather from behind her ear, a curling white plume that Julia knew was definitely not there when she'd tied it back that morning. '. . . to surprise them.' Robert placed the tip of the feather at Julia's neck, and traced a line across her chest, down between her breasts, and towards her belly. She felt the light tickling touch of the feather fluttering over her body and her breath started to quicken. Her nipples stiffened under her loose T-shirt. Was this a test to see if she'd storm out in disgust? Was he going to start fondling her now, in the interests of demonstrating how 'open-minded' he was? Julia wasn't sure if she was happy with the way the audition was going, and wasn't sure how to react. She stood stock-still, frozen with uncertainty and trying to stay looking calm, but there was nothing she could do about the way her nipples stuck out proudly.

'Cold?' Robert asked, casting a glance at her breasts. He smiled again. 'It is a little chilly in here.' He dropped the feather at her feet, and walked back to the chair.

Turned on, shivering and disturbed, Julia felt a rush

of adrenaline. As Robert seated himself again, she decided to play him at his own game. She was not easily shockable. In one movement, she pulled off her T-shirt. Underneath she was wearing a black sports bra, made with lycra netting. It held her breasts firmly in place while she danced, and was cut more like a cropped vest than seductive underwear. She removed her shoes and socks. Dancing barefoot was the way she preferred: it gave her a sense of freedom that she relished. Though her feet were tough and calloused, hardened after years of pointe shoes, they were also extraordinarily sensitive, able to feel the resistance of the floor and the minute shifts in weight that she needed to balance. Now, she felt the hard, cold surface of the concrete underfoot and realised this was her first chance to audition for a professional job. She had to make it good.

After a moment's hesitation, she peeled off her leggings too. Her knickers were sporty black thongs, cut high to accentuate her legs and firm buttocks. She glanced at Robert to see his response. His face remained impassive, as though he were looking at a painting in an art gallery. Slightly annoyed by his cool demeanour, Julia decided to perform a sequence she'd adapted from a *Chicago* number. It was the sexiest dance she could think of. May as well let your hair down, she thought to herself. She undid the clasp holding her hair back and shook out her curls. The tips of her black hair brushed against her nipples, which were still sticking out proudly.

She stood in front of Robert and inhaled, standing in first position to centre herself. She hadn't warmed up properly, and there was no music. This was certainly going to be a challenge. In her head, she conjured up the opening bars to a tango rhythm. Closing her eyes till she could concentrate on the beat, Julia started moving. She swept across the floor in a 'cat walk', aware all the time that Robert's eyes were following her. Rolling her shoulder and flicking her head, Julia looked straight at him. He was frowning slightly, his gaze fixed on her body. She felt suddenly weightless – the austerity of the space and the cold concrete floor now felt like a stripped-down, pure environment where she could vaunt her skills freely. Then she gave in to the dancing, forcing herself to concentrate.

She ran through her routine slowly, her movements fluid and sustained, hips swivelling and legs kicking high as she turned and spun. As her body warmed up she felt the familiar buzz of adrenaline enter her blood-stream mixed with a charge of sexual energy, dancing for this stranger, alone in a silent room. She executed switch leaps and *grands jetés* – the splits mid-air – with expert precision, breaking sweat and starting to breathe heavily.

Robert watched impassively, his arms crossed. Julia jumped higher, shimmied harder. No reaction, other than a faint smile. She was worked up now, flushed and letting out grunts of effort as she leapt and curled across the room, pounding her feet against the floor and slapping her ass to keep time, gathering dust on the palms of her hands and the soles of her feet. She moved closer to him, determined to elicit a response. When she was standing close enough to reach out and touch him, she turned her back, and reached up to undo her bra. As it fell to the floor, she felt a pulse of excitement flow through her body, flooding her with warmth. She knew she was sexy, and knew how to turn a man on. Robert couldn't fail to be aroused.

Holding her breasts cupped in her hands Julia turned to face him, shaking slightly with exertion and arousal. Her chest rose and fell as her breath came in ragged bursts. She looked up, her hair in front of her face. Robert was watching her, his chin in his hand. What was he thinking? Was she having any effect on him at all?

She let her hands fall to her sides as she stood in front of him, breathing shakily through an open mouth. She watched as his eyes dropped to her breasts and studied them. It was as though he was caressing her. Julia had to stop herself from walking the short distance between them. She wanted his hands on her, his mouth on her breasts. She imagined the feel of his stubble brushing over her skin, and his long fingers holding onto her hips. Most of all she wanted to see him shaken by desire, to see his calm amused expression shattered and see him lick his lips, blush, clear his throat – Jesus, anything!

Robert nodded. He looked at Julia as though she had just finished a standard ballet routine. She swallowed.

'Very good.' His voice was neutral.

Very good! Julia was stunned. She'd practically offered herself to him on a plate, stood near-naked in front of him while his eyes roved over her body, as though consuming her. Damned with faint praise, indeed. She stood there, still shaking from exertion and anticipation. As Robert turned his attention to his fingernails, she realised this would be all the reaction he would give her. Coldly, she turned on her heel and went to pick up her clothes. She dressed in stony silence, thrusting her arms into her T-shirt with furious movements. She felt humiliated and rejected. She'd been prepared for failing the audition, of course, that was par for the course in the competitive sphere of theatre. But to be teased like that, and then be turned down flat – it was not something she was used to.

'We start rehearsals in Brighton on Tuesday. Be here at 6 a.m. If you're up to it, that is. And you'll need to bring some more sensible clothing.' Robert spoke matter-of-factly, as though they had signed and sealed a contract. Julia turned to look at him, incensed. He was as laid-back as when she had first seen him.

'What, you're hiring me?'

Robert shrugged.

'It's not exactly what we're looking for, but I think your style has potential for development.'

'Development? That was . . .' *my best effort*. Julia finished the sentence in her head. Robert smiled at her, his face softening.

'We need a dancer, and I think you'll find the experience enlightening. The pay's not terrific, but the circus is . . . unique. We'll be touring all summer, so you'd have regular work.'

Regular work. The magic phrase. This reminder of just how precarious her existence was sobered Julia. Finding work as a dancer, of any kind, was no mean feat.

'I'll think about it.' She tried to imbue her voice with as much icy professionalism as she could muster. The last thing she wanted was to seem desperate.

'Good. You do that. And by the way, our dancers usually rouge their nipples before they go bare-breasted. It looks a little more dramatic.'

With that, he left the room.

Julia clattered down the stairs, cursing under her breath. She stamped back up the alley, still swearing. On the tube, she kept running over what Robert had said. As if she'd even consider signing up for more of his arrogant bullshit! Part of her winced when she remembered how she'd stood in front of him, practically naked and obviously aroused. At least she'd never have to see him again. She'd had enough humiliation for the moment.

She sank into her seat, feeling drained and miserable. A handsome guy in a denim jacket sitting across from her made eye contact and tried a smile. Julia glared back at him with as much hatred as she could muster. He withered under her 200-watt stare and Julia felt a small hollow sense of victory.

Back in her flat, she was still angrily clattering around when her flatmate got home. Karin picked up on the atmosphere immediately.

'So the audition didn't go well, I take it?' The question went ignored.

'Didn't get the job?' Karin asked again.

Julia looked at her grimly.

'Yeah, I got the job. But I'm not taking it.'

'Really? Why not? I thought it sounded like fun.'

'Fun? The man is a complete prick.'

'Oh. I see,' Karin said, nodding.

'What do you mean, "you see"?' Julia poured a generous measure of whisky into the cup and took a swig.

'It's just that you didn't complain about the job. You complained about the man. And interesting choice of descriptive phrase, by the way.' Karin was winding her up, but she couldn't help herself. She quite enjoyed watching Julia squirm in the throes of rejection for a change. Karin was very aware of the succession of love-lorn boys her flatmate had dropped so breezily, and just a little jealous.

'What descriptive phrase?' Julia snapped. This analysis session was doing nothing to improve her bad mood. Karin leant over and held her wrist.

'Julia. I've known you for four years.'

'Yes.'

'In all that time, I have never seen you drink whisky at –' she glanced at the clock – 'two o'clock in the afternoon. And I've never seen you so wound up.' She couldn't resist another dig. 'So what happened? Was the nasty man a lech? Did he try to get you to touch his "huge prick"?'

'Oh fuck *off*, Karin.' Julia stormed into her room and slammed the door behind her.

In the kitchen, Karin snorted with satisfaction. Julia was going to find it tough in the real world.

Lying spread-eagled on her bed, Julia stared morosely at the ceiling. What Karin had said had touched a nerve. She was upset precisely because he hadn't asked her to touch him, or even shown the slightest interest in her. And she'd stood in front of him practically fondling her tits! In her experience, just licking your lips at a man was usually enough. Robert had looked at her like she was some second-rate pole dancer! She snorted in disgust. Rolling over onto her front, Julia felt an uncomfortable pricking in her bra. She reached down her front and felt something against her fingers. Frowning, she pulled out the object.

It was the white feather. How the hell had he managed to get it in there? She remembered the feel of him brushing the tip of the feather down her body, and the teasing sound of his voice. 'If you're up to it . . .'

Suddenly everything clicked into place. This was a message he'd sent her. An invitation. A white feather, daring her to take him up on his offer. Perhaps he enjoyed a tease just as much as she did. Maybe his professional role forbade him from fucking her. Julia's imagination started working. She thought of his languid confident manner, and the controlled intensity of his gaze. She flicked at her nipples with the feather and imagined it was Robert's tongue licking her. The thought made her shiver. As she tickled herself lazily, she pictured him in front of her, reaching out for her tits. Oh she could make him lose his cool head, she knew she could. Julia sank into a daydream, lying back and letting her hand travel down between her legs. She thought of him getting turned on, beads of sweat breaking out on his brow. With one hand she started working at herself with her fingers. She closed her eyes. Dragging the feather over her face, brushing her lips, Julia arched her back and rubbed herself harder. In her head, she imagined the man quivering and helpless, begging her to let him fuck her.

Yeah, she'd make him beg. He'd have to be on the verge of crying before she let him so much as touch her. She'd have him on his knees.

As she pictured Robert kneeling in front of her, clutching her hips and burrowing his face into her, kissing her, trying desperately to get inside her clothes, Julia felt her orgasm approaching. Her body started to convulse and she curled up over her hand, one hand in her knickers and one still holding onto the feather. She clung to the bed, feeling the after-shocks subside, and pictured Robert on his back after she'd fucked him. He'd be lying there prostrate, arms spread-eagled. Breathless, sweating and utterly surrendered to her.

Julia smiled. She felt much better. And now she had a plan.

Julia put a Tori Amos CD on, loud, and stood in her room considering what to chuck and what to take with her. Her room was a chaotic fantasy land, strewn with clothes, knick-knacks and fake flowers, the walls strung with fairy lights and every surface cluttered with make-up, shoes, glossy magazines and CDs. Above the bed was a framed photo of Josephine Baker, the woman tipped upside down and balanced on the back of a male dancer, legs and arms flexed so she looked like a human Catherine wheel. It was Julia's favourite picture, Baker wearing nothing but a feather tucked between her legs and a magnificent smile. The image captured the explosive, vibrant moment that she first took the stage in Paris and rocked the world. It was Julia's inspiration.

She took it down from the wall and wrapped it in a soft wool sweater, placing it reverently in her suitcase.

She packed five pairs of dance shoes, stuffed with paper and carefully wrapped together by the ribbons. These were the most precious of her belongings. It took a long time to break her shoes in, banging them hard against the wall, walking round and round the house in them till the box at the tip eased enough that it wouldn't break her toes. Then they had to be prepared: the satin carefully snipped away round the toes; then darned and lacquered to stop it fraying; the soles sandpapered and rubbed with rosin. Even if she wouldn't be performing ballet routines at the circus, Julia knew she would have to keep training. Just a few days' rest meant her muscles would start to slacken and her joints stiffen up.

As she considered what clothes to take, Julia remembered Robert's warning that she should take more 'sensible clothes'. This was a problem – she didn't have any sensible clothes. Given the option, she'd wear silk and sequins every day of the week. In any case, she was plotting a seduction so there was no way she was turning up to rehearsals in trackie bottoms.

She smiled as she packed, thinking of just how much she was going to enjoy this. Robert was the first decent challenge she'd had in a very long time.

3

At 5 a.m. the following Tuesday, Julia was awake and dressing in the pale dawn light. Her eyes were puffy from lack of sleep and she was exhausted, but even so the thought of leaving to go on tour was giving her butterflies.

She'd been frantically busy since she decided to take the job: packing her stuff; clearing out her room; saying goodbye to friends ('Running away with the circus? Well, good luck . . .'). Through it all, she'd been considering how to approach her seduction of Robert. She'd spent Saturday shopping for a new outfit. This she had deliberated over carefully. Obviously, it had to make her look unbearably sexy. But it also had to look like she wasn't trying too hard – Robert wasn't going to fall for any cheap gimmicks. She had a feeling this game would be harder to win than that. After all, she'd stood in front of him virtually naked and he hadn't batted an eyelid. What she needed was an air of mystery that would fire his imagination: she had to look like she was almost unavailable.

Julia was used to dressing to shock – the idea of tantalising a man was an interesting new exercise. Eventually she'd bought a cute little flared skirt and a sheer top that fastened over her breasts, the loose floating fabric showing a sketchy glimpse of her body underneath. Her olive-toned skin seemed to glow under the pale fabric, and the curve of her belly showed over the low-slung skirt – so low the top of her knickers was peeking out. She'd also invested a small fortune in the provocative underwear: a lacy balconette bra and knickers that fastened at the sides with silk ribbons. A pair of kitten heels gave her a sexy wiggle. Last of all she'd had a bikini wax that left her nearly bare, just a strip of hair running between her legs and the rest naked.

As she dressed, she took pleasure in the feel of the clothes against her skin, the slide of the satiny fabric over her arms and the way the heels made her ass stick out, like she was displaying it. She'd liberally slicked herself with cocoa butter and fake tan. Her skin felt taut and smooth, and she was shivering with anticipation. Julia loved the build up to a seduction, the careful preparations and grooming. It all added to the excitement – dressing with the thought of fucking later was enough to turn her on. She wore her hair down, tousled and a little wild, letting loose curls tumble over her shoulders. At last, she looked at her reflection in the full-length mirror and gave a wide smile.

In the taxi the driver eyed Julia hungrily in the rearview mirror as he drove, casting longing looks at her cleavage and stocking-sleek legs. Julia noted his interest with pleasure – her charms were obviously apparent.

They drove fast – it was dawn and the streets were half empty. Julia was dog-tired, but the anticipation of seeing Robert was sending little thrills through her and making her a little shaky. She couldn't remember the last time she'd felt this nervous at the prospect of seeing a man. Dreamily, she imagined how Robert would react when he saw her. At the audition, she'd been unprepared. Now, perfumed, powdered, and dressed to the nines, Julia knew she was virtually irresistible. She pictured him smiling that skewed smile of his, pulling her into his office and starting to strip her, slowly. Squirming on the leather seat, she felt herself start to grow wet at the thought.

The taxi pulled up by the alleyway and the driver carried her case to the door, looking askance at the grotty surroundings. As she paid him he was still trying to sneak a look up her skirt. He left her alone in the alley, and Julia took the chance to prepare herself before she went in, pulling a cherry-red lip-gloss out of her handbag.

As she checked her hair in her pocket mirror the door burst open and Julia had to jump sideways to avoid the man backing out. He carried one end of a large crate, bent nearly double under the weight. She sized up his impressive bulk as he passed: a young muscular man with dirty blond hair and a T-shirt marked with dirt and sweat stains. Carrying the other end of the crate was a strange long-boned man, all awkward angles. His hair was pulled back in a grease-slicked ponytail and his goatee beard was waxed to a point. Julia met his eyes and felt the shock of his stare, an intense melancholic gaze that pierced right through her. Behind them, shouts, bangs and heavy footsteps echoed down the stairwell. Next the woman from the audition appeared in the doorway, hands on hips, apparently directing the move. She glanced at Julia.

'Ah. You're here. Late.' Julia was about to protest – it was still ten to six – but the woman dismissed the subject with a wave of her hand. 'No matter. I'm Rachel. You're travelling with the horses. Follow Joe.' She pointed towards the two men who had nearly knocked her over.

Horses? Julia turned to look at the men as they disappeared round a corner.

'Chop chop!' Rachel commanded, clapping her hands. Her gaze dropped to Julia's feet. 'And you'd better get yourself some decent shoes, darling,' she added. Rachel herself was wearing a black vest and jeans, dressed for work. Yet even in a pair of heavy lace-up boots she somehow managed to exude an aura of fearsome glamour.

'Shift your pretty little arse, princess,' she snapped, as Julia hesitated. Nonplussed, and feeling chastised, Julia lifted her suitcase and struggled after Joe. As she stumbled over the cobbles, she cursed her heels and then scowled, having proved Rachel's bitchy comment true within thirty seconds. Round the corner, the two men were loading the crate into a truck.

Julia groaned inwardly as she looked at the clapped-out old lorry she'd be travelling in. And where the hell was Robert? With bitter resentment, she pulled her suitcase towards the vehicle. Her efforts to look like a high-class libertine were going to be wasted on the navvies.

By 6 a.m. the truck was hurtling towards Brighton, where the rehearsals would start. Julia was wedged tightly into the small space between Joe and the bearded man, Henri. Joe drove fast and loosely, taking corners at high speed and spinning the wheel casually round with one hand. The truck was a rickety six-wheeler that shuddered and lurched along the road, making Julia's teeth rattle and throwing her against Joe at every turn – her leg pressed against his jeans and her shoulder knocking into his. She tried to hold herself upright, but there was nothing to hold onto other than Joe's leg, and in the end she gave in to the bumping and swaying of the truck. The other sticky area was changing gear. With three of them crammed into the cabin, Julia found herself sitting with the gear stick between her knees. She had to press her knees together every time Joe reached down to change gear, and every time he did so his hand would brush roughly against her thigh. She'd flinched the first time he did so, but he'd laughed at her as if she was a prim schoolteacher. He had a warm easy laugh, Julia thought. He chatted with a charming kind of playful forwardness, and his voice had a soft lilting quality to it. Joe was a full-blooded gypsy; his family were 'Rom'nies', as he told Julia, from a long tradition of horse-trading travellers. He'd grown up on the road, riding before he could walk, tending horses, doing labouring work. And then he'd joined the circus.

'To look after the horses?' Julia asked.

'Well, you could say that, I suppose.' Joe frowned. 'Though they're not exactly flesh and blood horses, you know.' He looked at Julia closely.

'You don't know anything about the circus, do you?' he asked, with a mischievous twinkle in his eye. 'Didn't you come see a show before you signed up?'

Julia suddenly realised that she did, in fact, know absolutely nothing about the circus or what her role would involve. She'd been so caught up in her plot to seduce Robert and so busy sorting out her life over the last week that she hadn't even considered what it was she would be actually doing once she was there. She shrugged and looked over at Henri, who gazed at the horizon with a distant expression.

Changing the subject, she leant over to Joe and whispered in his ear over the noise of his truck: 'Doesn't Henri ever speak?' Since they left, the other man had just stared at the road ahead, occasionally rolling a thin cigarette and smoking pensively. Joe gave Julia a wide grin.

'Henri is not a man of many words,' he said. 'But you wait till you see what he can do with a knife.' Julia flinched involuntarily, prompting another laugh from Joe.

'Henri's a knife-thrower. One of the best in the world. It takes a lot of skill, and a lot of concentration. Especially the act he does with the circus.'

31

Julia was becoming intrigued by the mysterious references to the circus. Just what, exactly, was it that made it so different from any other sawdust-and-clowns circus anyway? She tried to probe Joe for information, but he shook his head and told her to wait. He promised that once they got to the site, he'd show her round and introduce her to some of the 'crew'. At least there was one person who seemed to be friendly, Julia thought. And she liked Joe's laid-back rough and ready attitude. There was something refreshing about him, like a roll in a hay barn compared to her intense, infuriating encounter with Robert. Joe reached down to change gears, and this time he left his hand resting on Julia's knee. She felt him squeeze her leg, his hand rough and strong, rubbing the fabric of her stocking against his thumb. Casting an anxious glance at Henri, Julia quietly removed his hand, but shifted in her seat to feel the warmth of Joe's body closer to hers. She settled into the journey, reassured by the presence of a down-to-earth, horny young man.

The truck pulled into a field just outside Brighton and bumped over the grass to join various other cars, caravans and lorries that were parked in a circle. The field was already getting churned into a mud bath, most of the labourers having arrived the day before to set up. A small army of people were already putting up tents, raising poles and knocking pegs into the ground. Julia unfolded herself gingerly from the truck, her body cramped and sore. Joe ran round to help her down, apparently playing the gentleman, but not missing the chance to slip his arm round her waist and give her a stinging slap on the backside as he did so. While Julia tried to recover her composure he looked down at her shoes and shook his head.

'Now those'll be absolutely no use,' he said. 'Follow

me.' He strode off towards the group of caravans while Julia picked her way through the mud in his wake, her heels sinking into the earth with every step. Eventually Joe turned and watched her struggle for a bit before coming back to help her. Julia offered him her hand, but was taken by surprise when he grabbed her and swung her over his shoulder in a fireman's lift, leaving her upside down with her ass in the air and legs flailing. Weakly, she tried to protest, aware that she would not be making the most dignified of entrances slung over Joe's shoulder, but he ignored her. As he passed the other workers, they greeted each other with shouts.

'That the new dancer you got there, Joe?'

Julia winced, mortified at her ridiculous position and powerless to do anything about the whistles and jibes they attracted as Joe carried her across the field. Her underwear was digging in sharply, and she was rubbed and bumped against Joe's rough cotton shirt, irritating her tender newly-waxed flesh. All the blood was rushing to her head and her carefully primped hair swung wildly across her face. At last Joe let her slide down to the ground beside a caravan. He wrenched open the door and disappeared inside while she re-arranged her clothes, which had ridden up to expose her underwear and the lace tops of her stockings. Then she stuck her head inside the caravan, and found Joe rummaging in a cupboard.

'First rule of the site, Julia,' he shouted to her over his shoulder. 'Shoes off before you come in the caravan.' Julia complied, slipping out of her heels and climbing the steps in her stockinged feet. Once inside, she surveyed Joe's home with interest. The space was tiny, everything in miniature compared to Joe's bulky frame. It was also surprisingly tidy, the bed in the corner neatly made with a blanket tucked over it and the cupboards closed. It was a sparse home, everything functional and a little worn. Without doubt these were a man's living quarters. A postcard of a motorbike was tacked up over the sink as decoration, and a St Christopher hung from a nail over the bed. Other than these small decorations the walls were lined with neatly stacked shelves.

Joe turned to her, holding out a pair of cowboy boots in one hand.

'These'll do you better for rolling around in the dirt,' he said. As Julia sat down on the edge of the bed to pull on the boots, he came and stood close to her.

'In fact, I think you'll need to change your outfit altogether.' Julia looked up at him. 'I've got some old clothes in the cupboard there, if you'd just take off this.' He hooked a finger into the neck of her top, pulling it away from her body. Julia was aware that, standing over her, he could see right down her cleavage. And he was looking. She didn't pull away, enjoying the feel of his eyes on her, his playful confidence. She put her head on one side and looked sternly at him, meeting his forwardness with smouldering confidence.

'What have you got?' she asked slyly.

Joe visibly shook himself and went back to the cupboard. He returned with an armful of clothes – a check shirt and jeans – and threw them onto the bed next to her. She looked them over doubtfully.

'What, no cowboy hat?' she asked. Joe reached behind the door.

'It just so happens...' he said, producing a felt hat and tossing it to Julia, who caught it and smiled.

'A proper caballero, eh?' She let the hat dangle from her finger and grinned at him.

'Well, you know, I do work with the *horses*.'

'Yeah...' Julia frowned. She had the distinct feeling she was being wound up. Adopting a brisk tone, she tried to wrest the situation back to a more professional level.

'So, tell me where can I get changed.'

Joe spread his arms wide. His fingertips reached nearly to the walls of the tiny space.

'Feel free, babe. I'm not shy.'

'No,' said Julia, 'but maybe I am. Can't a girl have a little privacy?' She raised her eyebrow, letting the tension between them rise in the silence.

Joe licked his lips, obviously undecided just how far he could push it. He gave her a last lingering stare before bowing deeply.

'As you wish, madam,' he declared with mock formality, and left, closing the door behind him.

As she unzipped her skirt, Julia smiled to herself. The morning's flirting with Joe had warmed her up nicely. She had a little buzz between her legs that meant she was more than ready to go and find Robert.

She was unaware of the caravan window opposite her, or the fact that, outside, Joe watched her ghostly reflection disrobe with great pleasure.

Julia emerged from the caravan in the over-sized old clothes and stepped into a maelstrom of people all moving with purpose towards the centre of the site. She could hear hammering and shouts, and she followed the noise out past the caravan enclosure. In a wide open space in the centre of the field the company were erecting the tents. Julia watched as the central marquee went up. A couple of dozen men, sweating and grimy, pulled on ropes and the structure was heaved up to stand forty feet high. It didn't look like the circus tops she remembered. The marquee was entirely black. A woman draped black silk over the guy ropes, which were trimmed with purple flags. She watched a couple of guys climb ladders to the top and loop long strings of fairy lights round the crown. Towering over her, the dark canvas with its fluttering pennants loomed like a nightmare pirate ship. Julia felt a mix of excitement and anxiety as she looked around the site. The workers swarming over the site were a bizarre assortment of creatures. Each worked with intense concentration, the whole operation precisely co-ordinated. They had muscular, athletic builds and many of them were tattooed and pierced, with dyed hair tied back or shaved at the sides. They moved with a peculiar sort of grace, as though putting up the tents was a performance in itself. As a burly man brushed past her, Julia caught a whiff of body odour mixed with a faint scent of patchouli or hash – she couldn't be sure which. She saw Henri, winding a rope into a coil that he tossed into a crate. A slim delicate looking woman was sitting on another crate, stitching her costume. Julia walked slowly through the site, swerving out of the way as a young man, stripped to the waist, walked swiftly past on a pair of stilts. Behind her she heard the roar of an engine and turned to see Joe astride a black motorbike riding into the marquee. Motorbikes? She followed Joe into the tent, blinking as her eyes adjusted to the dim light inside.

The black canvas filtered the light to a sepulchral glow, turning the bright morning into twilight. The atmosphere had an intense dreamlike quality that made Julia feel she had entered a strange new world.

In here the workers swarmed like ants: hoisting a lighting rig into the rafters; unfolding rows of benches; hammering scaffolds in place in the centre of the tent. There was a smell of diesel and woodchips, and a sudden harsh burst of noise from the speakers at the back of the tent. Joe's motorbike leant against a pole and he stood watching the action. Standing in the centre of the ring was Robert. Julia recognised him instantly, a tall figure standing with his legs spread, directing people around him. Her stomach gave a little flip as he turned towards where she stood, but he seemed to look right through her. His brow was furrowed in concentration, and he was obviously totally absorbed in the preparations. As he moved around, inspecting scaffolds and giving instructions, Julia observed his calm, magnetic presence. She began to understand how he could hold a whole show together. He was the lynchpin around which everyone else was spinning. Without raising his voice, he summoned people to him and smoothly sent them off to their tasks.

Overhead, a rack of lamps was switched on, flooding the ring with a harsh violet light. The colours were suddenly inverted, and the scene resembled a photographic negative, grainy and indistinct. Julia walked into the ring to where Robert was bathed in UV, his teeth and the whites of his eyes dazzling against his blue skin as he looked upwards, peering into the dazzle. She felt disoriented, as though she had been flung into a surreal tableau. Would Robert even recognise her? She approached him as though moving underwater. When she caught his eye, he gave her a violet smile and walked over.

'So you made it,' he said, with genuine warmth in his voice. Julia felt a surge of relief that he knew who she was. Lost among a crowd of shadowy strangers, she was grateful to know at least one person. Even if their previous encounter had been a frustrating one, Julia felt a connection to him, as though they'd shared some intimacy as she danced for him. This time, though, Robert was obviously in his element. The languid suggestive manner she'd found so beguiling had been taken over by a focused exuberance. He was buzzing with energy, his movements vital and confident. He surveyed the interior of the tent, still awash with blue light.

'It's fantastic, isn't it?'

Julia looked around, seeing the dark structures of scaffolds, now being hung with heavy drapes, ropes looping overhead and rows of empty seats. Fantastic was right.

Abruptly, she was shaken out of her reverie.

'Sylvie,' Robert was calling, over her shoulder. 'Can you take – sorry, what was your name?' He looked at Julia, frowning.

'Julia. Julia Spark.' She was crushed that he didn't remember.

'Sylvie, can you take Julia to your caravan and sort her out please? Thank you.' He nodded at Julia, and turned back to his work.

Julia smiled weakly at Robert's back as a girl approached and led her out of the tent.

Back in the glare of daylight, Julia got a look at Sylvie. She was small and lithe, with a heart-shaped face covered in heavy make-up. Fast and graceful, she moved through the chaos of the site, leading Julia back towards the caravans. Following behind her, Julia admired the sculpted muscles of her legs, knowing how much effort it took to keep your body that sleek. Sylvie moved with a natural wiggle, and shimmied her ass as she climbed into a small silver trailer, beckoning Julia after her. Once inside, Sylvie sank onto the bed, lit a cig and let out a long sigh. Julia looked around in wonder. This caravan was a world away from Joe's sparse home. The tiny curved interior was a cornucopia of exotic fabrics and decorations. The bed was covered in a heavily embroidered Indian blanket, with mirrors and beads stitched over the surface, and a profusion of silk pillows. Sylvie lay back in these like a bird curling into her nest. Julia ducked her head to avoid crashing into the low ceiling, and felt feathers brush against her cheek. Dream catchers and mobiles hung around her, wind chimes rung tiny silvery notes. Sylvie nodded Julia to sit on the couch opposite.

'That's your bed. I'll get Joe to bring in your cases.' She spoke with a husky Eartha Kitt voice that didn't match her doll-like looks. Julia eyed her warily. Something about Sylvie was a little unnerving. She was a strange creature, by turns petulant and girlish, although Julia sensed in her proud posture and lithe body a confidence that could only come from long experience and devotion to her art. Sylvie did a high-wire act, 'and the contortionist thing,' she said, blithely. It was in the contortion act that Julia would start off.

'When I'm up on the platform, I need an assistant to dance around,' Sylvia explained. 'You know, that wafting stuff.' She waved her hands vaguely to show what she meant. 'Also to pour the wine over me.'

'Excuse me?'

Sylvie sucked her teeth, obviously impatient at Julia's ignorance.

'It's an Eastern theme. I'll be up on a podium, like a temple statue. While I'm rolling around and doing positions, you'll be brought on like a human sacrifice, in chains. In fact, maybe we'll make you crawl. Then, when I'm in position like this –' She pulled her leg round to flex behind her head and rested it on her shoulder. Pulling her other ankle round so she was delicately poised, she balanced on her hands. It took Julia's breath away. 'You put wine glasses here,' Sylvia nodded to the soles of her feet, 'here,' the palms of her hands, 'here and here,' her head and shoulders, 'and two here, on my breasts.'

Julia raised her eyebrows as Sylvie continued, getting into her stride.

'It's like we're doing some strange religious ritual. You'll be trying to bring me to life, under orders from Robert. He'll be the one with the whip, by the way. I'll move through several poses, you crawl round the stage, dance. I want you to move like you're lost in a sexual spiritual ecstasy. We'll have some acrobats moving around you – the guys playing temple guards. It's a fabulous set, lots of drapes and gold lighting. You'll love it. Anyway, then you're given a tall bottle. The sacred wine. You'll approach me and start to pour it all over. I don't spill a drop. At first. There's the drum roll, and so on. But this being the Circus Excite –' Sylvie paused and gave Julia a wink '– then you start to spill the wine all over me. Try to make it sexy, you know. You pour it all around; the music gets wilder. I'll start moving around, still holding the glasses up, striking more poses. You try to keep it from spilling, acting scared. Remember the guys behind you and Robert with his whip. The lighting will drop to just a spot on us, so it makes it all more intense.' Sylvie was lost in her description now, her voice a low purr. Julia watched as she leant back, smiling. 'The idea is that I am brought to life as you lick the wine from me. I'll twist into some more poses and we'll fool around. The act ends when we kiss, drenched in wine.' She looked at Julia, smiling. 'Then, bang! Lights out. Next act.' She held out her hands, palms up, striking a pose that reminded Julia of an exotic deity. 'As the contortionist – I'll just be doing the freaky bends. You're the one the audience will empathise with, so it's up to you to make it sexy.' Julia nodded, slowly. She thought she was starting to get an inkling of what the Circus Excite's unique angle was. She watched as Sylvie unwound her legs and lay back, stretching her muscles.

'Right. And the other acts?'

'What you'd expect, girl, in a circus. Skill and illusion, daredevil stunts and spectacular effects.' She looked at Julia curiously. 'You'll see. Of course Robert will show you everything. He's the one who can explain it all best. And he holds the whole thing together, of course. A natural showman, Robert. Even if his ideas are kind of bizarre, the show wouldn't exist without him.'

'The ringmaster.' Julia nodded, thinking of Robert in the centre of the tent, directing everyone.

'Oh, he's much more than a ringmaster. He's aware of the whole operation around him: audience, performers, the set, the sound. Even when he's in the middle of his tricks, he'll notice if just one of us isn't giving total attention.'

'He's a magician?'

'Well, he calls himself an illusionist. Worked all over Eastern Europe, a lot in Prague. Grew up with the stage and the darker side of the circus. I guess that's how he came up with the idea of Circus Excite.'

'Some kind of freaky sex show?'

Sylvie gave her a sharp look.

'Much more than a sex show, girl. It's all theatre. A circus, but darker than usual.'

'A circus with less clothes,' Julia guessed.

'Less clothes, yes. But we also use some shock tactics. Scenes that are a little perverted. We twist all the acts and get the audience turned on. Play with the danger.' She narrowed her eyes and an enigmatic smile spread slowly across her face.

'It's all about desire. You can see the audience squirming while they watch you. Trying to rub themselves off on the seats. You can practically hear them getting horny.'

Lying back on the cushions and drawing on her cigarette, Sylvie looked like an exotic throwback from 1920s Paris, luxuriating in her fantasy of strange theatre. The smoke from her cigarette rose in blue curls, filling the small space. Julia felt giddy. The atmosphere was faintly surreal – almost suffocating.

She wondered what she'd got herself into. The thought of being involved in the circus made her feel edgy, as though she'd joined a strange perverse cult. She'd be living in the midst of this highly charged scene, putting herself on display for an audience as an object of fantasy. It felt dangerous. At the same time a thrill of curiosity prickled her skin. She wanted to know how far she could go.

'Okay, dancing girl.' Sylvie roused herself from the bed and stood up, stretching. 'Time to visit Eva.' Julia raised her eyebrows. What now?

'Wardrobe,' Sylvie announced.

The wardrobe trailer was a fantastic world of feathers, sequins and billowing silk. A clothes rail ran the length of one wall, crowded with outlandish outfits on hangers. Hairpieces and bead strings hung from the ceiling. Julia trailed her hands over the costumes, feeling netting spring beneath her fingers, spellbound by the glitter and shimmer of the fabric. The wardrobe mistress looked her over critically.

Eva was in her forties, tanned and stately. She wore a loose blouse and heavy bracelets that clinked as she moved her hands, lifting Julia's hair and patting at her body under her clothes. She reminded Julia of one of her ballet teachers, her face weathered but beautifully composed, with sculpted cheekbones and perfect posture. She had an air of command that was both admirable and intimidating. Briskly, Eva moved round her, sizing her up. She was trying to gauge Julia's body through the baggy rolls of Joe's oversized clothes, feeling round her hips and boldly cupping her breasts, weighing them in her hands. Shaking her head, she stood back.

'Strip,' she commanded, bluntly. 'I need to see what I'm working with.'

Julia obliged, shedding her clothes on the floor and standing in her underwear under the critical gaze of Eva and Sylvie. 'You'll have to take all of it off,' Eva insisted, still staring intently at Julia's figure as though measuring her with her eyes. Reluctantly, Julia unhooked her bra and dropped it on the floor, then pulled her knickers off and stood naked in the midst of all the clothes, shivering.

'What's the theme?' Eva asked Sylvie, who was sitting in the corner with her legs crossed under her, smoking and watching Julia with amusement.

'I think white for this one. Pale, angelic. Pure. Make her look like a virgin slave. A little ragged around the edges. I'll be in gold. We can keep the lighting warm and use a bit of smoke on the floor. Everything will be totally decadent.'

Eva nodded.

'Roman-esque, don't you think?'

She flicked quickly through the rail of costumes, murmuring under her breath.

'Something billowy, a kind of wrap-around. I think we can adjust one of these.' She pulled a hanger from the rail, and handed the costume to Julia, who looked at it dubiously. It was basically a long strip of rough white cotton.

'Arms up.' Eva wound the cloth over Julia's shoulder, wrapped a strip tightly over her breasts and round her back, letting it drape round her hips. She pinned it in place and stood back.

'Something like that, Sylvie?'.

Sylvie cocked her head, watching Julia.

'See what happens when you move around, girl. Is it loose enough?'

Julia looked at herself in the mirror. The fabric just skimmed over her nipples, her breasts threatening to spill over the top. It covered her pubis, but only just, leaving one hip entirely bared and the crease of her buttocks showing. If she walked you would catch a glimpse between her legs with every step, and if she leant forward her arse was bared like an animal display-ing its genitalia. Although Eva had pinned the costume together, she'd have to be careful not to let the whole thing slip off her shoulder. Julia whirled around, and the fabric brushed against her body. The cotton fell in ragged folds, chafing against her, winding round her legs. It excited her to think of an audience full of men watching her move in this, trying to get a look at her naked, tantalised by the possibility that the whole thing could unravel in front of them.

'I like it,' she declared. 'It needs trying out onstage though, there's no room to move in here.' Sylvie nodded in agreement. 'What about the hair?' she asked Eva. 'Make-up?'

Eva considered for a minute.

'Full body, I think. Maybe a bit of powder. We can tie her hair up and keep it simple to start with. You want to keep the innocent character going, so don't make a fuss about her face. She should look blank almost, like a statue come to life. Then when you've got your twisted, bizarre poses next to her it'll provide good contrast. Anyway, they're going to be looking at the curves –' Eva ran a hand down the cotton to where it hugged Julia's hip '– and the flesh, not her face.'

'In fact, we must use white paint all over,' Sylvie joined in, standing and approaching Julia. 'Do you mind, sweetie?' She pulled aside the cotton swatch to show Julia's pubic hair. Before Julia could move, she was reaching down to the strip of hair between her legs, tugging gently at the tufts. 'I think we need to get rid of your muff,' she said, frowning. 'Eva can wax you tomorrow.'

Julia was stunned, feeling totally vulnerable as the two women pulled and prodded her. She was also uncomfortably aware that she was turned on; Sylvie's pulling at the hairs had sent a surge of blood between her legs that made her knees weak. Blushing, she drew back from the women, her heart hammering. Sylvie, totally unconcerned, sensed her discomfort and smiled wickedly.

'Excellent,' she purred. 'That's exactly what I want. A blushing virgin who can't help getting turned on.' She turned to Eva. 'You're a genius. Now we can get started on the practice.'

Walking across the grass with Sylvie, Julia felt relief at being clothed again and out of the charged atmosphere of the wardrobe trailer. The site was still buzzing with people carrying equipment into the tent. Radios were playing music and the day was heating up. Most of the men were shirtless, and many of them turned to give her a lingering stare as she passed. Before, she'd felt like she was invisible on the site as the company focused intently on their work. This time, she and Sylvie attracted attention, and Julia was a curiosity. She felt scrutinised in a way that was almost hostile. This feeling was only made worse when one of the men called something to Sylvie that made her laugh out loud; a rough dirty laugh that Julia suspected was directed at her.

'What's so funny?' she asked, bristling. Sylvie looked at her with her round cat-like eyes, considering whether to explain the joke.

'You're a stranger, Julia. You're a "first of May", you know? A townie.' She shrugged. 'It's a hard life, and we stick tight together. Some of the roustabouts don't trust outsiders; it's just in their blood. They're probably going to hate you. Either that or they'll be trying to fuck you.' Sylvie looked Julia over. 'You'd better keep your wits about you, girl. You go around shaking those big titties at the labourers, and you'd better be prepared for the consequences.'

'I can handle myself'.

'Maybe with the pretty boys in college. But this circus is kind of a magnet for outsiders, you know.'

'What do you mean, outsiders?'

'People who are drawn to extremes. Who like to experiment. They like to play games, Julia. You need to understand the rules.'

'And they are?'

Sylvie laughed, a squeaking shivery laugh that made her whole body shake in delight.

'Nobody tells you the fucking rules, Miss Ballerina!' She made her eyes round and wide, mocking Julia with an expression of dazed innocence. 'Just presume this place is full of dangerous perverts with kinky ideas, okay?'

'And what if I have some kinky ideas of my own?' Julia asked, rising to the challenge. At this, Sylvie threw back her head and howled, laughing like she'd inhaled helium. They'd reached the caravan, and she climbed the steps shaking her head at Julia's naiveté. As she opened the door she turned to Julia, her small frame still quivering with laughter.

'Okay, sweetheart, you play your own games.' She winked. 'Just don't let the ringmaster catch you fucking behind his back. He likes to keep a very close eye on our antics. You'd be surprised at how much he sees – it's like living in a peepshow, this place.' She delivered the last line in a stage whisper, as though she were letting Julia in on a dirty secret.

Julia imagined Robert's intense brown eyes watching her as she flirted her way round the circus. The thought of his attention gave her a delicious glimmer of nerves, the same butterflies she had when she performed. She was struck by a vision of the circus itself as a sexual theatre, everyone a performer, everyone a watcher. From the steps of Sylvie's van, she turned to look round the site. Amongst the cluster of vehicles and tents, she imagined every corner filled with writhing couples, lewd acts hidden behind curtains and furtively enacted perversions. Watching everything with a penetrating gaze was Robert, spying zealously on his workers while the site buzzed with simmering, artful eroticism.

Julia let the vision wash over her, certain that in such a place her desires and talents would thrive.

'Hey, daydreamer,' Sylvie called from inside. 'Get your ass in here. We've got a dress rehearsal to prepare for.'

4

'HEY! What's the game?'

'Hit the lights, for fuck's sake!'

'I can't see a thing – will someone get those sparkies moving? We're trying to work down here!'

'Can we get some light onstage please? White floods will do.' Robert's voice cut smoothly through the confused darkness of the tent. The stage was smothered in velvety blackness and tangles of cables were heaped haphazardly among the equipment, making moving around a dangerous operation. Julia was tucked in behind the curtains at the back, wearing her slave-girl wrapper and watching intently. The tent was a chaotic industrial scene, with the muscular roustabouts and stage crew busily adjusting the scaffolds and working on the next set. The vast circular platform of the stage, covered with stretched canvas, sat resplendent in the midst of the racks of folding seats. It could be seen from almost every angle, and Julia was aware that when performing she would be enclosed by a ring of strangers, rather than facing the audience as she was used to. Her performance had to be flawless – she would be totally exposed.

This afternoon, the first dress rehearsal, the audience consisted of other performers and the circus workers. In some ways they were more daunting than the public – Julia had noticed the rough brutal attitudes of the people on site. They wouldn't spare her feelings if she messed up. She was also keenly aware of Robert's presence. Hs attention was focused sharply on the stage, as he paced round the tent checking every aspect of the show. He moved fluidly through the chaos, occasionally shouting brusque orders at the performers. Julia could feel the tension building around her – the outraged shouts as the lights cut were just part of the intense urgency that permeated the whole circus. Behind her, Sylvie was stretching, warming up her muscles. She caught sight of Joe, deeply involved with the lighting rig, his face grim and sweating. Backstage there was no laughter; only abrupt exchanges and occasional arguments as the performers clashed with the stage crew. Sylvie had barely spoken to her, just given her a critical stare and pulled at her costume so that more flesh was exposed. Julia had submitted with sulky reluctance, letting Sylvie push and prod at her till she was just about spilling out of the wrapper. She had a bad feeling in her stomach; not the usual pre-show butterflies but a nasty twisting sensation, as though she was about to enter a nightmare.

She had spent a difficult few days with Sylvie practising their routine. The other girl was quick to anger and even more demanding than the strictest ballet master. If she sensed even the slightest reserve in Julia's performance, she'd bark insults at her – 'With feeling, girl, for Christ's sake. Don't you have any imagination?'

Julia didn't respond well to such scathing criticism, especially from someone with none of her formal training. She'd danced solo routines en pointe – gyrating sexily around the stage was sure to be a breeze. The more Sylvie pushed her to learn the movements precisely, the more Julia resented taking orders from an arrogant little nymph. After endless repetitions of the act, the sequence still wasn't flowing perfectly. Backstage, she ran through the steps in her head, secretly hoping she could rely on improvisation. There was no escape now though, and time was running short. They were on after the next act.

Onstage now, suddenly bathed in flat white light, were the tigers. These were, in fact, three lithe and curvy girls, kneeling or lying on plinths. They trailed their hands languorously on the floor, like sleeping cats. Julia recognised the blonde girl. Sarah had shared a smoke with Julia the night before and seemed friendly in a rough aggressive manner. The set was based on a carousel, a crazily ornate Baroque backdrop, gilded and strung with lights, the whole central dais revolving at a languorous pace. Sawdust was scattered in drifts over the stage, adding to the sense of an old-fashioned fairground. As the lights gradually came up, a hush fell over the workers and attention focused on the glittering, lush spectacle. Julia watched as Sarah and the other girls held their poses, crouched on the floor in tiny bikinis.

'Will they be in costume tomorrow?' she whispered to Sylvie.

'Not exactly. They'll be painted. Naked, but made to look like they're tattooed in black stripes. Eva does them. And the way she does it, there's something vicious about the faces, you know. Like they really are bloodthirsty animals.' Sylvie laughed, looking at the tableau onstage as the speakers whined with feedback.

'I love this act. So does Robert, in fact. Look at his face.' Julia sought Robert's tall slim figure and found him in the shadows opposite; his hand stroking his chin, a thoughtful, hungry look in his eyes. She knew instantly that she wanted him to watch her like that. He was eating the scene in front of him with his eyes, and she wished she were there onstage, letting his gaze stroke over her, showing him the beautiful curves of her body.

Julia's attention was drawn back to the stage as music poured from the speakers in a sudden rush. The sound was a loud raunchy tune that suggested old-fashioned circus – a squeezebox and mewling violins. It sounded like an old record playing, with all the scratches and crackles of vinyl. The tent suddenly seemed European, rich and Bohemian in atmosphere, as though they were thrust back into a vintage big top smelling of sawdust and sulphur.

She watched as the lights came up on the performers, spotlights whirling over the stage and flecks of light from mirror-balls cascading over the bodies of the tiger-girls. They lay curled over the plinths, bodies frozen in pose, totally unmoving as the opening bars played out. Then there was the shimmer of a drum roll, and the girls came to life, twisting and stretching. At the same time, Julia had to leap to the side as four burly guys charged past her, poles resting on their shoulders supporting a canvas litter. Sprawled on top was the tamer – Rachel, dressed in top hat and tails, fishnet stockings and viciously high stilettos. A long leather whip trailed from her hand, and she flicked the tip of it idly over the shoulders of the men carrying her. Her face, vividly made up and thickly covered in white panstick, wore an expression of sultry arrogance. As she passed Julia she aimed a kick at her with the pointed toe of her shoe and sat back laughing as Julia recoiled, bewildered.

'Rachel has a fairly competitive streak,' Sylvie said behind her. 'She likes to discipline people.' Julia raised an eyebrow, shaken by the unprovoked attack. 'She's one of Robert's oldest colleagues. They devise the scenes together – though I reckon it must be a hell of a fight before they agree on anything. Especially with all their history.'

'History?' asked Julia, feeling a sudden cold pang of jealousy. 'Are they together?'

'They're not lovers, at least not in the way you'd normally describe a relationship. Robert doesn't do that kind of thing.'

'Surely he's not celibate?' Julia said, incredulous. She couldn't imagine a man so deeply involved in eroticism leading a monk-like existence. Robert's whole *raison d'être* was sexual arousal. The thought seemed kind of perverse. She wanted to ask Sylvie more, but the show onstage was starting to heat up and her attention was drawn back to the performance.

'This is where Rachel licks the girls into shape – look, you mustn't miss it, Julia.'

Rachel had been carefully lowered onto the stage, and was now parading around the circumference, rolling her hips and strutting so that her costume displayed her G-string under the hem of the fitted jacket. She was buttoned up to the neck, but you could see the tight fit of the coat, the swell of her breast underneath. The brim of a top hat hid her eyes – her appearance had an almost military air to it, Julia thought. She held her shoulders rigid and the purposeful strides she took in her four-inch heels could have been a march. Now she stood with her back to Julia, legs spread wide and arms akimbo. In front of her the tiger-girls paced warily on all fours, baring their teeth. The pallbearers stood aside with arms folded and faces impassive, awaiting their orders. Rachel nodded to them, and used the handle of the whip to point at Sarah, singling her out for attention. The men approached, now carrying heavy black ropes and a net. This they threw over Sarah, who screamed and struggled wildly as she was scooped up and carried to the side of the stage where Rachel stood waiting.

The men dropped the net at her feet, sending Sarah sprawling across the floor. She craned her head back at Rachel, a mix of fear and anger in her eyes as Rachel lifted the whip and flexed her arm. She gave a shout and brought the whip down with a sharp crack, flicking it away inches from Sarah's back. Julia watched fascinated as Sarah, on all fours, panted and arched her back, flinching as the whip cracked above her. The scene was surreal, but there was something in the attitude of the two performers that meant Julia couldn't look away – the tamer had an edgy drive about her that suggested she was restraining herself from actually letting the whip cut Sarah's flesh. Her ass jutted out as though part of her wanted to feel the stinging punishment of the whip. The atmosphere between them had a buzz of cruelty and Sarah's whimpering and trembling was real enough to make Julia wonder if there wasn't more going on than just acting.

'Sarah tried to make a move on Robert last year,' Sylvie whispered to Julia, answering her unspoken question. 'It hasn't been forgotten. Rachel is very protective of him.'

'She won't let him get involved with another woman, even if they don't sleep together? That's crazy,' said Julia.

'This circus runs on frustration. And Robert just encourages it. He won't ever flat out refuse anyone – he'll tease you till you're dripping, but he'll never touch you. I think that's how he gets off, in fact, just letting his women fight among themselves, watching the tensions build and meanwhile just staying above it all.'

'But if everyone knows that, how does he get away with it?' Julia asked.

'He's a sexy man. You know how charismatic he is; I've seen you look at him. What he likes best is to watch, and what do all performers want most of all?'

Onstage now, Rachel had locked the tiger-girl in a cage, which was hoisted high into the air. Sarah writhed pathetically, reaching her arms through the bars and snarling at the empty space below. The music was grinding on around them, punctuated by the cracking of the whip and shouts from Rachel as she goaded the other girls. Julia heard a sinister tone in the fairground music now; the plaintive notes of the accordion seemed to turn sour and dark as the tigers cowered, shrinking back from the vivid figure of the tamer. Julia suddenly wanted them to turn on her, wanted to see Rachel stripped of her power and stopped from her relentless tormenting of the tigers. Though she knew it was a fantasy, she sensed that Rachel enjoyed wielding her whip and intimidating people. Julia hadn't forgotten the vicious kick she'd tried to give her earlier. She saw Robert, leaning over a chair and watching with a twisted smile, and felt as though the two of them were implicated in some strange sadistic game.

The music continued relentlessly as Rachel, served by the silent muscle men, rounded up each of the girls and had them hoisted aloft in cages.

Within a few minutes she was standing triumphantly alone on the podium, striking poses with the whip and showing her teeth in a grotesque smile. She curled the leather strip around her legs and let it slide up her thigh as though she were caressing herself with the tip of it, working her hips as she pulled the whip closer to the tops of her stockings. Julia watched unbelieving as Rachel started stroking the whip between her legs, all the while arching her back and opening her mouth in a half-laugh, still celebrating her dominion over the animals.

'She's an utter bitch!' Julia couldn't help herself.

Sylvie let out a blurt of laughter, and pointed upwards. 'You really are a gullible little girlie, aren't you? Watch the tigers.'

In the cages, the girls had stopped trying to escape. Instead they were now rubbing themselves against the bars – Sarah had her legs spread in the splits over the wire floor of the cage, displaying her crotch to the burly man standing underneath. In another cage, the girl was pushing her breasts out from the bars, squeezing them together and making low purring noises. The tigers were purposefully displaying themselves to the men below, pushing their asses upwards as though they were animals that wanted to mate, licking their lips, pawing at the bars. The scene was starting to change, and as the men hungrily watched the girls in cages, a new beat started to creep into the music.

'This is where things start to turn around,' Sylvie said, nudging Julia.

While Rachel gyrated unaware on the podium, still playing with her whip gleefully, the men were lowering the cages. As they opened the doors a driving seductive beat started playing, weaving insidiously through the tent. The tigers slipped easily out of the arms of the men, running into a huddle downstage before turning to where Rachel stood exposed in the centre of the stage. Julia felt a little rush of delight as Sarah crept up to put a clawed hand on Rachel's leg, catching the whip in her other hand. As Rachel looked around, horrified, the tigers placed themselves in position around her, quietly teasing her. Julia had to admit she had a fantastic stage presence. Even as the tigers pulled her down from the podium and pawed at her clothes, she kept her attitude of pained arrogance, refusing to beg for mercy.

Now the girls circled Rachel and knocked off the top hat, letting a long swathe of auburn hair spill over her shoulders. Carefully, Sarah crouched in front of her and pulled at the buttons on her blazer-style jacket. Julia felt the air thicken with desire. Now the whole tent was watching the action onstage and even the stage crew had stopped in their preparations. Someone whistled as the jacket was stripped roughly from Rachel's body, exposing a corset and the creamy-white skin of her décolletage.

'What we've been waiting for,' Sylvie noted. The tigers pulled at the corset, growling excitedly as it came undone and fell open. Rachel's body was sprawled over the podium, her breasts exposed and her legs bent apart as she struggled weakly against the tigers' efforts.

'Kind of kinky, isn't it?' Sylvie suggested to Julia. 'I hope it's getting you heated up, girl, 'cause we're on in five minutes.'

It was a jolt to Julia's system – she'd almost forgotten her own act while the tigers played out in front of her. She felt another wash of sickly nerves rush through her. She'd be at the mercy of the audience, which, she now realised, would include the terrifying Rachel. She watched the tigers mauling Rachel with a mixture of admiration and despair – how was she going to follow this? As the act reached its climax, the music developed into a deep, pulsing house track and the lights were turning blood red over the bodies onstage. The tigers were now pulling at Rachel's limbs in a frenzy of lust, their bodies tangled around her as they rubbed themselves against her and ran their tongues in long licks over her skin. The tamer lay surrendered, giving herself up to the animals as they feasted on her body and growled with pleasure. From the people watching in the wings and round the tent there was appreciative applause, some shouts of encouragement. Julia saw Robert bang on the flat of the seat in front of him, giving a whoop of approval and clapping hard. There was a gleam in his eyes that she knew meant he was turned on. Julia felt her knees grow weaker as she imagined his pleasure.

Julia was at the edge of the stage. Round her neck was a collar and chain, Robert holding the end of the leash. The foreboding she'd felt earlier was turning into a storm of nervous shakes. The more she tried to calm herself, the more wretched she felt. She couldn't quite understand why she was so overwrought – she'd taken part in enough shows to be able to put on a professional attitude even when she felt less than confident. Deep down, she knew it was something to do with Robert's proximity, and his dark languid attitude that made her feel herself melting even as she struggled to concentrate on her moves.

The tigers' set had been struck and the scenery for the contortion act had been swiftly changed over. The stage was now an opulent fantasy of an ancient temple. Stone columns lined the walkway, adorned with flickering torches and lit with an unearthly blue light. At the foot of each pillar stood burly temple guards, shaven-headed and clad in loincloths. The bronzed sculpture of their muscles contrasted sharply with billowing swathes of white fabric, so that it almost seemed as if they themselves were carved out of stone.

An altar stood in the centre, on which Sylvie would perform. The music was a low, echoing drumbeat accompanied by trance-like chanting, enhancing the sombre ritualistic atmosphere. Dry ice drifted slowly over the stage, its smoky acrid smell stinging Julia's eyes and drying her mouth. She waited for her cue, staring blankly at the floor and trying to control her breathing. Robert stood inches from her in his tailored suit and braces. His presence was awe-inspiring; Julia was almost painfully aware of his magnetic command of the show.

In front of them, Sylvie climbed onto the altar, under cover of the dark set. As the lights came up, she sat straight-backed on the stone slab (in fact, artfully painted wood). Her legs were folded into a lotus pose, and her body was burnished with gold paint. Sitting totally still, her doll-like face impassive, Sylvie looked like a life-size effigy.

Without looking back at Julia, Robert started walking onstage. The chain tightened, and Julia was pulled along behind. She tried to move in time with the languorous beat, settling into a loping stride while she rolled her hips and curved her back. She'd practised this movement with Sylvie leading her, trying to lend sexiness to her movements without showing too much flesh. Now, with Robert tugging at the rope, jerking her forwards, Julia felt as though she were too obviously intrigued by this man, too willing to let him drag her around and humiliate her. She imagined suddenly with a little panic that the other performers watching her knew how she'd tried to seduce Robert. Did she look pathetic following him across the stage? She felt herself cringe as she imagined their knowing laughter, and was struck with a sudden burning desire to run away. As Robert pulled her past Joe, who stood rock-solid in his role as temple guard, Julia felt her humiliation turn into rage. Fuck this man and his sadistic flights of fancy – she didn't want to be paraded around likes some idiotic sycophant. Dancing was one thing, but submitting to his perverse power trip was sticking in her throat.

Halfway across Robert turned back to look at her, and the critical expression on his face made Julia falter and hesitate. He stopped in his tracks. Around them the music continued; the low insistent drumbeat and hollow chants the only sound in the cavernous dark of the tent. The temple guards looked on implacably, and below them circus workers in the rows of seats watched with lazy curiosity, some smoking, some with their arms folded. Julia felt eyes on her as she held her breath and waited for Robert to continue.

Instead, he marched back to her, and her heart sank.

'Julia, you know the character, don't you?'

Sylvie had explained the story of the slave-girl and the goddess as they rehearsed. Julia should know her role; after all, it was hardly a Shakespearean drama. All she had to do was 'waft' around and show some flesh.

'Yes.'

'And what do you feel?' Robert leant down further to her. 'You're a slave, here against your will. About to be made a sacrifice to the goddess of lust and sensuality.' Julia watched him warily, unsure of how to respond.

'I guess ... she's scared,' she faltered, her rebellious thoughts dissolving as she quailed under his ferocious gaze.

'Scared? How perceptive, Julia. I thought they taught you this stuff at dance school.' He straightened up again, and Julia saw his eyes were as dark as thunder.

'We don't have time to develop this here and now. I'll see you after we finish. Just for now, let's concentrate on moving that arse of yours to centrestage. At least make an effort to look sexy, okay?'

Julia felt her heart skip in her chest, and a blush prickled at her cheeks despite her efforts to stay calm. She fixed her eyes on Robert, trying to ignore the snide ripple of laughter coming from the workers sitting in the shadowy depths of the tent. She felt the lights hot on her skin, as though she was burning up with shame and uncertainty.

Robert gave a sharp tug on the chain and started walking again. Julia had no choice but to try to slink along the stage, stretching her arms and legs out in long, swaying movements, trying to keep a hold on her feelings as she felt a mix of hot fury and embarrassment boil inside. Willing herself to concentrate on the routine, she approached the stage and allowed Robert to push her onto the steps of the altar. She lay sprawled over the steps, waiting for her cue and feeling her heartbeat pound as she felt Robert watching her with displeasure. The fabric wrapped around her revealed the curve of her thigh and the fold of her ass, every inch smeared with white body paint. She knew if she moved her legs too far apart she would show a glimpse of her newly waxed sex, hairless and also whitened with panstick. She had dabbed the paint gingerly onto her pussy before the show, advised by Sylvie that any skin let unpainted would stand out naked and pink. Careful to pat the sponge gently over herself, Julia had duly made up every crevice and fold of her sex, feeling a strange pleasure as she did so, as though she were putting on the most insubstantial underwear in the world. The paint covered her whole body, smeared over her limbs, belly and breasts. Last, she covered her face, even brushing a fingertip over her eyelashes and working the paint into her hair so that it hung in clogged grey strands, as though it were carved marble. Sylvie had applied the paint to her back, rubbing it on roughly with great speed. She was practised at her craft, knowing in detail every tiny ritual of preparation and able to perform her act flawlessly every time. Next to her exquisite, precise body, Julia had felt clumsy, as though she were starting to learn all over again.

Now she was aware of the sweat building under the greasy make-up, and the fact that her body was intimately visible under the spotlights. How much could Robert see? Could he tell that she had been waxed and painted even deep between her legs? She lay on the steps with one arm flung over her head and her legs bent out, trying to give an air of lust and abandon, even though the position was awkward and uncomfortable.

He approached now and as planned pulled Julia to her feet by her hair. As he reached for her, she saw the brutal look on his face and flinched, scared he would in fact grab her hard by the hair. She saw a flicker of some human feeling in his eyes as she drew back, and he winked at her.

'Relax, it's all theatre,' he whispered, as he slipped his hand under the back of her head so gently Julia was taken by surprise. Giddily, she clicked back into her role and rose to stand in front of him, holding her head back as though he really were pulling on her with all his force. As he thrust her forward up the steps, Julia wanted badly to turn and search his face for another sign of warmth, to see if he had softened his opinion of her, but she knew she had to concentrate on the next part of the dance and forced herself to focus on her performance.

She swayed upwards, climbing as though she was approaching an alluring but terrible fate, sometimes stumbling as she mounted the steps. Behind her, she knew the whole tent was watching as she approached Sylvie, whose motionless figure, covered in shimmering gold, was lit by the flickering torches.

Sylvie wore a bikini that was sewn to make it look like filigree metal, the embroidered and beaded bra cupping her breasts with flame-like tongues of gold fabric. She wore a headdress worked in metal wire and sprayed with gold, a beaded belt that wrapped round her belly and hung down to the strip of brocade that she wore between her legs as a simple thong. Her gaze was heavy-lidded and unblinking as she stared impassively into the dark distance. Julia approached as though she were worshipping an idol, and sank to her knees in front of the altar, stretching out before Sylvie in a pose of utter surrender. She rested with her hands spread palms down, her back to the audience, shoving her ass in the air and arching her back so that her body had the curved pose of a supplicant. She imagined herself begging for mercy at the feet of a goddess.

Now Sylvie started to move with fluid and graceful precision, stretching out her arms as though she were a bronze statue. She struck several poses, one flowing into another as she pulled her limbs into breathtaking contortions. The first time she saw it, Julia had thought she had bones missing. Her joints could turn in ways that looked utterly wrong – curving her legs backward over herself to rest her feet on her shoulders like a scorpion's tail; rolling forward and coming into the splits; lifting her legs to gracefully frame her face as she hooked her knees behind her head. While she did all this, Sylvie made it seem totally effortless – in fact she moved as though she loved it, twisting her body with an expression of immense pleasure, as though she possessed an unnatural control over herself.

As she went through her sequence of slow, strange positions, Julia was to dance as though bringing the idol to life with her devotions. She used moves that suggested the dances of ecstasy of Sufis, throwing her body forward and pulsing back and forth as though heaving with huge breaths, brushing her fingertips along the stone, rolling along the altar and reaching up to stroke Sylvie's legs. Around the foot of the altar, the temple guards were starting to roll and tumble in acrobatic sequences, framing the tableau of the two women under the spotlight with dynamic flourishes.

Julia moved with a rhythmic sensuality, aware all the time of her costume constantly slipping from her shoulder and the danger that her breasts would fall from the loose confines of the dress. When they'd rehearsed the moves, Julia had felt breezily confident that she could dance like this easily. Now, onstage before the critical presence of Robert and the other workers, she felt uneasily as though her moves were faked, as though she were putting on an act that was transparently contrived. Julia ran her white hands over the lines of Sylvie's body, trying to tease her to move further, aware that her hands were shaking. She had a feeling that she was pleading with Sylvie to move faster, to get the act over with so she could run back to her caravan and curl up in bed. She wanted to hide herself, painfully aware that with every move she was showing her nakedness to strangers who had treated her with rough indifference. Desperately, she kept circling Sylvie, trying to remember her moves from rehearsal but aware that she was missing cues. When she met Sylvie's eyes the harsh fury in them gave her a lurch in her stomach that she knew meant she'd fucked up. To someone as obsessively, proudly professional as Sylvie, failure would be unforgivable. She gritted her teeth and continued to dance, going through the moves mechanically and as well as she could manage while feelings of shame washed over her.

The music grew in volume as they approached the finale. To Julia, the loud drumbeat was ominous and forbidding. She positioned the glasses as they'd practised, aware of the cold hostility emanating from Sylvie, who nevertheless continued to move flawlessly through her routine. Her hand shook as she placed a glass on Sylvie's breast, and she heard a sharp grunt of anger from the woman's throat, making her even more recklessly despairing. As the chanting in the background became faster and more intense, Julia lifted the clay bottle of wine she was to pour over Sylvie, knowing that in a few moments she would have to try to kiss this woman, who probably wanted to kill her and might actually do so after the show. They'd practised the moves several times, and Julia had secretly enjoyed the feel of Sylvie's soft skin under her hands, the heat of her mouth and the lingering kiss that they finished the act on. She wasn't prudish about being intimate with a woman and found the whole routine quite surprisingly tender, liking the feel of Sylvie's breast in her hand and the thought of the audience getting horny.

Now, though, it had all gone wrong and Julia knew leaning down and kissing Sylvie was going to be a terrifying experience. She swung the bottle hopelessly towards Sylvie and watched, horrified, as she caught her arm against a glass and it tumbled to the ground, crashing sharply on the floor and shattering into a hundred shards. The drumbeat continued, but Julia stood frozen behind Sylvie, unable to move as her worst nightmare became real.

5

Julia stood outside the caravan, wearing Joe's old shirt over her costume and feeling as though she were waiting outside the headmaster's office. Her act had been a disaster, she was painfully aware of that, and Robert had summoned her to see him after the rehearsal. She was glad to have an excuse to avoid Sylvie's furious reprisals, but the thought of a dressing down from the ringmaster was painful. After the debâcle onstage, Sylvie had abruptly stormed off and only Joe had shown any kindness to her, offering her his shirt and wrapping it round her shoulders in a tender gesture that had only made her feel closer to tears. Robert had said little to her, but gave her a tired look that Julia interpreted as disgust, before he turned back to the show to concentrate on the next act. She'd felt wretched since then, as though awaiting a court appearance with Robert as her judge.

His caravan was a sleek silver lozenge, sitting right on the edge of the site slightly apart from the others. Inside, a light shone dimly, and Julia could hear the low sound of music playing.

She knocked tentatively, curious despite herself to see what his living quarters were like. When the door opened, she was greeted by the sweet smell of incense and Robert standing in bare feet, inviting her in. She entered the caravan with a mix of trepidation and excitement – it wasn't how she'd wanted to get him on his own, but the thought of a private audience in such a tightly confined space was stirring her blood.

'Would you like a drink, Julia?' Robert was reaching into a cupboard and bringing out glasses. The sight of them reminded her instantly of her ham-fisted performance earlier, and she cringed inwardly. Nodding dumbly, she took a look round while he poured red wine for them. The sitting room was a microcosm of a circus tent – silk drapes hung across the windows and the wood was painted with intricate dark designs like an old gypsy caravan. Stretching over the sofa was a well-packed bookshelf, and more books were sitting on a stack on the table. She took in elegantly carved wooden marionettes hanging from a cupboard door and the small framed pictures hung on the walls. Julia studied one, curious that a man should live in a space so beautifully decorated. It was an Indian painting, a delicate working of a couple lying under a star-filled sky, the woman with her legs spread wide, the man approaching with a huge curved erection. Julia looked with fascination at the exquisitely painted figures, the serene expressions on their faces, and the patient attention that the painter showed to the minute intricacies of their flesh.

'The beauty is in the detail, don't you think?' Robert handed Julia a glass of wine and stood behind her calmly studying the picture. 'Never fails to inspire me.'

Julia thought she heard a teasing edge in his voice, and hoped fervently that he could be distracted from the events of the afternoon. When she turned back to smile at him, however, he was slumped in the sofa, rubbing his eyes distractedly. 'Have a seat, Julia. We've got a lot to discuss.'

Julia obeyed, sitting on the couch opposite. The deep cushions were so soft she was forced either to sit ramrod straight or sink back till she was almost lying supine. She sat up, crossing her legs awkwardly under herself and trying to look attentive, aware that Robert was

observing her thoughtfully as she fidgeted. His choc-
olate-brown eyes studied her as though she was a chess
piece and he was considering his next move. He let his
gaze follow the line of her shirt buttons, down to the
nervously restless hands in her lap.

'What is it you're scared of?' Robert spoke with the
lazy intensity Julia remembered from the audition, and
she felt suddenly as though she were under the same
powerful scrutiny. His easy confidence both unsettled
and aroused her, and she felt his question creep under
her skin. With a shiver, she was reminded that under
Joe's shirt she wore only the thin white wrapper. She
felt as vulnerable as if she were sitting naked under
Robert's eyes.

'Getting it wrong?' she asked hopelessly. 'I'm scared
of missing my cue, and fucking up the whole show, I
suppose.'

'Julia, without being cruel, one nameless dancer dropping a glass will not fuck up the whole show.' The
comment stung. 'What will, however, let the show
down, is if one of our performers is up onstage going
through the motions. I couldn't care less if the whole set
came crashing down around you.' He paused. 'This circus is about arousal, Julia. About getting horny. What I
want from you is a mind-fuck. You can't just wriggle
your ass and turn me on.' Julia felt the white-hot shock
of his words, so intimate and direct. Was he still talking
about the show? Was he bluntly telling her he didn't
want to fuck her? Robert seemed to read her mind:

'What you fear is often the source of your most
powerful sexuality. What makes you angry, what dis-
gusts you, even. What were you thinking of, this afternoon? What is it you really desire?'

Julia hesitated, her mind racing. How should she react
to this? She didn't know if Robert was offering a challenge or asking a rhetorical question. As she sipped at

her wine, playing for time, she remembered the photo of Josephine Baker, curling over on her back with an expression of tense joyous sensuality. The image of a woman so explosively sexual, so dynamic and vibrant, was what had driven her through dance school.

'I want to blow everyone away,' she heard herself blurt out.

Robert remained silent, waiting, it seemed, for Julia to elaborate. When she stayed silent, feeling embarrassed, he spoke in a voice so soft Julia wasn't sure she'd heard him right.

'Take off the shirt, Julia.'

She felt a thrill of uncertainty run through her, and her stomach flipped with shock. A delicious buzz of warmth started between her legs as she raised her eyes to Robert's, questioningly.

'Take it off.' He nodded at her, locking his eyes on hers.

As if mesmerised, Julia reached for the top button of the shirt and worked it loose. She held Robert's gaze as she undid the buttons, feeling as though she were stripping for a teacher. Something told her it was wonderfully, dangerously wrong to be undressing for Robert alone. He sat relaxed in his chair, impassive, as he had during her audition. Julia pulled the shirt off and sat in her revealing wrap, now crumpled and ridden up. She had wiped off the panstick with cold cream, but traces of it remained in the folds of her skin, white rims of paint rubbed into her fingernails and between her toes. She knew that under the short fringe of the wrap, her pussy was still brushed with make-up, and she thought of her painted clit with a frisson of desire as she wondered what Robert would ask of her next.

'Close your eyes.'

Julia complied, giving in to the irresistible feeling of being under Robert's control.

Robert stood up, placed his glass on the table and disappeared through the curtain that separated his bedroom from the living area. Julia felt disorientated, able to hear his footsteps but unable to see what he was doing. She waited, feeling her breath start to quicken and the tightly wound fabric of the wrap crush her breasts with every inhalation. The friction against her nipples was fantastic, and she felt them stiffen with pleasure, hoping Robert was getting a good look at her as she sat nearly panting on his couch. As she heard Robert re-enter the room and move around, she pressed her thighs together as tightly as she could, feeling her muscles clench against her naked clit and send a warm pulse through her body. She suddenly noticed how hot the caravan was; after a June day the temperature inside one of these metal boxes was close and intense. A film of sweat was building on her top lip, and she licked it away, wishing she could feel Robert's mouth on hers. She was aching to feel his skin against her.

'You're getting hot, aren't you?' Robert's voice was coming from the sofa again, commanding her to agree. She nodded, shivering, as even the sound of his voice was a caress against her skin. There was an agonising moment of silence while she waited for his next move.

'How do your tits feel?'

She wanted to open her eyes and move towards him, dying to cross the space between them. The tension of being watched and questioned was almost unbearable, forcing her to admit her feelings to a virtual stranger. Still, wanting to prove herself willing, she played along.

'They're aching. My dress is rubbing against them.'

'Good. Concentrate on that feeling. You really have got beautiful tits. I like to think of them aching. Now tell me about your pussy.'

Julia let a low moan escape from her half-open mouth, not knowing how to respond. She wished he would just touch her, let the tension ease a little – but realised this was what he wanted, to observe her as she got more and more turned on and less able to control her reactions. She rocked back and forth gently, trying to press herself against the cushions.

'Are you wet?'

Julia nodded, unable to admit her state of arousal in words.

'Now open your eyes.' Julia was expecting to see Robert opposite her, and instead was shocked to find a full-length mirror facing her, her own dishevelled reflection looking back at her with startled eyes and flushed cheeks. She saw just how exposed her costume made her, the full curve of her breasts straining against the low, slashed bodice, one nipple peeking from the top, a sliver of a rosy-pink crescent. With her legs folded under her, and in the soft lamplight of the caravan, her sex was hidden in the shadows, but it was apparent that she was free of underwear.

Robert was holding the mirror upright, watching her with amusement.

'Pull up your dress, have a look at yourself.'

Julia hesitated, feeling as though she were being pulled into one of the perverse games Sylvie had warned her about. But Robert was watching, waiting for her. If she refused she'd be conceding defeat, and she had the feeling it could be the end of her circus career.

Leaning back, Julia slowly lifted the hem with one hand, exposing the hairless V of her mons, letting Robert examine her as she lingered over her reflection in the mirror. She was delighted with how slutty she looked, like a slave-girl displaying herself proudly.

'It's a beautiful sight, Julia.' Robert took a sip of his wine, looking down at her as she admired her reflection. 'The audience is your mirror. You have to treat them as a lover, a mass of lovers. When you're up there, I want you to be as wet as you are now. I want you to be so dizzy with wanting you can hardly stand. If you break a glass or make a wrong move, let the fear turn you on more. Imagine Sylvie's anger. Play to it, play with it. What the audience wants is intimacy, they want to understand you: why, how ... and *whom* you desire. If that includes your darker emotions, it only makes it more intense. Don't be afraid to show your true feelings.'

As Robert spoke, Julia felt he was drawing out her essence, relaxing her and at the same time exciting her further. Was he goading her into admitting that he made her horny? She wanted to spill out an admission of her desire now, show him clearly what she wanted. It was obvious how ready she was for sex, how much she needed to be touched, felt and fucked. Could she ask him now, simply, to put an end to this tortuous arousal and lay her down on the couch?

'And the last secret of the circus, Julia.' She looked up at him, her eyes hooded, sultry, heavy with longing. They smiled at each other, understanding what must come next. Julia reached up to unfasten the clasp that held her wrap, feeling the heartbeat bouncing in her chest and willing Robert to come to her.

He laid the mirror to one side and approached slowly. Julia could see the size of the bulge in his trousers, knew his cock was stiff with longing. She couldn't wait to touch it, feel the heat of his arousal in the palm of her hand. As he reached her, Robert reached down and cupped Julia's face in his hands. Her mouth watered as he leant in to whisper to her.

'The last secret is that we never give it all away at once.'

She felt herself suddenly bereft as he dropped his hands and walked away, letting the atmosphere hang terribly between them, a humid, empty silence that made Julia want to scream with frenzied frustration. He busied himself clearing the table, putting away the mirror, while Julia felt the fury rise in her yet again, and whether she was shaking with want or anger was immaterial.

'Impatience is something you need to learn to get over, Julia. I want you to go to bed now. Fall asleep and dream about fucking.'

Julia was a blur of white as she stumbled across the site, not knowing where she was going but just aware she had to move, fast, get far away from Robert and his games that had left her nearly deranged with frustration. She headed blindly into the dark, taking deep lungfuls of the cold night air and shivering as the breeze brushed over her skin. Ahead of her a knot of the circus people sat round a small fire, their voices a low murmur in the dark. Julia veered away from them, desperate to avoid meeting anyone, thinking vaguely she might dive into the black tangle of the forest that edged the site and lose herself in the night.

She didn't see the tall figure break away from the fire and follow swiftly behind her. When his shout rang out across the site, it pulled her up short, but she turned to face him with all the built-up tension of the past hour still coursing through her veins. He caught up with her, breathing heavily and swearing as he struggled through a patch of thick mud. His face was obscured by darkness, but Julia recognised the lingering smell of diesel and the burly outline of Joe's figure.

'I'm going for a walk,' she snapped, aware that she was taking out her anger on this blameless guy – the only one in the company who'd shown her any real warmth. 'Is that a problem?' She couldn't help the waspish sting in her voice, at that moment she wanted to hurt someone – preferably Robert, but Joe was easier.

'Actual fact, I don't give a fuck what you do. But I'd like my shirt back.' Julia realised she'd left it in Robert's caravan when she stormed out, and that Joe was standing in front of her shirtless. Against the faint light of the campfire she could see his muscular silhouette, the taut curves of his biceps as he crossed his arms and waited. The firelight flickered over his skin, and Julia felt a familiar pang of desire to feel a man's hard smooth skin against hers.

'Am I supposed to hang about here half-naked all night, or are you going to give me it back?' he asked sharply, matching the tone of her voice.

'I don't have it,' she admitted, feeling smaller. 'I left it in Robert's caravan.'

'Oh, I see.' Joe sounded amused.

'See what? We were discussing the show.'

'I'm sure you were. And I'm sure he got you all worked up. I know how he operates, Julia.' Joe came closer, so Julia could smell the mix of sweat, diesel and wood-smoke from him. 'I bet you're panting for a fuck.'

Julia couldn't deny it. Goosebumps were rising on her skin with the chill of the night air; Joe was so close she could feel his warm breath on her face.

'I think he's got you so wet you're dizzy. Has he, Julia? I bet he didn't even touch you.' With this, Joe reached out and traced a line over Julia's face with his finger, running the tip across her mouth, pressing against her bottom lip. Without thinking, Julia opened her mouth and let him slip his finger inside. Being touched was such a welcome shock that before she knew it she was sucking on it hungrily. She hardly cared that he tasted of ash and metal, the roughness of his fingertip a harsh abrasion against her soft, wet tongue.

'He's a head-fuck, that man. Nothing more. You'll not get to feel his cock in you.' Joe pulled his finger from her mouth and dragged his hand down her neck, towards

the top of her breasts. 'He could talk to you for hours.'
Julia felt the back of Joe's hand stroke the front of her
wrap, teasing her nipples to stiffness. His voice was a
melodic accompaniment to his touch, his low soft
brogue lulling her into a trance-like state as he pulled at
her tits, kneading them under his workman's hands.

'Did he tell you his theories, Julia? About how you
should feel when you're being watched?'

'Yes.' Julia's voice was a low growl, half resentful of
Joe's presumptions, yet enjoying the fact he was talking
about Robert as he worked at her nipples. 'He wanted to
see me turned on.'

'And did he?'

Wordlessly, Julia took Joe's wrist. She lifted the hem
of her dress and moved his hand to her sex, letting him
feel for himself how wet she was. In the blanket of
darkness, she could only see the murky outline of Joe's
bulk, but the sensation of his fingers reaching into her,
slipping into her pussy and gently curling inside her
was magnified to an even greater intensity. She felt the
pressure of his thumb against her clit as he worked it
over, circling the hard nub of her excitement.

Though Joe's fingers were thick and agile, she still
felt an ache of want in her pussy, and knew she needed
the whole length of a cock inside her. She'd spent the
night in a state of almost unbearable arousal, and
thought if she didn't get to relieve the pressure soon she
might go insane. Her whole body was tensed with desire
and she moved onto Joe's hand so that his fingers
pushed deeper into her, stifling a moan as she did so.

'Oh, you are ready for a fucking, aren't you, girl?' Joe
seemed to read her mind. 'I think I'm going to have to
take you right here on the grass.'

'Yeah?' said Julia. 'So close to the campsite? What if
we get caught?' She threw a nervous glance towards the
fire, where she could hear the voices of the workers

laughing and chatting, the wood crackling as it burned. Even so, her knees were weakening and she knew she wouldn't argue if Joe pushed her down into the mud and fucked her in full view of the whole site.

'I'm going to unwrap you first, or Eva'll have my balls on a plate.' He reached to unfasten her dress and pulled the cotton roughly down so that her breasts bounced free and she felt the cold night air stimulate her skin. She gasped at the sudden change in temperature, feeling totally vulnerable as she stood naked in the open air only yards from the company. Joe was running his hands over her, turning her around and pushing her gently but firmly to the ground so she dropped onto all fours. She felt her knees sink into the wet mud as she waited impatiently for Joe to satisfy her, spreading her legs wide and pushing her ass against his thighs. Behind her, he knelt down and grabbed her by the waist, holding his stiff, fat prick and guiding it towards her freshly shaved slit. As she felt the cold earth under her hands, Julia dug her nails into the mud and bucked against Joe, feeling the rod of his glans slip against her and nudge at her wetness.

'I need you to fuck me.' Julia was in charge now, impatient to be filled with the swollen weight of his cock, heedless of the cold and the dirt underneath them.

As his length slid suddenly into her, Julia inhaled sharply, a rush of pleasure taking over and compelling her to lean even further into the mud, wanting to feel her face against the wet grass, to feel herself sink into the earth and be surrounded by the sensations of hot flesh, cold earth and black night. She lay her cheek on the ground and let him fall into a hard urgent rhythm as he fucked her, the only sound now the noises from the campfire and Joe's low grunts, his body concentrated solely on pumping into her, pulling her back and forth on his cock.

'This is what I need.' Julia felt words spilling out of her open mouth, a desire to hold a conversation with Joe welling up in her, wanting to hear him talk again as Robert had, with that authoritative perversity that had got her so horny. 'I want him to watch while you fuck me, Joe'.

She felt Joe bang hard against her hips, grinding his cock into her, her words seeming to encourage him to fuck her even deeper, as though he wanted to drive Robert out of her head with the force of his thrusts. Though he was silent he gave her all the answer she needed with the relentless pounding of his hips, working gradually faster. Julia felt him stiffen inside her and knew he was on the brink of coming.

'Think of him and play with yourself,' he said, voice low. In the dark, a twisted smile grew on Julia's lips as she reached to finger herself, imagining Robert watching as she crouched naked on the ground, mud smeared over her knees, pushed under her fingernails and smudged on her cheek as she rubbed her face against the ground. As Joe slowed his movements and started fucking with huge drawn-out thrusts, she pictured Robert's face, intense with jealousy and burning to watch her come. Would he talk to her as he fucked her?

'Are you thinking of him? While I fuck you? Do it. Think of him and bring yourself off.' Joe's voice was commanding and Julia felt herself rushing into a well of dark ecstasy as she lost herself in her fantasy, rubbing her clit roughly while Joe heaved into her, whispering encouragement, willing her to join him as he reached his climax, the two of them thinking of the ringmaster, working each other to a point of frenzy as they shared their fantasy.

As Julia came she stretched forward, sprawling face first into the mud, her hips writhing against the ground and Joe's cock pulsing into her as he shared her orgasm, both of them barely managing to conceal the noise of their climax as they fell together, each holding tight to the hard warm body of the other and clinging on, rolling into the dark on a wave of oblivion.

They lay together panting for a moment, Julia feeling the grit digging into her hip as she regained awareness, realising she was now covered in mud and grass stains. Shakily, she reached behind them to where Joe had dropped her wrap on the grass, suddenly feeling the cold breeze again and anxious that someone might have seen them. She held the wrap round herself and turned to Joe who lay on his back, breathing heavily.

'I guess that makes two favours I owe you,' she said. 'You're some performer.'

'Star of the show,' he replied, pulling Julia down to give her a warm, affectionate kiss. 'I'd like to see Robert follow that act.'

'With some constructive criticism, no doubt,' Julia agreed grimly. 'In fact I think I'd rather have a hot shower and an early night.'

'Ah yes, you'll need your beauty sleep, darlin'. First show tomorrow.'

Julia sighed, remembering the real reason she was stuck in a field near Brighton. The memory of her disastrous rehearsal was still a sore point.

Joe propped himself up on his elbow and put his arm round Julia's neck.

'Sweetheart, you'll knock them dead. All you need to remember is how angry Robert got you tonight, and how much I'll want to fuck you again after the show.' He looped a strand of her hair behind her ear. 'We'll be watching you, babe. Don't forget.'

6

People had been arriving since half eight. Buses from Brighton Pier pulled up at the entrance, emptying crowds of flamboyant audience members at the gates. People filed through the box office before being released onto the site, rambling through the sideshows and beer tent. A growing, excitable babble built up. The crowd was a varied mix of Bohemian queens, trendy art students and dressed-up partygoers; many wore feather boas, glitter and false eyelashes. Everyone was hyped-up and mischievous.

The backstage area was separated from the public gaze by a tall fence, behind which the circus people were still working, making last-minute adjustments to costumes and stage lighting. Julia noticed a subtle difference in the atmosphere – since the patrons had started arriving she felt for the first time less of an outsider. She sensed an underlying jubilance among the crew, noticing that even Rachel allowed herself a sultry smile as she surveyed the crowd. The other performers curtly acknowledged her presence, their earlier curiosity vanished now that it was show night.

As she hurried from her caravan to the tent Julia peered curiously through the wire grid at the audience outside. She caught the eye of a couple of guys in check shirts standing by the fence, who nudged each other and whispered loudly as she hurried past. She was secretly delighted at their reaction, as though she was part of a mysterious secret cult that the world stared at in fascinated awe. She couldn't help giving her ass a sexy little wiggle as she passed them, a tease just to intrigue them further.

Long before the show started the circus was already in full swing, people spilling from the beer tent to wander round the sideshows. Small tents around the midway housed 'teaser' acts – pole-dancers and fire-eaters working the crowd up with mini-performances. Meanwhile 'Butchers' – cigarette girls in mini-skirts and bobbed platinum wigs – circled the crowd. Trays hung round their necks, carrying glossy programmes and chocolate kisses, while their low-cut tops afforded tan-talising glimpses of flesh. The sound of loud dance music floated around the field. Although the warm evening sun still lingered, lights glittered over the tent and the whole site had taken on a lively dangerous feel, as though the game of teasing the audience had just started. Julia felt her senses sharpened with the excite-ment she only got before a performance; as though everything were more vivid, colours brighter and sounds louder. It was a similar thrill that she felt when pre-paring to meet a new lover, nervous energy making her wide-eyed and shaky, while her mouth watered and tingles rushed over her skin. At the thought of writhing about onstage half-naked, she felt another lurch of nerves, this time a sexually charged jolt that made her clench her thighs together and bite her lip. Her fear had turned into impatient anticipation. A fresh, jittery sense of daring seemed to have appeared within her, as though her fear were compelling her to reckless confi-dence. When Sylvie reminded her sharply that she had to make it perfect tonight, Julia smiled and blew her a kiss. It was all a matter of attitude, she reckoned.

The air was close, hot and perfumed. Hubbub from the audience, occasional whistles and claps interspersed the music that throbbed from the vast speaker stacks. With a live restless audience cackling and shouting, the stage waiting and lit up, and Sylvie ready on the altar, Julia felt a sudden change. Waiting in the wings, she could virtually feel the desire emanating from the audience. She knew exactly how she must move, exactly how her body should feel. It was as though the expectation of the audience gave her new courage.

As Robert dragged her on she felt the white-hot lights on her skin, the stirring of the audience as curious eyes fixed on her pale white figure. The music infused her movements with a wanton sensuality, compelling her to let the wrap slip further over her shoulder, enjoying the sense of transgression as her naked breast threatened to spill out. A murmur from the audience rewarded her daring, and she managed to slip a wink at Joe as she passed his motionless oiled figure, waiting to start the acrobatic sequence. With a flicker of recognition, he acknowledged her new confidence by raising one eyebrow. The gesture was imperceptible to anyone else, but to Julia it meant she was on track for a dazzling performance. Tossing her hair back, she approached the altar, ready to dance.

Julia stood over Sylvie, holding the wine jug high over her body, letting a thin trickle of liquid pour into the glass below. Not a drop spilt. Sylvie held her pose perfectly as Julia filled each glass; both of them tense with the knowledge of what would follow. A roar of applause started, filling the tent as Julia poured the contents of the wine jug over Sylvie, one hand loosely on her hip as she slowly started over-filling the glasses, allowing the liquid to spill over and run down Sylvie's skin in dark red rivulets. She let the noise of cheers and whistles wash over her, enjoying the response and the energy of the crowd who had been fired up all night and were now letting go uproariously. The volume grew as the drumming increased in tempo and pounded out over the speakers, the act approaching its climax as Julia liberally glugged wine over Sylvie's body and elegantly reached down to lick it from her skin. As she did so she met Sylvie's eyes and the barest flicker of a satisfied nod passed between them. Julia allowed herself a surreptitious smile as she put her lips to Sylvie's in a lingering kiss, knowing that the performance had been a well-oiled machine. As the girls sank into their kiss a raucous barrage of heckles swelled with the applause. Julia could taste the powdery make-up on Sylvie's lips and the slight tang of salt from her sweat, and the heady sensation mixed with the clamorous reaction from the crowd tasted like the sweetest success. The girls held the pose as the lights dimmed and darkness veiled their intertwined figures. In the shadows, still bent over Sylvie's body and panting with exertion, Julia felt the adrenaline speed through her veins and a vast surge of pride well within her. She had not disgraced herself – in fact, she had excelled. The drawn-out applause from the pit confirmed what she already knew, and she left the stage with a joyful bounce in her step.

Backstage Sylvie rewarded her with a furious hug and an earnestly whispered 'Bravo, girl', before she left to clean the make-up from her body and change costume. After the interval she was on again, this time on trapeze. Julia knew that as the new girl she was being broken in gently, only appearing in the temple act and the finale. For the moment, it was all the excitement she needed. She sat on a crate in the wings and allowed herself to relax, feeling the sweat dry on her skin and her heart rate return to normal.

She cracked open the beer Henri handed to her as a congratulatory drink. The cold fizz had a welcome, refreshing taste, and it could have been champagne as far as Julia was concerned. She'd made it. Her first professional performance, with Robert, Joe and three hundred strangers watching closely. Just as it had the day before, the act had turned her on. Only this time, she'd had the howls of a full house to raise the temperature and keep her pushing herself to give the sexiest performance of her life. She could see now why Sylvie loved it so much. From her perch in the wings, Julia watched, as thrilled as the audience to see the daring and skill of her fellow performers.

Even if Robert was a strange sadistic control freak, she had to concede he knew how to put a show together. Every act revolved around a theme, involving massive set changes and elaborate costumes, each time drenching the stage in a new atmosphere and intense, lush surroundings. Robert himself was the thread that pulled the whole thing together, and Julia grudgingly admired his charisma as he played with the audience, whipping them up to fever pitch as he narrated. Around him, the performers worked so hard the sweat dripped from their bodies.

The act that followed the temple scene was based on acrobatics, a towering human pyramid growing gradually from centre stage. It was built of a solid wall of muscular guys standing on each other's shoulders, bodies oiled and glistening. Julia watched with a tinge of envy as Sarah ran past her, to somersault onstage before being caught and hauled hand-over-hand up the pyramid, passed between the men. She obviously enjoyed feeling their strong arms enwrap her and roll her towards the top, planting her feet on their bare chests and sliding slowly upwards. Robert walked round the pyramid, cracking a whip and shouting incitements to the men to hold firm. Julia admired the grace of the men as well as their physiques – although they must have been straining under phenomenal weight their faces remained utterly impassive, tense and stock-still, proudly staring straight ahead. She craned her neck back to see Sarah reach the top of the pyramid, where she sat on the shoulders of the two men beneath her and stretched languorously, before suddenly flipping over, tumbling through the air and landing square on her feet.

Henri's knife throwing act blew Julia away. The lighting was strong and dramatic, catching the angular planes of Henri's face, throwing his silhouette into striking relief. Rachel, in a long red dress, was strung up on a six-foot square target, bound to the metal slats with black silk scarves at her ankles and wrists. In the dark pooled shadows around the stage motorbikes circled, the riders hooded and wearing fingerless leather gloves, revving the engines loudly. Everything was black and red – the scene reminded Julia of a modern vampire flick; Henri with a floor-length cape and high collar, strutting around with a cool unflappable demeanour. Dry ice filled the stage and drifted round his ankles as he opened his cloak to show a row of glittering knives tucked into the lining. Rachel twisted in her bonds, as if fearfully trying to escape, while Henri stood tall and erect, taking aim.

He threw the small thin-bladed knives with incredible precision. The silver shafts glinted cruelly as they sped through the air, slicing through the silk of Rachel's dress and falling to bury themselves in the stage. Henri's gaze never wavered. Julia watched, rapt, as he slowly cut Rachel's dress from her, slicing the fabric across her thigh to reveal her stocking-clad legs but never scratching her. As the bikes circled closer and closer to the target, Rachel was finally left hanging with just a few scraps of red silk covering her body. With the last four knives in Henri's hand and his eyes fixed on his target, the stage fell silent, the bikes' engines a low purr.

Then he threw the knives in rapid succession, their

blades flashing as they flew towards Rachel, hitting the four points where she was bound to the target, slicing instantly through the scarves. She dropped from the scaffold only to be caught, gracefully, by Joe on his monstrous black Ducati. From backstage, Julia watched closely as he held her curled against him with one arm, steering with the other. She wasn't jealous exactly, but the sight of Rachel's half-naked body lying across Joe's saddle raised her hackles. The bike circled the stage one more time, Rachel clutching Joe with a smug smile on her face as the audience whistled and shouted. Then Julia realised they were coming straight for her as Joe rode his bike towards the curtains to exit.

As they passed, Joe caught her eye and gave her a conspiratorial wink. She inhaled the mix of diesel fumes and sweat, and it gave her a delicious reminder of Joe's skin and their last encounter.

'Oh, the ballerina!' Rachel shrieked, picking up on Joe's wink. 'She's a little gauche for your tastes, Joe, surely?' Clinging onto Joe, Rachel gave Julia a catty smile.

'Hi, Rachel,' Julia responded, as sickly-sweet as she could. 'Great act. I just loved watching Henri throw knives at you.'

Rachel narrowed her eyes viciously. 'And it was great to see Robert dragging you around. He's really got you hooked, hasn't he?' She slid off Joe's lap and came closer to Julia, putting an arm round her shoulders. Julia did her best not to recoil, unwillingly letting Rachel turn her towards Robert, who stood backstage preparing his next entrance. Rachel took hold of Julia's chin, forcing her to look.

'That man, my dear, is one of the best ringmasters in Europe. He's put on shows for royalty. He's worked with the best performers, in the most extreme and exotic shows ever staged. What the hell do you imagine you can offer him?'

Rachel let Julia go and walked off, her spike heels giving her a slight sway. Julia watched her go, angry yet fascinated by the power and force of the woman. Her body was long and sinewy; she moved with a controlled energy that expressed a darkly potent sexuality. The scraps of red silk clinging to her revealed a long complicated tattoo rising up her thigh, thorns and roses tangling across her skin. Julia noticed there was a black snake curled around the rose stem, a forked tongue flickering upwards towards Rachel's sex. A formidable enemy. As Rachel passed Robert she placed her hand on his stomach and reached up to kiss him on the cheek. Julia was quite aware she was marking him as her possession – it was a warning.

It was nearly 3 a.m. before the circus was finally finished. After the crowds had left, shuttled back to Brighton by the busload, the crew had a solid two hours of clear-up before they could relax. Julia was assigned to clean the seats, and found herself on her knees wiping up spilt beer in the small hours of the morning. Though exhausted, she knew she was still being given the soft jobs. As she mopped the red plastic seats, she listened to the noises of the stage guys clearing the arena and prepping for the next show. Their shouts echoed round the tent, and Julia found the empty tent's atmosphere strange after the lush, extravagant spectacle that had been the show. A slight mist of dry ice still clouded the air – it smelt like smoking bonfires, spent fireworks. The show had been an explosive success. The whistles, howls and stamping feet of the audience when the show finished had testified to their enjoyment, and Julia's ears were still ringing from the noise.

'That'll do for tonight, Julia.'

She looked up to find Robert standing above her in shirt sleeves. His hair was damp with sweat, and he held two cans of beer in his hand.

'A celebratory drink? Only you'll need to forgo the glass.' He offered Julia a can, looking at her with a wry smile. 'You did well tonight. Time to relax.'

Julia stood and took the beer, dropping the cloth into the bucket with great relief.

'I was starting to think no one in this circus ever relaxes.' She popped open the can and drank a long draught, aware that Robert was watching her movements. Buoyed by her successful performance, she swallowed and looked straight back at him.

'So, how was your first show?' he asked.

'Intense.' Julia nodded. 'You've got some incredible performers here. Just a shame some of them seem to be arseholes.' She thought bitterly of Rachel.

'You think so? I heard you'd been making friends already.' Julia caught the tease in his voice and fought to stop herself from blushing. Had Robert been told about her encounter with Joe?

'Your people aren't what I would call welcoming,' Julia said defensively, and remembered Rachel's hissing, the hard stares of the roustabouts. She thought of Robert's game playing the night before and felt a mix of arousal and shame as she remembered how she'd lain, naked and exposed on his couch. After the rush of the show, her emotions were volatile and she felt like confronting Robert, letting him know she couldn't be so easily manipulated.

'In fact, I'd call them twisted. There's not a sane person in here.' She controlled her voice with difficulty, trying not to let Robert see her agitation.

'Nothing you can't handle, Julia. It's an intense environment, and not an easy way to live. I understand that.' Robert was talking in a reasonable honeyed tone as though Julia were a teenager throwing a tantrum. She felt herself bristle.

'You'll understand, with time, what it's all about.' Robert reached out to rub a smudge of paint from Julia's hairline and the tenderness of the gesture totally disarmed her. She was once again speechless in front of him, her body pulsing with adrenaline and her mind unsure of whether she wanted to fuck him or hit him.

'It's been a long day. Why don't you unwind with the rest of the crew? They'll be having a drink after the clear-up. Good chance to get to know them better, now that the first show's over and everyone's more relaxed.'

He lifted his can of beer to toast her, before turning and walking back to the exit. As he left she suddenly felt herself go limp, the tension of the day overwhelming her and leaving her with a mild buzz of exhaustion. Half of her wanted to follow Robert and slip into his caravan, sneak into bed beside him and press her body against his. But she couldn't stand the thought of being rebuffed yet again, and instead walked listlessly towards the arena where the crew were stretching out on the crates and sitting on the edge of the stage. Julia slipped quietly into a seat aside from the chatting crowd, happy to watch from the sidelines for the moment.

The circus folk turned up gradually, dropping into seats and greeting each other with playful claps on the shoulder or kisses. Julia looked around. For the first time, everyone seemed relaxed. A warm glow was cast over the stage by the remaining house lights, bathing everyone in soft amber light. Sylvie sat cross-legged onstage, chatting with one of the trapeze girls. Half of the performers were still in costume, with T-shirts thrown on over the top and make-up half removed. Laughter rang out in the high vaulted space of the tent and Julia felt a pleasant buzz from the beer as she slouched in her seat. Feeling a little left out, she noticed Henri sitting by himself, staring vacantly at the floor between his feet. Julia approached him tentatively.

'That was amazing, Henri. Really close to the edge with the knives.'

Henri looked up and smiled a little sadly, nodding. He had a soulful quality to his eyes Julia hadn't noticed before, a kind of softness to the pale blue irises that was almost hypnotic. When he smiled, Julia saw the razor sharpness of his cheekbones soften, and a playful expression dance over his face.

'To be honest, I wouldn't have been all that unhappy if your hand had slipped,' Julia admitted, feeling somehow that she could spill her secrets to Henri without fear of him betraying her. He laughed, the sound surprisingly deep and throaty. His freakish angular appearance reminded Julia of a gawky teenager, only with some deeper mystery to him that fascinated the eye.

'Something tells me Rachel has not made a favourable impression?' He whispered this to Julia so that the others couldn't hear. 'She can be a little challenging, Mizz Jones.'

As she sat there, feeling Henri's wiry long-boned body next to hers, Julia found herself surprisingly drawn to his awkward personality. Though his silence and gaunt appearance had been alarming at first, she found that now she thought of him as complicated rather than intimidating. After seeing the utter focus of his knife-throwing and watching his muscles flexing delicately as he threw them, she had new admiration for his slim, bizarre body. She felt she was in the presence of a skilled artist.

'So, is Rachel like that with everyone?' she asked.

'She's a firework. She likes to cause trouble.'

'You could call her a firework. Or you could just call

her a bitch.' Julia couldn't keep the bitterness from her tone.

Henri looked at her, amused. His dark eyes raked over hers, and she felt like some deep gentle force was probing her.

'She really hurt you,' Henri said, his voice more amused than sympathetic. Julia clenched her teeth, refusing to admit all the anxieties that seethed in her heart. She had performed well, but the circus was testing skills other than her dancing ability. Living among these people she felt she had to be constantly on the alert for games and traps.

'Julia, this isn't just a summer job.' She looked up confused. Henri turned and surveyed the crowd who surrounded them, the tattooed, muscular men and the lithe women who laughed with deep throaty amusement as they sipped beer and discussed the night's show. He nodded at the people in the tent.

'We live this way. When we put on a show, it's not merely work. It's just the time we invite strangers to watch us. To watch us play our games.' With a long, white-knuckled finger, he pointed at Sarah.

'Take Sarah. When she's climbing the pyramid, rubbing up against all those lovely glistening bodies –' Henri raised his eyebrow at Julia, teasing her '– she's not just acting a part, Julia. She's doing it for her love of the feel of skin against skin, the desire to climb to the height of sensual experience. They developed the whole act around that idea, the slipperiness of oiled skin, the way you climb over your lover's body as you rise higher.' Henri's voice was low and musical, and Julia felt a shiver run over her skin as he talked. 'When I'm throwing knives at Rachel, it's not an exercise in marksmanship. It's a courtship.'

He paused to see if she had understood. She looked at him, the confusion evident on her face. He smiled, and again Julia saw an expression on his face that seemed tinged with some kind of sadness.

'Will it be easier to understand if I tell you I've wanted Rachel for years? Since she joined us.'

'She knows that?' Julia was startled.

'Of course.' Henri shrugged. 'It's a one-way street, the way I feel about her. But if I didn't feel for her, we couldn't perform together. It's playing out our desires. I want to undress Rachel, but I never will without trickery. And she loves to tease. Power play, you know.' Julia saw the hunger in Henri's eyes, and realised his gaze was fixed on Rachel across the stage, where she was sharing a cigarette with Joe. 'I throw knives with anger as well as lust.' He sighed, dropping his eyes to the ground.

'It's the sweetness of pain, Julia. Part of life's rich tapestry. Why do you think you're acting the part of a slave-girl?'

Julia's face darkened as she considered Henri's suggestion.

'Robert thinks I'm a slave.'

'Not unwillingly, Julia. You're an acolyte of Sylvie.'

'What do you mean?'

'Sylvie is the goddess of sexuality. You've been brought to worship at the altar. Robert takes you to Sylvie to awaken your own desire.'

'This is bullshit.' Julia felt herself growing angry again. 'It's a sex show, Henri, not some philosophy club.' She was taken aback by Henri's raucous high-pitched laughter.

'No, my dear, it's not a philosophy club,' he said. 'But you'll understand more if you stop trying to fight everyone. Play the game.'

'Game? I thought you said it was all for real?'

'Oh the game is real, Julia, very real.' He gave her an enigmatic smile. 'What else is there? Take the two of us, just now. You are a beautiful girl, so brimming with possibility, so full of sexual energy that your own desires confuse you. I'm a strange man offering you my own freakish ideas.'

'What?'

'Play the game, Julia. At the moment, I have the power, you are the one who is lost.'

Julia saw the strength in Henri's body all of a sudden, the years of training and learned skill focused in his lithe sinewy muscles. His eyes were cold, deep and magnetic. Julia felt herself drawn into them.

'But if I tell you that I suffer because of my desire for Rachel, you see how the game changes?'

Julia saw the sadness in Henri's eyes again, and noticed his craggy asymmetry, his singular ungainliness.

'It's all a matter of perception, Julia. Learning to play the hand you have.' He leant in close and spoke in a low voice. 'What if I tell you that I like the pain?' Again, Julia sensed a subtle shift in the atmosphere between them. Henri was looking at her with a strange expression. She sensed a charge to his words.

'There is more to sex than straightforward fucking, Julia. There's a darker side too. Did you ever ask what turns you on?'

'A horny man with a good body usually does it for me.' Julia tried to keep the tone light, but Henri wouldn't relent.

'Is that so? What constitutes a good body? Would you call me horny?'

Julia felt suddenly like she had been trapped in a spider's web – was Henri trying to seduce her? He was regarding her quizzically, lying back and propped on his elbows, with one long leg bent at the knee. Julia now realised she could see the tight crotch of his trousers. He licked his lips.

'Did we cross the line, Julia? Is there tension between us now? Can you imagine me making love to you?' With one bony white hand, he reached out to touch Julia's thigh. The feel of his hand, cool and dry on her skin, was disturbingly intimate, and as he tickled his fingers slowly over her thigh, dancing towards her lap, Julia struggled to stop herself from slapping him in the face. His wheedling tone and the sparse angular beauty of his face fascinated her, but she was almost horrified to think of him trying to fuck her. A mix of repulsion and excitement surged within her – there was a perverse allure to Henri, but he was –

'You don't find me attractive? Does that disgust you? Make you angry?'

Henri seemed to be reading her mind as his hand reached higher, creeping towards the hem of her white wrap. Julia was on the point of pulling away, but something kept her frozen, mesmerised by Henri's actions. She'd never experienced a conversation like this, so direct and intimate that it made her squirm with discomfort.

'How does that make you feel? If I asked to lick your feet, what would you say? Would you hurt me?'

'Hurt you? I don't want to ... I don't want to sleep with you.'

She was aware how feeble her reply sounded, but was still shaken by Henri's reaction: he laughed again, throwing back his head and squealing with a horse-like whinny. She noticed a few heads turning, as the two of them caught the attention of the crowd. She saw Sylvie, leaning with her head on her hands, watching them intently. A silence had fallen in the tent and Julia realised she and Henri were the centre of attention. Across the stage, Joe leant against the scaffolding, sipping at a beer and smiling at her grimly. As her eyes met his he gave her a wink.

'What are you doing to Robert's protégée, Henri?' a girl's voice called out at them, prompting a ripple of laughter in the crowd. Julia felt herself stiffen as she looked warily round the tent. She noticed the bodies lying prone in the heat, still slightly damp with sweat and brushed with stage make-up. Sarah was lying across the lap of one of the roustabouts, her bustier pushed up so that her breasts were loose, almost spilling out of the corset.

'Trying to find out what makes her tick?' Rachel cut in, walking across the stage to where Julia and Henri were sitting. 'You could ask Joe.' Another ripple of laughter. Rachel stood in front of them and put her hands on her hips. Julia felt herself prickle with distaste, looking up at the woman as she stood proudly over them.

'Did you tell her what you really want, Henri? What you enjoy?' Rachel slowly bumped her hips side to side, waving her crotch in front of Henri's face. Julia saw his eyes darken, whether with anger or lust she couldn't tell.

'Give her a bite, Henri,' another voice called out from the back of the tent. Henri ignored the comment, and Julia watched transfixed as he looked up at Rachel's sneering smile. She thought he was almost begging Rachel, though there was a coldness in his face too.

'You want to be careful you don't make me lose concentration, Rachel.'

'In case the knives slip? I know you wouldn't do that to me, darling.'

Rachel leant down and kissed Henri, their faces so close to Julia she could hear the smacking noise as their mouths touched. She saw Rachel's tongue dart between Henri's thin lips and run over his teeth, and heard his sharp intake of breath as Rachel caught his bottom lip between her teeth. Julia knew she was biting him, hard. She heard the softest of moans escape from Henri's throat before Rachel released him and stood back laughing.

'It's a piece of cake, girl. You want to hook someone, all you have to do is find out where your desires meet.' Rachel looked triumphantly at Julia, while Henri reached out to stroke her ankle, his pale hand touching the leather of her boots with almost reverent fascination.

'I like to hurt Henri, and he enjoys the pain.' Rachel spoke with leisurely cruelty, ignoring Henri's caresses before kicking his hand away sharply. 'What's your pleasure, Julia?'

'I like some competition,' Julia hissed, aware once again she was letting Rachel antagonise her. 'Helps me rise to the challenge.'

Her dislike of the woman sent heat coursing through her veins, provoking her to react without thinking. She felt cornered between Rachel's poisonous antagonism and Henri's twisted overtures. Both of them were watching her intently, along with half the performers, who were fascinated at the prospect of a catfight to entertain them. The atmosphere between them crackled electric, neither woman breaking the silence.

Henri finally stood up to whisper something at Rachel. She spat with disgust, but Julia knew his words had defused the situation when Rachel's haughty posture relaxed by a fraction.

Rachel continued to stare at her, one eyebrow raised as though sizing up the competition. Julia held her gaze.

'Fabulous,' Rachel declared finally. 'In that case, let the games begin, sweetheart.'

7

Motors roared into life, engines revving loudly, till the field was full of noise and fumes. Trucks and caravans circled the field before leaving one by one for the motorway. Behind them tyre tracks criss-crossed over the grass, the only remaining sign of the circus's two week occupation.

Julia settled into the passenger seat of Joe's truck cab, ready for a long and deliciously flirtatious drive to Birmingham. Better prepared for the road this time, she wore sandals, a vest top and short denim cut-off skirt, her body lightly tanned from days of practice in the sun, her muscles already stronger and her body leaner than when she'd arrived.

'Been a good run here,' Joe remarked, looking over the site one last time. 'I'm almost sorry to go.'

'Yeah, I'm guessing you've developed a particular fondness for that patch of grass by the fence.' Julia grinned.

'Fuck the grass, girl. I was thinking of a different area entirely. The one you're sitting on, in fact.' Joe had to raise his voice over the old truck's engine as he gunned it over the verge and onto the tarmac road. He swore as the gears crunched, working the accelerator with his foot and pulling hard on the wheel. Julia could see his skin glistening and smell the sweat from him.

'It's a beast to drive, this thing,' he said. 'Be better once we're on the open road and can cruise. You up for a game of I-spy?'

'I can think of better ways to pass the time, Joe.'

'Discussing politics and art, you mean?'

'Of course.'

'Well don't get any funny ideas, young lady. We're in convoy and on a strict schedule. There'll be no rest stops, I'm afraid.'

'Who said anything about stopping?'

Joe grinned his lazy grin, eyes still focused on the road ahead.

'Just as long as you don't distract the driver. We've got a long way to go.'

As they gathered speed on the wider road, Julia felt a rush of exhilaration at the prospect of moving on. Touring life had its drawbacks – cramped conditions and a severe lack of privacy, to say the least – but she relished the chance to pack up and change the scenery every few weeks.

'So you're sure you want to stick with us, babe, or should I drop you off at London?' Joe asked.

'You mean, am I sure I'm cut out for the circus? I thought I was doing okay.'

'Oh, you're doing fine. Just wondered if the freakshow hadn't put you off.'

'You forget I've spent years in the theatre, Joe. I can handle a few tantrums.'

Joe nodded, still concentrating on the road ahead.

'You're enjoying it, then?' he asked.

'I love the show.'

'And the people?'

'They certainly aren't easy,' Julia acknowledged. 'But they are ... fascinating. I think it's a learning curve. And,' she added, 'I've spent the past week so horny I can hardly sit still.' Her words were calculated to prick Joe's interest.

He glanced over to where she was curled on the seat. She had her legs tucked underneath herself like a Buddha, and was pushing her tits up against the seatbelt, letting the hard black strip press into her nipples. She rubbed gently against the edge of the seatbelt, looking up at Joe from half-closed eyes. His gaze dropped again to her nipples – from the way they stuck out proudly through her cotton top, Joe could tell she was aroused.

'It's a treat seeing you strapped up,' he said, playfully. 'You keep rubbing yourself, babe. I could use a little in-flight entertainment.'

He suddenly turned to look in his wing-mirror.

'Shit,' he swore, and slowed down to let Robert's black Merc pull up level with them. Julia felt a warm breeze float in as he wound down the window, and heard Robert shout something she couldn't catch. Joe gave him a thumbs-up in response.

As the Merc revved and speeded up to pass them Julia noticed Robert was alone in the car. Unlike the rest of the crew, crammed into lorry cabs and backseats, Robert obviously didn't like to share his journey with anyone else. She watched as he slowed at each driver's window to pass on his message, finally taking up the head of the convoy.

'What's happening?' she asked.

'You'd better hold on tight, sweetheart. There's rain forecast for this afternoon so we need to gun it up there as fast as possible.'

'You're worried about the weather?'

'You ever tried to put up a tent in a storm?' Joe was concentrating firmly on his driving now, and Julia slid back in her seat to watch the countryside slip past in a green blur, frustration making her clamp her legs together. She was dying to lean over and turn Joe on, but wasn't sure if he'd rebuff her. Since their encounter last week he'd been friendly, but she was pretty sure their relationship wouldn't be anything more serious than the occasional boisterous fuck. He'd flirted with her pretty openly, but Julia had the sense that he was holding back somehow. One afternoon, as he was teaching her to juggle, he'd started by holding her hands out in front of her and pressing his length against her back, so she could feel his cock bobbing lightly against her arse. It had been a struggle to keep her co-ordination, wrapped in his bear hug and trying to concentrate on throwing. Just as she thought things were going to get seriously dirty though, Joe had dropped her arms and moved away. When Julia looked up, surprised, she saw Robert walking away from them. Had he somehow told Joe to back off? Julia remembered Sylvie's warning – about Robert keeping 'a very close' eye on them – and felt a familiar prickle of anger at the his manipulative ways.

'Does Robert have some kind of "no fucking" rule?' she blurted out.

Joe was changing gear as the convoy approached a roundabout that would take them onto the motorway. He flicked on the indicator before turning to her.

'Of a kind. But there's ways round it. It doesn't matter what we do in down time, so long as the show doesn't suffer. Basically he wants to keep us all simmering. Thinks if people develop relationships it'll spoil the show dynamics.'

'So we're to be celibate for the whole tour?'

'No, not quite, babe. There's exceptions to the rule.'

'Such as?'

Joe pulled the truck onto the slip road and Julia felt the cab shake as he accelerated, slipping into the slow lane behind another of the circus lorries. He racked up the speed again before answering. Julia studied his glowing, tanned skin and the curve of his biceps as she waited for his response. The man could have been a pin-up, a rough and sexy lumberjack type with three-day stubble and those big rough hands with dirt ingrained under the fingernails. It made Julia want to jump on him, and to hell with the Highway Code. Finally, he answered, voice hoarse.

'The unspoken law is that you can do what you like so long as there's more than two people present.'

'Really? So I can fuck you if someone else is watching?'

'Yes. Particularly if the someone is Robert.' Joe's voice was emotionless, and Julia couldn't tell what he thought of this idea. Julia gasped, incredulous.

'He likes to watch? He never joins in?'

'No.'

'What is he, then, some kind of peeping Tom?'

'I think you might call him a voyeur. And he likes to explore the darker side. Likes to keep all his workers open to new experiences.'

Julia paused, thinking this over. The thought of fucking under Robert's watchful eye was giving her a rush of adrenaline. Her mouth was watering and her heart rate speeding up. She was taken with a sudden desire to test Robert's rules to the limit.

'Joe,' she said, slowly.

'Yes, mademoiselle?'

'How fast can this crate go?'

'You'd be surprised at the horsepower, actually, darlin'.'

'Good.'

Julia struggled to push the seat belt down around her waist, leaving her top half free. She pulled her vest off in one movement, so she was sitting in her bra, a hot-pink lace concoction trimmed with small bows and underwired so it pushed her tits upward.

'You'll make quite an impression if we get pulled over, you know.' Joe was eyeing her greedily, watching as she pulled open the buttons of her skirt and exposed the sheer net of her matching cerise knickers. 'Now that is a sight for sore eyes.'

'Watch me, Joe.' Julia hardly needed to encourage him, but she felt the sudden need to give him instructions. Talking as she stripped could be a real turn on for Julia, especially as she needed to tell Joe what to do next. Outside the car, the road was heavy with traffic as they approached the exits for Gatwick. Joe was keeping a steady speed up as he turned to watch Julia.

'You liked watching me strapped up, you said?'

As he watched, she stretched out one leg and carefully slid the belt so that it ran between her legs. Leaning forward and holding the belt so it was tightly wedged between her thighs, Julia stretched out to undo Joe's flies. He gave a nervous glance at the traffic beside them, but Julia ignored it. She had no intention of rushing this encounter. It was the first time in days she'd been alone with a man, and she was determined to draw the experience out as long as she could.

She lay back, letting the strap dig in deep between her legs, lazily watching the motorway landscape blur past.

'I love motorways,' she said dreamily. 'There's something kind of sexy about the road, don't you think?'

'Julia, you are honestly the first person I've ever met who'd describe the M23 as sexy.'

Julia ignored him again, slipping into her daydream as they moved fast through the flat landscape, watching the long grey strip of road spin out ahead of them.

'Play with yourself, Joe,' she said quietly, her voice hardly audible over the buzzing and rattling of the truck's engine. Beside her, Joe obeyed silently, and pulled his cock from his fly so that it rested on his lap while he kept one hand on the wheel. Slowly, he ran his hand over the shaft, glancing at Julia as he started to rub himself. Julia felt her throat tighten as she watched, imagining the feel of his skin as he hardened in his hand. There was something fantastically sexy about the surreptitious sex play they were conducting in broad daylight. Around them, cars sped by, intent on their destinations, the drivers and passengers oblivious to the dirty antics of the two people in the truck. The cab was a good two feet higher off the ground than most cars, so Julia knew that only their top halves were visible. As Joe slowly played with his cock, letting it stiffen and bulge to its full length, Julia bent her knees and braced her feet against the dashboard. She let her knees fall open, so that the crotch of her knickers was exposed to the breeze coming in from the wound-down window.

'I love the feel of the wind against my skin,' she said, knowing that Joe was acutely aware of her movements. She could hear him struggling to stay in control, breathing hard through his nose and slowing the movements of his hand.

'I think I'm getting used to having a bare pussy,' she mused, pulling her knickers to the side so that her slit was covered only by the wide black band of the seat belt. The edge of the belt pressed tightly into her skin, exciting her further as she rocked her hips gently to feel the webbing brushing against her clit. Since Eva had waxed her, Julia had been blown away by the increased sensitivity. The slightest movement, even walking, produced a gentle friction on her skin. She would feel a slight tingle every so often to remind her of the smooth, tender flesh between her legs and it gave her a little thrill of exposure. Now, lying back on the slippery faux leather seats of Joe's Bedford, she felt the air – warm, and laced with dusty exhaust smoke circulate around the folds and crevices of her cunt, stroking her as lightly as Joe's eyes were. He was half driving and half watching Julia, curious to get a glimpse of how wet she was.

'Eyes on the road, cowboy,' Julia admonished. She was enjoying her slow torment of Joe as much as the feel of being naked while surrounded by oblivious motorists. 'I want you to concentrate on driving for a minute.' Although Joe was in the driver's seat, Julia knew that she was the one in control. She instructed him to speed up and overtake the vans in front. As they sailed past the dozen or so trucks carrying the circus north, Julia studiously ignored their drivers. She knew they could see her wearing just a pink bra and an enigmatic smile, and was tickled at the thought of their imaginations running wild as they watched her and Joe steadily move forwards up the convoy, till they were running alongside Robert's black Merc.

'Keep us level with him, Joe.' Julia looked to the side to make sure Robert was aware of them. He was. She could see him staring up at her as he kept at a steady sixty miles an hour, hands calmly resting on the steering wheel, face impassive – but definitely interested. Now Julia felt her heart beat faster. Did she dare to play this game? Their truck was straddling the middle lane, she could hear the engine straining to keep up speed. If she was going to make her move she had to do it now.

Keeping her eyes locked on Robert through his closed window, she reached down and with deliberate slowness peeled back the lacy tops of her bra cups. Her breasts were squeezed upwards by the restrictive fabric, nipples jutting out like two glossy cherries.

'Julia, you're going to get us arrested.' Joe sounded more turned on than anxious. 'Or fired.'

Julia turned to give him a smile, licking one finger and letting it trail down her chin, dragging it slowly over her chest and feeling a cold trail of moisture on her skin. Joe's face had darkened, and his expression became intense with arousal, sweat beading on his upper lip and his Adam's apple jerking up and down as he swallowed repeatedly. His flies were still unbuttoned, his cock once again springing to attention as Julia played her intimate game of striptease. When she nodded towards his lap, it didn't take any more prompting for him to grip himself firmly and start working the shaft of his cock.

'Keep it going, Joe. I've got a little audience here to entertain as well as you.'

Robert's Merc had windows that were slightly tinted, and through the dark turquoise glass she couldn't tell if he had a hard-on or not. No matter, she thought, I'm going to get off even if he doesn't. Looking down so that she was sure Robert would get an eyeful of her tits jiggling away with the vibrations of the engine, Julia pinched each nipple with her moistened fingers and rolled them between her fingertips till they were hard. She let her mouth fall open, licking her lips so that they were as pink and shining as the stiff points of her nipples.

Outside, Robert had locked his eyes on her, throwing frequent glances to the road to make sure he wasn't slipping over onto the hard shoulder. Julia felt like a siren, luring the two men from steering their course and captivating them with glimpses of her secret treasures. The only frustration was that she couldn't touch either of them; a middle seat, not to mention the gear stick and brake, separated her from Joe. If she slid over to his side of the cab Robert wouldn't be able to see her. And she very much wanted him to be watching.

As she moved one hand down between her legs and felt the merciful pressure of her fingers against the seatbelt, a movement from Robert distracted her. Joe let them drop back slightly and she realised he was indicating. Irritated, she looked ahead to see what turn-off he was taking.

A tall blue sign up ahead announced SERVICES.

'Follow him,' Julia said instantly, guessing with a thrill that Robert wanted to get a closer view of her and Joe's peepshow.

They pulled into the large car park to see Robert getting out of his car and walking at an easy pace towards the low featureless concrete building that passed as a truck stop. Julia pulled on her vest, her hands shaking. As Joe cut the engine and silence rushed in around them, she had a sudden moment of panic. They were in the middle of a busy area, not hidden away in the magical atmosphere of the circus enclosure. It was broad daylight, people were coming and going and the noise of the motorway traffic was a brisk rushing just a few hundred yards away. What if she'd misjudged Robert's reaction?

'We can always say you just desperately needed a piss.' Joe seemed to read her mind, but although his words were casual, Julia caught the undercurrent. What he hadn't said was – *'If we go in there and Robert doesn't want to watch us fuck'*. Julia shivered, trying not to break the mood with questions. It was a chance she was willing to take, if it meant getting closer in some way to the strange fantasy world that was the inside of Robert's head.

Jumping down from the truck, she felt how shaky her legs were as she straightened them. It was half from sitting awkwardly in the cab and half from anticipation of what they might be about to do.

Inside the antiseptic tiled foyer of the truck stop, Julia looked around her. She could see no sign of Robert. Heavy-set truckers in sagging denim passed them, giving Julia an appreciative once-over as they did so. She'd forgotten that her breasts were pulled out the top of her bra, hastily covered by her vest. She didn't realise the very obvious outline of her stiff nipples would magnetically attract the roving eyes of everyone who walked past. Accustomed to male attention and used to bathing in the feel of being a lust-provoking woman, Julia barely noticed their hungry stares.

'In here.' Joe's voice sounded tight and urgent, and he took hold of Julia's wrist to pull her into the gent's toilet.

It was a large room, white-tiled and lit with harsh fluorescent tubes that glared down on their reflection. One wall opposite the cubicles was mirrored, and Julia saw Robert leaning against the sinks, hands folded in his lap. Waiting patiently. He looked up as they approached him, unsmiling and silent.

Julia's heart was hammering so hard she was sure the other two men could hear it. The tension between them was so high you could almost touch it. Joe was hanging back behind her, eyeing Robert warily. In her head, she pleaded with him to break the silence. Instead, he stood back and inclined his head towards the sinks, seeming to direct Julia to move that way. Was she about to be unceremoniously sacked? She moved to the sinks and propped herself against them, feeling the ice cold of the china against her buttocks.

Robert leant back against the wall and folded his arms. Julia had a sudden flashback to her audition as she waited anxiously for his reaction.

'I think it'll be easier here to show me what you were trying to do in the truck, Julia.' Was there a trace of admonition in his voice?

'Joe, why don't you help her get started?'

Tentatively, Joe approached and stood facing Julia. She looked at his face. The swarthy complexion and sky blue eyes gave him a look of such intensity that she caught her breath.

Wordlessly, Joe reached for her vest and peeled it up. Her tits were pulled upwards before they jumped free of the cotton and hung sweetly over the top of her bra. Next he leant down, his bulky frame moving with surprising delicacy as he gently lifted the hem of her skirt to expose the small triangle of cerise net that half obscured her pubis.

'Turn her round, Joe. Let's get a look at that peachy arse of hers.' Robert spoke as though he were asking Joe to fix scaffolding, his voice betraying not the slightest tremor.

Julia felt Joe's big spade-like paws grip her waist and push her slowly round. Now she was facing the mirror, her half-naked body lit by the white glare of the overhead lights, and her face flushed. She noticed the feverish shine in her eyes, and Joe leaning back to appreciate the round curves of her bottom, the thin strip of her G-string cutting in between the cheeks of her arse. A few feet behind them, Robert was simultaneously admiring her rump.

Julia could hardly breathe. The sterile atmosphere of the washroom and the faint stinging smell of male urine added to the impersonal, almost scientific feel of the moment. She had the fleeting impression she was being examined by doctors, her most intimate parts under their intense scrutiny, her arousal clear for them to see. Joe tugged at the elastic of her flimsy knickers, letting them fall around her ankles. Now she felt more exposed than ever. Anyone could walk in. She imagined the rough gazes of truck drivers raking over her, reaching deep between her legs to the wet pink flower of her sex.

As she watched Robert in the mirror, standing motionless behind them, Julia felt the softest touch of a finger stroking down the cleft of her arse, to dip into the opening of her sex. Bucking against Joe's hand, she gasped with an urgent need to feel something inside her. With pleasure she felt his index finger sink in and rub around inside her, reaching as deep as it could. Julia leant forward so her tits were hanging over the sink, spreading her legs wider so as to almost beg Joe to fuck her.

There was a moment of suspense. Julia listened as a

zipper was undone and Joe pulled himself free. She took a deep breath as he removed his finger, only to replace it with the head of his cock, nudging it roughly against her lips, then sinking slowly deep inside her. She heard herself groan with relief as his wonderfully thick member filled her cunt. Pushing her ass up in the air she let him angle himself into her and braced herself against the sink, gripping hard on the slippery porcelain as Joe started to rhythmically thump into her. His balls slapped against her as he fucked her deeply, and she felt the corresponding jolt in her tits as they swung freely over the sink.

Getting lost in the feeling of Joe and her swaying together, grinding his cock in and out till she felt like she was being thoroughly fucked, Julia watched hypnotically in the mirror as Robert approached. Was he going to join in? Touch her? Julia craved to feel his cock on her, his mouth against hers, his tongue running over her lips. Perhaps he'd abandoned his strict principles for the first time; he was so close to them, close enough for her to smell the sweet fresh tang of his aftershave. Robert leant in over Julia's prone figure and she almost wept as he stretched out his arm. Her nipples burned in anticipation of his touch.

Instead of grabbing for her tits, though, he was reaching for the tap. Before she knew what was happening, Julia felt the sudden shock of icy water explode over her breasts, making her nipples shrink to rock-hard points as Joe reached round and plunged his hands into the stream of water, groping for her nipples and tweaking them hard. It was an unbelievable dual feeling, the numbing cold of the water combined with the strong pressure of Joe's fingers. Rivulets of water ran down her front, trickling into the cleft between her legs and soaking the front of her skirt. The sudden freezing splashes of water made her skin tighten with goosebumps and her heart pound even harder. Julia thought she might pass out with the intensity of the sensations, and was only dimly aware of reaching down to frig her clit, feeling the cold dampness of her wet clothes contrasting with the heat under her hand and the insistent thump of Joe's hips against hers as he drove his cock into her as deep and hard as he could. Feeling herself on the brink of oblivion, she looked up desperately, to see Robert standing beside them, calmly studying the look on her face. In the mirror, she could see her own frantic, wild expression as she broke apart, the vivid hot pink of her bra pushed aside and the exuberant cascade of water still gushing from the taps and spilling over her front.

She couldn't prevent the cry escaping from her throat, never mind who might walk in on them. She felt as if she was being broken into a thousand pieces and fizzing like the explosive water from the taps as she came. She wasn't even aware of Joe's grunts as he pulled his cock out of her and came all over her back, hearing his guttural expletives as though they were made by someone a million miles away.

Sinking onto the cold china, she was letting the shattered fragments of her mind come back together as Robert leant in and quietly turned off the taps.

He disappeared, giving Joe time to straighten up and take a few deep breaths, before coming back with a handful of tissues and giving them to Joe.

'Clean up with these. We'd better get back on the road ASAP.'

Joe nodded dumbly, turning to wipe Julia's back as she lay still sprawled over the sink, panting and confused. How the hell could Robert be so cool? Didn't he have any hormones? What would it take to get him to touch her?

'The storm's approaching. We need to be in Birmingham by three.' Robert turned to leave, already pulling his car keys from his pocket.

'Oh, Joe, I almost forgot.'

'Yes?' Joe's voice was shaky and hoarse.

'Drive safely.'

8

Rumours had started by the time they reached Birmingham. Joe's truck finally pulled onto the site to find the troupe already working frantically to raise the tent before the rain started. Julia noticed eyes turning to watch her as she crossed the grass. Their diversion had not gone unremarked, and Julia realised she would have to tread carefully if she didn't want to make enemies. The complex and invisible lines of power that crisscrossed the site were a mystery she could only guess at, allegiances and grudges that had been playing out long before she'd arrived. The air was thick and heavy, and her body was limp from the afternoon's adventure. She wanted a hot bath more than anything, to plunge herself neck deep in scalding water and wash away the clammy sticky residues of lovemaking and humid weather.

There was no time. The entire circus had still to be put together: the tents and stages; seats and lights; generators; fences; flags and signposts. This time Julia was not spared from the work; she spent the afternoon dragging heavy boxes of equipment from the trucks to the stage. By five o'clock the thunder had started and by six they were working in a monsoon, feet slipping on wet grass that was rapidly churned into mud. Julia worked alongside Sylvie, feeling that she'd be wise to keep out of Robert's way. Sylvie was working in a check shirt that swamped her tiny frame, hair tied back with a silk scarf and make-up still applied. Julia was quietly amazed at her strength. Though she still moved with insouciant gracefulness, Sylvie could haul weights like an ant. Squaring her shoulders, she draped herself with coils of rope and gave Julia casual instructions, seemingly unaffected by the driving rain and ominous growls of thunder.

'Lift with your knees,' she snapped briskly when Julia struggled to carry a box of sound equipment. 'You move like an elephant, girl.'

Although they'd been sharing a caravan for a week now, Sylvie still referred to Julia as 'girl'. Usually her dismissive attitude grated on Julia's nerves, but since Robert had supervised her illicit shag with Joe she felt she had transgressed some boundary, and Sylvie's blasé insults were reassuringly familiar. She kept her head down and worked as hard as she could, the ice-cold rain soaking her to the skin and the increasingly treacherous ground underfoot forcing her to struggle through the mud, sinking to her ankles.

Within three hours most of the circus was set up, and Sylvie at last declared they would surrender for the night. The two girls dragged themselves to their small caravan, and Julia found she was looking forward to a shower in the cramped minuscule bathroom. Most of all, she wanted to collapse on her narrow cot and let her aching muscles relax. Although their caravan was tiny and her bed uncomfortable, Julia was starting to see it as her haven in the fraught world of the circus site.

Unfortunately when they reached the caravan they found the rainstorm had not only turned the ground to a sea of mud, but also seeped through the roof and flooded their quarters. She looked dismally at the puddles on the floor, the soaking bedcovers and the rivulets of rainwater that were cascading down the walls, and felt exhausted despair wash over her. Sylvie was swearing energetically, bustling around trying to find a dry patch to move her precious costumes into. Julia stood helplessly watching as Sylvie shoved quilts and clothes into a suitcase and pushed it under the bed. Julia had hardly unpacked yet – feeling she couldn't yet make the place her own – so had left her belongings stashed under her cot. The bed she'd been longing for was now a damp chilly swamp and Sylvie snapped that she mustn't use the electrics. No shower either.

With a ferocious sigh, Sylvie disappeared back into the rain to find somewhere else for them to sleep. Julia slumped against the wall, hardly aware of the drips falling on her head. She was already soaked and too tired to care.

She let her eyelids close for a moment and felt the aching in her arms and thighs – partly from carrying heavy loaded crates and partly from the standing fuck she'd had earlier. Her mind wandered over the events of the past week – the high-octane blur of their nightly performances and the ever-present tensions backstage. She thought of the dance studio at uni, her daily training sessions. It was weeks since she'd practised. Instead, she'd been learning how to juggle, working on her 'slave' routine with Sylvie, and trying to find a way to fit in to the strange environs of the circus. In the background, her desire for Robert was a constant irritation that kept her restlessly turned on, and threatened to push her to dangerous stunts. Using Joe to try to entice Robert had been a risky move, one that could jeopardise her position in the circus, but Julia had been almost unable to control her horniness. The frustration had given her a reckless feeling that bordered on the deranged. Robert seemed to want to turn her into a toy for his pleasure, not a dancer. Julia remembered his face in the mirror that afternoon, interested but not involved – as though he were watching a performance for aesthetic curiosity rather than arousal. The thought of his dispassionate regard sent a flush of shame through her, mixed with a shock of arousal. No matter how he humiliated or angered her, it seemed Robert touched a nerve that connected directly to her sex.

Sylvie wrenched the door open and greeted Julia's startled face with a wicked little smile.

'Better bring your nightie, Julia. We're going to a sleep-over.'

'Where?' Julia felt a surge of relief. She only hoped she wouldn't be sharing with Rachel. The thought of it made her seriously consider climbing into her bed, cold and wet though it was.

'We got lucky, girl. Tonight we are the guests of the ringmaster!'

The rain drummed on the tin roof of Robert's caravan, a steady noise that Julia found strangely comforting. She thought of submarines and ships sailing through the night, Robert's sitting room a warm dry cabin sealed off from the stormy world outside. Music was playing when they arrived, sodden, bedraggled and dripping onto Robert's Persian carpet. Julia didn't recognise the tune – some relaxed jazz number with a muffled piano playing long aching notes. Though she'd approached the caravan with trepidation, not knowing how Robert would react after the service station scene, Julia found she was so drained she hardly had the energy to worry about his attitude. In fact, all three of them were so shattered from the heavy unpleasant day's work that the atmosphere was one of sheer and overwhelming relief. Sinking down in soft cushions and nursing large glasses of red wine, all three sat for a while without talking, letting their muscles relax and the music drift over them like a soporific smoke.

Robert had handed them towels when they arrived, and Julia at last dragged herself to her feet, desperate for a hot shower to warm her chilled skin. Like all the caravans, Robert's had a bathroom about the size of a coffin, with a shower that hummed as the water pump worked. It wasn't luxury accommodation, but Julia was grateful to peel off her clammy skirt and top and breathe in the clouds of steam that rose from the water. She left her soaking clothes in a ball on the bathroom floor, and stood under the shower. The trickle of warm water flowing over her chilly skin felt like a small piece of heaven. Closing her eyes she listened to the murmur of Robert's voice from the couch. She couldn't make out what he was saying, but she heard Sylvie's smoky laughter and prayed Robert wasn't discussing her. As she soaped herself, rubbing the blood back into her limbs, Julia remembered Henri's advice. Living in the circus, there was no such thing as privacy. There were no secrets. The cramped caravans and the intensity of the work meant intimacy was virtually inevitable. Surely, Julia thought uneasily, Robert wouldn't share the details of his voyeuristic exploits?

As she soaped herself she noticed two small bruises on her hips, marks left by Joe's thumbs where he'd gripped her that afternoon. She rubbed thoughtfully at the small purple shadows, wondering at their significance. A kind of badge of initiation into Robert's world of experimental sex. For a moment she felt proud to have taken the initiative that afternoon, showing Robert that she was more than capable of transgression and not afraid to venture into dangerous territory.

She turned off the shower hurriedly and wrapped herself in Robert's purple silk robe. It smelt faintly of cedarwood, a warm, musky scent that made her feel like it was Robert himself wrapping his arms round her and caressing her with a slippery touch. Shivering, she stepped into the sitting room and found Robert stretched on the sofa, glass of wine in hand. Sylvie was cross-legged on the floor beside him, and it seemed obvious that she should sit on the chair facing them. The same chair, she remembered with a flush of shame, in which she had exposed herself the first time she came here.

The conversation had stopped when she entered the room, increasing Julia's anxiety. She sat stiffly on the edge of the chair, holding the robe tightly around herself. Of course, both Robert and Sylvie were intimately acquainted with her naked body, but in the tiny space of his living room, Julia felt acutely aware of the fact she had nothing on underneath. As the silence stretched out, Julia listened to the sound of the rain on the roof, wishing that someone would speak. At last, Sylvie broke the silence.

'Nice and relaxed now, Julia?' She looked at her with amusement. 'We were just discussing how you've been settling in.'

Julia didn't respond, her mind racing through the possible conversations they may have had.

'How do you feel about your act, Julia?' Robert said. 'About working with Sylvie?'

Julia's throat was dry and her heart was starting to speed.

'It's been ... interesting,' she managed to stammer.

'Really? Can't you be a little more expansive?' His voice had that teasing edge to it. 'How do you feel about touching her? Kissing her?'

Julia suddenly had a vivid flash of the softness of Sylvie's lips, the throb of the drumbeat increasing in intensity as she leant in to kiss her, the whistles of the audience goading her on. She couldn't deny that she'd come to enjoy their act, the way their bodies slid against each other, the contrast of Sylvie's petite frame with her own more voluptuous charms. She met Robert's eyes, seeing the tease of his smile. He was daring her, trying to embarrass her.

'Sylvie's very skilful, and very beautiful. But I'm not into women.'

'You mean it doesn't turn you on? Don't be ridiculous, Julia. I've seen you afterwards.'

'And the way you kiss me isn't exactly cold,' Sylvie added, leaning forward to pour Julia a glass of wine. Julia lifted it gratefully and took a long sip. She was playing for time.

'Whom you choose to fuck is your business, Julia,' Robert said. 'But in this show, we need to keep everything fresh. Most of all, you must enjoy performing.'

'You're not happy with my work?' Julia felt resentment and confusion rising in her chest. 'You've hardly given me a chance to show my skills.'

'I don't know you well enough yet, Julia. If you do well with Sylvie, I'll consider ways to put you to use more ... effectively.'

His words were provocative; a thinly veiled allusion to the afternoon's events, and Julia knew it. Was he offering a deal? As she wondered how to respond, she took another gulp of wine. They hadn't eaten since lunch, and she could already feel the alcohol going to her head, the rich strong wine making her a little woozy.

'So what's the secret, Robert? You think I'm lacking something?' Julia had a dim sense that the wine was giving her Dutch courage, but she couldn't help rising to Robert's challenge. She lay back in the seat, at last releasing the robe and letting it fall open enough that Robert and Sylvie could see the swell of her breast underneath.

'I think your routine is very polished, Julia.'

''S a good thing, isn't it?' Julia said, letting Sylvie refill her glass. Sylvie perched on the arm of the chair, closer to Julia.

'It's the least I'd expect.' Robert's voice was calm and measured. Julia looked at his casually stretched out legs and wondered how the man managed to stay so cool every damn minute of the day. He was leaning on his elbow, watching the girls, and only that hint of fire in his dark eyes expressed anything like excitement.

'A flawless act is fine. What I'm looking for, Julia, is passion. We need to draw you out, Julia, find out what turns you on.' Robert nodded gently at Sylvie, who quietly set down her glass of wine and turned to face Julia.

'Robert and I thought it might help if we acted out the scene,' she said slyly, openly staring at the gap in Julia's bathrobe, letting her eyes run over Julia's body and back to her face. She smiled, letting the tip of her tongue moisten her lips.

'It's safe in here,' she said. 'We won't be disturbed. How about we let Robert see how far we could take it?' Her voice was low, her large eyes hooded as though she were drugged. Julia felt a tremor of excitement rise in her, as she realised what they had been plotting while she showered. It was another of Robert's games. This time he wanted to see her with a woman and Sylvie was obviously pleased to entertain him.

Though Julia was happy to act out a little Sapphic role-play every so often she hadn't ever really imagined making love to a woman. The wine and the thrill of being on the verge of forbidden territory sent a flush to Julia's cheeks, and she felt dizzy, half in a trance as she set down her wine and placed her hands in her lap. She was horrified to find she was shaking.

In the dim soft lighting of the sitting room Julia hoped no one else would notice her nerves. A small lamp on the shelf spilled light over the girls, leaving large pools of dark shadow and Robert only half visible. She was nevertheless very aware of his presence as Sylvie stood and wriggled out of her work clothes, stepping gracefully aside to leave them puddled on the floor.

She wore a luxurious black velvet bra that pushed up her small breasts into high curves, a frivolous piece of underwear that suited her quirky manner. Her knickers, too, were black velvet, frilled and ribboned like a fifties bikini. They skimmed across her buttocks, the folds of her curved cheeks peeking out from underneath. Julia was used to seeing Sylvie in her gilt metal costume, and the sight of her in normal feminine underwear seemed somehow far more intimate. Besides, they were doing this for pleasure, not work. The difference was palpable.

Sylvie stretched like a cat, pushing her breasts upward and curving her back. Turning to kneel in front of Julia, she ignored Robert as though he weren't there.

'Undo me?' she asked almost shyly, and Julia found herself disarmed by the usually forceful Sylvie surrendering to her. She leant forward, putting her chin on Sylvie's shoulder and hearing the other girl breathe right next to her ear, fast and urgent. Julia leant her face into the fine hairs at the nape of Sylvie's neck and smelt her rose-water scent, the sweet girlish smell of her skin.

Reaching down, she unhooked Sylvie's bra, pulling it gently over her shoulders and letting the garment drop to the girl's lap.

Now Sylvie caught her hands and pulled them to her breasts, letting Julia's fingers brush over the soft mounds of her tits, catching on the nipples that were stiff little points, hard against Julia's palms. Silently, Sylvie moved Julia's hands back and forth, letting her rub against the nipples and massage her breasts. She was petite – her breasts were no more than a handful for Julia, who felt with pleasant surprise the delicacy of the flesh she was rubbing. Is this what a man would feel, the shock of such softness? She wanted, suddenly, to feel Sylvie's breasts in her mouth, but before she could move, Sylvie had moved in close and was burrowing her head into Julia's bathrobe, searching with her mouth and tongue for Julia's naked skin.

When she felt Sylvie's quick, wet tongue darting against the swell of her own breast, Julia was almost scared by the strength of her reaction. She felt as if a small hungry animal were sucking on her, almost nipping her with tiny white teeth, clawing at the robe and pulling it open. When Sylvie's mouth finally found her breast and sucked hungrily at the nipple, Julia was so overcome with the sensation that she forgot Robert, and saw with a shock when she looked up that he was pointing a camera at them. While she let Sylvie lick long trails across her breasts and drag her tongue slowly over her belly, Julia eyed Robert. It was a small silver digital camera; there was no flash and only the faintest of electric clicks as the shutter blinked. Otherwise there was no noise but the soporific jazz playing on the stereo and Sylvie's ragged breathing as she wound her way further down. Meanwhile, Robert watched them through a lens.

'Keeping a memento for later?' she asked, the bitchiness in her voice overtaken by breathless arousal. Her senses were almost drowned by the languorous sense of Sylvie licking slower and slower, letting Julia squirm in her eagerness to feel Sylvie's head between her legs. Still, part of her remained conscious enough to try to draw Robert into their scene.

'I'm just taking these for reference,' Robert replied, raising the camera to Julia's face and taking a shot of her as she stared at him, her eyes glazed and her cheeks burning.

'It's a hobby of mine.'

With this, Robert stood and moved closer to them, kneeling down on the floor behind Sylvie and pointing the camera at Julia's lap.

'Sylvie, can you pull that wrap out of the way?' he said, once again directing the action. Sylvie obeyed immediately, laying the fabric at either side of Julia's thighs so the pale skin of her shaved mound was exposed to the camera.

'Pull her legs open.'

Julia felt the strength in Sylvie's arms as she firmly gripped her knees and drew them apart, spreading her legs wide so they could both feast their eyes on her slit. She felt the tension in the room so strong it was almost unbearable – she was being displayed to Robert like an exhibit, as though she were their toy to be manipulated until she lost control. Desperate to feel some friction, she clenched the tiny muscles of her sex, willing Sylvie to put her face there, to kiss her and use her lovely quick tongue against the swollen clit. Without being able to stop herself, she raised her hips up imperceptibly, bucking towards Sylvie.

'Oh, you're an excitable one, girl,' Sylvie said with delight, her eyes still fixed on Julia's pussy. 'Let's see, is this what you want?'

Delicately, with the slowest of movements, she dipped her head down to within a few millimetres of Julia's flesh. Julia could feel her hot breath against her inner thighs and groaned with the dreadful tantalising sensation as Sylvie blew against her pussy, the gentle caress of her breath sending a buzzing through her sex that threatened to tip her over the edge. She knew she was wet, could feel the slipping sensation inside herself, and wondered if it was visible. Robert was leaning in close, taking more pictures, and Julia imagined her sex lips shining with moisture, the dark pink of her most intimate place a shockingly lewd sight between the whiteness of her thighs.

Then she abandoned all thoughts of the pictures Robert was taking as she felt at last the deliciously hard tip of Sylvie's tongue flicking against her. It was a fabulous torment, to feel that little muscle working against her clit, licking deftly around her and nudging inexorably towards where she most wanted to feel it. She imagined Sylvie fucking her with her tongue, and knew how good it would feel – but at the same time she wanted to feel a cock inside her more. She was almost far gone enough to beg Robert to join in, but not quite. On the edge of her consciousness she heard the camera shutter clicking.

'Is this what you want, Robert?' She echoed Sylvie's question, letting the girl explore her with her tongue as she sank further into the seat, looking directly into the lens of the camera. Robert was raking over the bodies of the two girls with the viewfinder, framing shots of Sylvie as her mouth worked steadily at Julia's lap.

'You want home-made porn?' Julia kept pushing Robert, wanting him to admit he was involved in the session. As she felt Sylvie press against her legs, rubbing her breasts against her thighs and reaching down to play with herself as she brought her closer to orgasm, Julia grabbed the girl's hair and gently pushed her head further towards her core.

'How are you enjoying that, Julia?' Robert answered her questions with one of his own. 'How does it feel to have her tongue inside you?'

'It feels fucking good,' Julia managed to answer, although her head was filling with a warm buzz, rising from where Sylvie was turning her on to the point of explosion and suffusing her whole body with the rushing pulsing feel of approaching orgasm. Sylvie kept licking, her tongue firm and darting like a cat lapping at milk, her breath hot against Julia's skin and her free hand holding her legs firmly apart so she could reach in deep. As she drew near to her climax, Julia heard the shutter of the camera clicking repeatedly, Robert snapping a volley of images as she lost control and threw her head back against the chair. She clung to Sylvie, her hands buried deep in the girl's tangled hair, still wet from the rainstorm and tumbling over Julia's thighs, her face locked on Julia's pussy, tongue jabbing insistently at her clit. As she started to rock with the waves of orgasm, she pulled Sylvie's head hard against her. Tipping over the edge, she heard the short high gasps of Sylvie coming too, and the two girls hung on in their moment of oblivion, letting Robert snap away furiously as they rocked together, bodies convulsing with the little spasms of pleasure.

At last they fell back, breathing hard, muscles limp from the release of tension. Sylvie looked up at Julia from where she sat on the floor. There was a new quality in her expression, a complicity. Julia knew she had finally earned the respect of the more experienced woman, in the most pleasurable way possible. Just by letting Sylvie make love to her, Julia felt that she had crossed some invisible line. It was as though she got closer to the inner circle of the circus every time she transgressed her own limits.

Next to them, Robert was turning off his camera and laying it on the table. He fetched the half-empty wine bottle and filled the girls' glasses, handing them their drinks with a deference that Julia had never felt from him. She sensed somehow she'd passed a test.

'That was very illuminating, girls. Thank you.' Robert spoke as though they'd performed some experiment on his behalf, but there was a warm humour in his voice that let Julia relax.

'I think it'll only help you develop the act.'

Julia, despite feeling languorous and spaced out, saw her chance and jumped in: 'You mean, I could dance more?'

Robert shook his head.

'I don't think the "slave" act needs more dance. What I'd like to see is the two of you drawing out the love-making at the end.'

Julia felt irritation pulling at her, as once again she was denied the chance to put her professional skills to good use.

'I can do a lot more than writhe around like a pole dancer, you know, Robert,' she said bitterly. Her post-orgasm bliss was disappearing rapidly, as was the sense she had risen a notch in Robert's estimation. He still saw her as a cheap diversion or an erotic curio, and she was suddenly filled with unease about the photos he had stored on his camera.

'And what are you going to do with the pictures?'

'I told you, Julia. They're for research. Or you could call it inspiration.'

'Uh-huh.' Julia nodded, hoping he wanted them for himself. Not only would it lessen the chance he wanted to threaten her with them later, but also she relished the thought of him looking at her for kicks. If she could turn him on, even as a model in his dirty picture collection, surely that meant he was attracted to her?

'You see, Julia, I have an idea,' Robert continued. 'I want to bring in a new act. A headline act, just before the final curtain.'

Julia looked at him, hardly daring to believe what he was telling her. Sitting curled up on the floor, Sylvie gave her a wink and grinned. She obviously knew exactly what Robert was about to tell her.

'I want a dancer, Julia, to play the part of my lover. It's a tough routine. Take a lot of rehearsing, and the timing needs to be perfect.' Robert was speaking casu-ally as usual, but there was no doubt that what he was saying was deadly serious. He looked at her with his film-star expression, a dare glittering in his rich brown eyes.

'So what do you say? Do you think you can handle it?'

9

The dim house lights were on, the thump of dark electro music sounding as the tent lay empty. Julia hung in the wings, watching as the first few people moved, raggle-taggle, into their seats. She was still wrapped in her bathrobe, face scrubbed and bare of make-up. There would be more than three hours before she was onstage, Robert's new act taking the prestigious 11.30 slot, the last before the midnight finale. The programme was designed to end with a bang, and Robert wouldn't perform early on when the audience was still restless. Only once the other acts had warmed up the house would he present his most breathtaking skills – the magic and illusion that he was renowned for. Now Julia would be appearing with him, playing the role of his 'object of desire'. With his mastery of timing and suspense, Julia understood implicitly that this meant she was being offered a chance to make her name in the circus.

She was well aware of the added kudos this act offered her, and the unspoken but tacit pressure to pull it off. If she missed a cue, or fell out of synch with Robert's precisely co-ordinated routine, she could blow the whole thing. It was more tension than she'd felt before. She looked down to see her hands were shaking with nerves. If she didn't know better than to drink before going onstage, she'd be downing a large brandy.

From outside came the roar of engines, and Julia heard the shouts and laughter of the audience approaching the tent.

The buses had arrived, disgorging crowds of drunk and excited Mancunians onto the site. They were a rowdy babble, dressed sharp and smelling of fresh after-shave, beer and cigarettes. Julia loved watching the changing landscape of their audiences, hearing the different pitch and lilt of the accents as the circus moved further north. While the people who came to see the show tended to be of a certain type – young, liberal, decadent – she noticed the certain flavours of each location. There had been a riotous celebratory atmosphere in kitschy Brighton. Tonight the crowd seemed bawdier; Julia heard rough throaty laughs from men grouping together in almost predatory fashion. Women were dressed in dazzling ghetto-fabulous style, squealing and teetering as their heels sank into the soft mud of the midway between the sideshows and the main tent. The bar tent was packed, empty glasses already littering the grass around the door, and Julia heard chants of encouragement as a line of young guys at the bar downed shots of tequila.

Behind her, Henri stopped and peered over Julia's shoulder at the scene outside. He watched the raucous crowd for a moment, his deep implacable eyes taking in the debauched atmosphere. Finally, he grunted his judgement:

'A tough house tonight, Julia. They'll be baying for blood.'

He looked at her with an expression that could have been forbidding or challenging. Julia was never sure how to read him, knowing how his thoughts tended to perverse contradictions.

'They're just up for a good time, Henri,' she shrugged, silently hoping she was right. The circus trod a difficult line between exciting the audience and causing riots. Julia was never entirely sure this wasn't Robert's secret aim – to drive the audience out of control, to shake them up and disturb them until the lines between the stage and the crowd blurred. She knew how he loved playing games, distorting things, most of all provoking people till they were shaken into questioning their taboos, till they wanted to break the rules. As Julia spied surreptitiously on the crowds outside, she realised she was acting out this role-reversal herself.

'Looking for secrets out there?' Robert had appeared suddenly at her elbow, and seemed to be reading her thoughts. 'What are you hoping to find, Julia?'

Julia had no intention of joining in with his philosophising. She just wanted to focus on her performance later, make sure she was psyched up for it.

'Just checking out the crowd,' she replied stubbornly, determined not to be drawn into another situation where Robert had the upper hand. She nodded at the beer tent, trying to divert his attention. 'They seem to be gearing up for a wild night.'

'Like animals,' Robert observed, looking absently at the crowd. His voice was neutral. 'The more noise they make, the less power they actually possess. The ones you need to watch, as they say, are the quiet ones.' He nodded at a couple of men who stood apart from the crowd, sipping from bottles of beer. 'Those two.'

'What, those are the ones who'll start throwing Molotovs halfway through the first act?' Julia said contemptuously, scrutinising the pair.

'I didn't say that.' Robert had moved closer to Julia, so his mouth was inches from her ear. His breath was warm against her face as he stood behind her and they both gazed at the men. 'Look at the way they hold themselves.'

The men were relaxed, one of them in a black leather jacket, the other in a T-shirt, both dark-haired and well built. Julia noticed a subtle confidence in their manner, as though they were waiting for something to happen.

'You know what they're here for, Julia.' Once again, she felt that desperate lurch in her stomach, the strange mix of revulsion and allure that Robert effected on her. He was whispering to her now.

'What do you think they want to see? D'you think they're just after a display of your tits, or do they want more than that?'

Keep cool, Julia told herself. Play the game. She leant against the curtain, pulling the perished velvet closer around herself so she was wrapped in it, the fabric coiled tightly round her arms.

'You could bring them in here now. Look, they're just a few feet away. Don't you feel like giving them a little preview?'

'I don't want to spoil the surprise, Robert. They'll see me later.'

'What are you going to show them?'

'Just what you told me to show them. Not enough.'

'And afterwards? I know how you get after a show, Julia.' Robert pulled the curtain tighter round Julia's shoulders, till it constricted her ribs and she couldn't move her arms. He held on to her, forcing her to face the men.

'I know you get wet when you're dancing. I've seen how you walk after you leave the stage.' Julia's heart was hammering in her chest now, the curtain and Robert's arms making it hard to draw breath.

'You're suffocating me,' she said quietly, trying not to struggle in his grip.

'I'm showing you what you want,' he replied. 'Wait here.'

Abruptly letting go of Julia he moved swiftly out onto the site, heading straight for the men standing by the beer tent. Julia watched as he hailed them and started chatting amiably. He pulled a deck of cards out of his back pocket, and unfurled them in a fan, offered them to the men. She noticed the swaggering ease that the man in the leather jacket displayed, choosing a card with a casual gesture, a half smile. He wouldn't allow Robert to overawe him. As Robert shuffled the deck, Julia saw him questioning the men, deferring to them. He was buttering them up. There was a barely perceptible tension between them, the two townies macho and assured, Robert playing the part of strange conjuror. Julia knew just how well he could anticipate people's reactions.

Robert pointed to the man's friend, asking him to find his card, which had miraculously transferred itself into his back pocket. The men relaxed, laughing, and Robert drew them in closer, as if about to tell them a secret. Julia tensed, suspicious. The three men turned to where she hid in the shadows, and she shrank back behind the curtain, withdrawing from their curious stares. What the hell was he up to? She retreated, running to hide in her caravan.

Sylvie was outside, warming up for her performance. Leaning against the bumper of the caravan, she continued stretching, regarding Julia's approach from her bent-over position.

'You got nerves, dancing girl? On your big night?'

'Robert's up to something again.' Julia wished there was someone in the circus she felt she could totally trust. She got the feeling Sylvie was jealous of her being chosen to perform with Robert – she'd been acting coldly ever since they'd arrived in Manchester. Right now, though, she was the only person Julia had to talk to.

'Oh Robert ... he'll break your heart, baby. Nothing but games with that man.' She straightened up. 'What has he done?'

Julia frowned, not sure if Robert had actually done anything. At least, not yet.

* * *

At quarter past eleven Julia emerged from her caravan, costumed and in full make-up. Eva had devised a tailored forties suit for her; black pinstripe with patent leather shoes. She wore a pillbox hat at an angle, fixed securely to her hair with long pins and Kirby grips. It was a bizarre outfit in the muddy site, and Julia struggled to walk the hundred yards to the tent. Her make-up was a garish parody of glamour – white pan-stick caked her face in a thick layer, her eyes were heavily outlined with dramatic black liner and false eyelashes curled up to her brows. She had painted her lips a violent shade of red, as crimson as blood, and smudged grey shadow in the hollows of her cheeks so that her cheekbones stood out razor sharp. Hidden by the mask of her make-up, she felt the buzz of pre-show anxiety transform into adrenaline as she heard the noise of the crowd inside. The motorbike engines screamed as they left the ring, and Julia slipped into the backstage pen.

Robert was waiting for her, also clad in stage gear, dressed in a costume that was modelled on a private dick from a film noir. His face was whited up and a smear of five o'clock shadow shaded his jaw; hair slicked down and shining with grease. His eyes, like Julia's, were rimmed with black. In a white shirt and braces, pinstripe trousers and brogues, he had a seedy, dangerous look to him.

'And here's the lady we've all been waiting for.' His lips curled in a smile that intimated cruelty. 'Ready?'

'Sure,' she said, forcing a hard crimson smile in his direction. 'Raring to go. How's the show been so far?'

'The townies are loving it. Particularly John and Mark. They're especially looking forward to seeing you perform.'

Julia knew instantly Robert was referring to the men he'd been talking to before the show. 'Really.' She kept her voice cold, one eye on the curtain. 'Why would that be?'

'I told them you just loved to meet your fans. I've invited them to come backstage after the blow-off. They seemed very keen.' Robert could barely suppress his smile. Julia shook her head.

'I'm not getting involved in more of your games, Robert.'

'Oh, Julia, please. This is turning into a very interesting adventure. You're going to be the centre of attention tonight. Don't let me down.'

As the whistles and shouts from the audience reached a loud crescendo, Robert strode out onto the stage, leaving Julia alone in the wings. She listened as the music started up, a raucous jazz number full of blaring saxophones and snare drums. There was no time left to argue. Even though her nerves were frayed by Robert's baiting, Julia had to push her feelings to one side and focus on the show.

The act started with a single spotlight, Robert slouched on a chair, a cigarette hanging from his hand, wreaths of smoke surrounding his shadowed face.

Julia danced onstage with staccato pointed steps, moving like a film star up the Hollywood red carpet. She circled Robert, drawing herself up haughtily and looking down at him with disdain. This part, as he'd explained to her, was an illustration of her power – she would tease him, lifting the edge of her skirt to show the top of her stocking, a rich girl playing with the desire of a down-at-heel drifter. As he craned forward and reached out to touch her, she'd whirl away from him, miming laughter. They danced around each other, Julia making suggestive movements, pulling her jacket off and rolling her shoulders, Robert by turns trying to catch her and feigning disinterest.

Every time Julia showed a little more flesh, the audience responded with howls and whistles, willing Robert to grab her and force her to strip. But the point was to show virtually nothing, and although she pulled down her top and bared the curve of her breast to Robert, the audience would see nothing. They could feel the vicarious thrill of Robert's arousal as he ogled Julia, but they were presented with a view of Julia's back, and no more. Julia could feel the hungry eyes of the crowd fixed on her, hear them murmuring and whispering. The entire tent was turned on.

Julia kept up the dancing flirtation with Robert, enjoying the feel of him lusting after her even if it was only an act. As he became yet more frustrated by her coquetry, Robert's movements became sharper and angrier. She draped herself over him and stroked his thigh, only to pull away moments later, and finally he drew a gun from his pocket. The music was suddenly cut dead. A crack of gunfire was made offstage, and Julia dropped, lifeless, to the ground.

This was where the trickery came in. Under her, a trapdoor opened and a dummy figure was hoisted up. While Robert acted out his remorse, Julia slipped under the stage and left the dummy lying in her place. Now she had to work quickly. Henri was at hand to help her rip off the suit, held together with Velcro to speed up her change. Underneath she was wearing elaborate silvery-grey underwear, over which she pulled on a suit identical to the one she had been wearing, only grey. She shielded her face, trying to get her breath back while Henri emptied a handful of talc over her hair, and her ghostly appearance was ready.

Out in the tent, the aerial girls were spinning overhead, looping out of the dark shadows of the tent, flying round Robert as he sat on the floor, head in hands as though despairing. A slow heartbreaking lament played from the speakers, and the lighting was softened to a pale glow. Now the stage had an ethereal dreamlike appearance, the girls trailing wisps of gauze behind them as they floated around Robert.

In the wings, a second, false stage was hidden by darkness, and it was here that Julia slipped back into position, carefully aligning her body with chalk marks on the floor. Between her, the stage and the audience was a diagonal sheet of glass, and a footlight now rose to shine on Julia. The audience saw a ghostly vision of her, reflected on the glass screen, superimposed over the tableaux on the main stage.

The trick was an old one: 'Pepper's Ghost'. It was simple but striking. Every move was timed to exactly coincide with Robert's. As he raised his head to see Julia's ghost float to her feet, Robert followed the music to coordinate with her. What now appeared to the audience was a slow misty apparition of Julia, dancing slowly in front of Robert. This time her provocative gestures were half obscured by the reflection. The noise from the audience died gradually, and the tent was filled with only the slow seductive music as Julia dropped her jacket to the floor. She slid out of her skirt and stood, pale and unearthly, clad in lacy silver under-wear and stockings. She counted two bars, and leant forward, poised over another chalk mark on the floor. At the same time Robert lifted his hands, and the audience saw him fondling Julia's breasts, reaching to touch the mirage of her body. Someone in the crowd gave a low whistle, sending a shiver down Julia's spine. She was dancing alone on the second stage, but imagining Robert responding to her – as though dreaming the whole sequence.

As she felt the tension build, Julia straightened up smoothly, and released the clasp of her bra. It fell to the floor soundlessly, and the audience shifted in their seats to see the hazy outline of her breasts, a maddeningly slight vision of her body. She shook herself gently, just giving a little jiggle of her tits to provoke them even more. Now, as Robert reached up to stroke the imagined side of her body, she pulled off her G-string, her movements timed perfectly so that she stood naked at last just as a pall of dry ice rose around her. All that was visible was a pale silhouette, the suggestion of her curves and the shadowed seam between her legs, the stage filling with smoke, and the dark shape of Robert reaching to touch a body that didn't exist.

Around them the girls on silk ropes twisted and spun, wrapping themselves in the fabric and pulling themselves higher into the vaulted ceiling of the tent. Sheer body stockings revealed pure angelic bodies underneath, the pale fabric contrasting with the dark fathomless black of the stage, lips and nipples rouged as bright spots of colour against their slight ghostly appearances. The rippling motion of the aerial act flowed around Julia and Robert, the two of them playing caresses back and forth, Julia rolling her figure over Robert's desperate arms, passing through them even as he tried to catch her. It was the most maddening of sights, a man so aroused he was chasing a voluptuous dream, snatching at Julia's limbs, letting his hands hover over her breasts, hips, ass as though trying to tickle the apparition into existence. Occasionally their images would overlap perfectly and the audience saw Robert join Julia in a deep kiss, heads close together and bodies limp with ecstasy, only to break apart again seconds later.

As she danced this luminous insubstantial tease, Julia felt she was acting out her feelings for Robert; the two of them able to fuck only in an imagined scenario, her sexual exploits a mirror of her desire for him. She danced alone on the hidden stage, assuming the positions she longed to share with Robert, allowing the audience to see the deepest of her secret fantasies. On her knees now, so that her rounded pert ass was displayed to Robert's shadow-image, she closed her eyes and imagined him kneeling behind her, stroking the softest part of his fingertip along the line of her crack, teasing her pussy and clit as if he was mesmerising her. She started to sway and rock, knowing that the audience saw her reflection being taken by Robert, hands on her hips. She could tell from the hushed restlessness of the audience that they were fixated by the sight now unfolding: Robert miming his fuck, moving his hips as though sinking his cock into her, slowly increasing the tempo of his thrusts as the aerial display whirled ever faster around the stage. It was a stylised fuck, an exquisite and graceful simulacrum of the sexual act, and Julia knew it only aggravated the sexual longing of the audience. They were now agitated with a mix of pleasure and frustration, in the same state as Julia would be after the show, so keyed up and sensitised that every movement seemed heavy with suggestion. She let her breasts sway gently under her as she and Robert moved, together but far apart, providing a perfectly synchronised display of erotica for this house full of strangers.

She moaned as she moved, her voice lost in the loud cocoon of stirring music that accompanied the climax of the act, strings swooping as the girls unfurled the fabric and tumbled to the ground, where they writhed like fallen angels around the stage, their dramatic movements surrounding the tableau of ringmaster and dancer, rocking steadily in a final spasm, sharing their imagined orgasm with the crowd.

10

As she walked over the grass towards her caravan, a figure in a leather jacket stepped out from the shadows.

'Hello there, beautiful.' His voice was unfamiliar, and Julia froze, trying to make out his face in the inky blackness.

'Who's that?'

'Your most ardent fan. My name's John. This is Mark.' His friend materialised beside him, a provocative smirk on his face. Julia suddenly recognised them – it was the two men Robert had spoken to before the show.

'We've been waiting to see you.'

'Yeah, loved the show.' Mark spoke for the first time.

'Only, it's left us feeling kind of cheated.'

'But that's the whole idea, boys.' Julia was shivering, cold after the sweat from dancing had dried on her skin. She was wearing her costume suit, and hugged the thin fabric round herself in an effort to stay warm.

'Surely you know the deal with a strip show?'

John nodded. 'Yeah. Cheap tricks. It's not that which was bothering me. It's more what your manager told us before the show.'

Mark was moving in closer to Julia while John talked, slipping his arm round her shoulders.

'My manager?'

'The guy with the cards. He said you always needed to unwind after a show.'

Mark played with the hair at the nape of Julia's neck, curling a strand round his fingers. He leant in to her ear and whispered, his breath tickled her neck. Julia caught a whiff of beer and smoke.

'We thought you might fancy a little trip. Help you relax.'

'Show you the sights. There's a lot to see round here.'

Julia laughed. 'Cow-shit in the dark? It's not my idea of fun, guys.'

'A bit further than the next field, we were thinking.' He held up a set of car keys and shook them.

'We can promise a night to remember.'

Julia looked at the glittering keys, wondering if she was entirely insane to even consider the offer. John had a tightly packed, compact body that bristled with an aggressive sexuality. His attractiveness was amplified by his arrogance and the boldness of his suggestion. Mark appeared a darker, yet more enigmatic presence, less inclined to bravado, more likely to quietly insinuate himself into a situation – as he was now calmly slipping his arm round Julia's and pressing his fingers into her flesh. Julia felt as though she was being coerced, and for a minute the very danger of the situation appeared tantalising.

'Don't pretend you're not tempted, Julia.' Robert's clear voice was a sudden shock, and as he appeared from the shadows she felt as though she'd been caught in a trap. The three men stood waiting to hear her response as she stood shivering with uncertain excitement in the cold night air.

'I'll be coming along too,' Robert added, as though the decision had been made for her.

'How could I refuse?' Julia finally answered, meeting the challenge in Robert's eyes.

John's car was a sleek black Audi that made the road melt under them. Julia didn't even notice when they hit 100mph, especially with the distraction of John's hand on her knee and the driving house music that thumped a heavy bass line from the speakers. Mark cracked open cans of beer as they drove, and Julia felt a warm buzz overtake her, the night flashing by filled with traffic and a reckless feeling of escape. After half an hour on the motorway they were pulling onto the slip road, Robert's car a short distance behind them. When Julia caught a glimpse of the signs, she burst out laughing.

'Blackpool? You're taking me to Blackpool?'

'Valhalla, babe, Valhalla.' John gave her a wide smile, and in the dark Julia saw his teeth gleaming.

The three of them spilled out of the car and straight into the carnage of Blackpool on a Saturday night. It was one in the morning and the seafront was littered with smashed bottles and chip wrappers, among which groups of drunken revellers staggered, shouting and singing. The neon signs and lights dazzled Julia, suggesting a lurid carnival of debauchery. A strip club blared raucous music into the street from a pair of tinny speakers, the sign promising 'Girls, Girls, Girls! Live action!' She could smell the reek of the night – the vinegar from the fast food vans mixed with the smell of vomit and piss from alleyways. Overhead seagulls circled and shrieked, beating their wings against a stiff sea wind.

Julia was still in her costume, shivering with the blustery cold. John wrapped his jacket round her, Mark slipped his arm round her waist, and they meandered down the street swigging beer. She felt herself carried along by the two men, hunched under John's arm, with Mark kneading her hip, the three of them bumping pleasantly against each other as they walked. Behind them somewhere, she knew Robert was following. Resisting the impulse to check for him, Julia relaxed into the company of her two new admirers, enjoying their attentions as they playfully flirted with her.

Ahead of them a stag party crashed out of a pub onto the street, a dozen guys reeling with drink and full of vim. One of them caught sight of Julia with her twin escorts draped over her and bellowed at them. Within a minute the whole gang were whistling after her, making animal noises and cackling with laughter. John casually gave them the finger, pulling Julia closer in to him as though claiming her.

'I think it's time we took you somewhere a little more private, sweetheart.'

'What, like a hotel room?' Julia wasn't sure if she was into the idea.

'No, like a long, dark ride.'

The Pleasure Beach was a vast city of roller coasters and fairground rides that stayed open long into the night, and Julia passed through the turnstile into total sensory overload. Rides looped under and around in a crazed tangle of tracks, everything covered in 200-watt light bulbs and fluorescent paint. After the sleek black tents of Circus Excite, Julia felt that she had entered a huge cheap spectacular. In the circus they worked to keep a tightly sophisticated atmosphere of erotic tension, playing with dark illusion and restrained desire. This place was an explosion of cheap thrills, a cheerful mess of blatant kitsch and high-tech special effects, the gargantuan Big Dipper sitting monstrously above it all.

John and Mark pulled her through the arcades to where a hundred-foot high cliff face rose forbiddingly. Julia felt a pang of trepidation as they approached the small wooden station, behind which a waterfall roared. The entrance was carved in the shape of a huge Viking skull.

'Told you I was taking you to Valhalla, didn't I?' John jumped into a wooden longboat that rocked on the current of an underground river. He held out his hand. Julia hesitated, wondering if she should wait till Robert was near. Before she could speak, however, John had grabbed her and pulled her down to sit next to him on the bench.

'I'm not getting left out,' Mark said, squeezing himself in next to them. Julia was trapped in the middle, jammed in tightly.

The boat moved off, the surly ticket seller barely glancing at the party before they disappeared under the jaw of the Viking skull. Once inside, they were plunged into darkness. The cave-like tunnel was cold as the tomb, echoing with the splashes of the boat as it drifted further into the murky shadows. Julia gripped the padded handrail with a feeling of fluttering disorientation as they moved into unknown territory. Beside her, she felt John slip his hand under her top and caress her back. His fingers were so cold they made her shiver.

'What happens in here?' she asked, only half wanting to know.

'Thrills and spills,' John replied, reaching his hand down the back of her skirt and working his way under the elastic of her G-string. Julia jumped as lightning sparked over wires around them, prompting laughter from Mark, who put his hand on her knee as if to reassure her.

'Scared?' he asked, leaning in to try to kiss her. 'You want to sit on my lap?' He pulled her over onto his knees, while John shifted round in his seat to face her. The pace quickened while around them projections of fire rolled over the walls. Julia felt the boat start to spin and rock as Mark manoeuvred her closer, holding her firmly by the hips and pushing his hard-on against her.

Julia wriggled, wondering if the whole boat was about to turn over.

'Move your legs further apart,' John instructed. 'It'll help you balance.'

'And let you get your hand up my skirt,' Julia observed, realising the men intended to take full advantage of the pockets of darkness inside the caverns to get their kicks.

'It would be a temptation,' John said, reaching inside her jacket to stroke at her tits. 'But I really would like to get a look at what we didn't see onstage.'

He pulled at her buttons, uncovering the silver lace bra underneath, while Julia kept a firm grip on the handrail. Any minute they could turn a corner and encounter another boatful of people, and she craned her head trying to hear the approach of any other voices.

'Just relax, baby. I only want a look at your tits. They looked so gorgeous from a distance. Let me pull this down.' John tugged at the bra, pulling her breasts free to spill over the lace. Julia felt surrounded by the two men, Mark slipping his hands over her thighs and between her legs, John working away at her tits. He bent forward to take a nipple in his mouth, and Julia moaned, leaning back to let Mark nuzzle at her neck. She felt two pairs of hands swarming over her, and the delicious, terrifying feeling of being trapped in the dark without knowing what would happen next. Part of her wondered what had happened to Robert.

Suddenly the boat plunged without warning over a steep drop, into a rolling dark mist. Julia struggled frantically, thinking suddenly that they were underwater as the spray hit her, that they'd overturned and she was being plunged into the depths of the river. Mark held her firmly round the waist, taking the opportunity to unzip his flies and help Julia pull up her skirt.

Water was sloshing over the sides of the boat now, and Julia felt the cold shock of it at the same time as John ducked his head down to her lap. As he flicked his tongue over her, she relaxed, realising that they were slowly rocking down a tunnel, the walls a cascading curtain of water. Oblivious to the changing scenes around them, John licked hungrily at her while Mark nudged the head of his cock against her ass insistently.

The ride was a rolling shadowy journey, twisting through more caverns where flames licked up the walls. Julia was lost in a dark fantasy, balanced precariously in the boat as it dipped and tilted, as she was rubbed and manipulated by John and Mark. She felt a rising need to take Mark's cock inside her, her sense of urgency spurred by the approaching sound of a waterfall, another drop.

'Stop the boat,' she said urgently, pushing John away. He grabbed hold of the wall, forcing the boat to spin close against the side. There was a scraping, grinding noise as they hit the wall, and then he turned back to Julia, who was breathing heavily, crushed against Mark's body. The boat continued to grate against the wall as the three of them moved silently into a position where Julia could sit on Mark. She was still aware there was a danger of another boat happening on them, so their movements were furtive and they made no noise, other than the sound of their breathing and the suck of the water lapping at the boat. Julia felt like a teenager stealing a sordid grope, caught up in a filthy huddle between two strangers. All thoughts of Robert following them had disappeared as she felt the urgent need to fuck overwhelm her.

She eased herself down onto Mark's cock, and started moving slowly up and down, letting the whole shaft push deep inside her with a wonderfully insistent force. Because the boat was unstable, gently rocking with their motions, the sensation was almost gentle, but the intensity increased with John's attentions. He buried his head between her legs again, and the double feel of being fucked while he licked her threatened to send Julia over the edge almost immediately. She felt herself pushed forward onto John's tongue as Mark gripped her waist and moved her hips hard against his, the three of them locked in an awkward but irresistible embrace. As Julia braced a foot against the side of the boat, biting her lip and screwing her eyes shut, she didn't notice they'd drifted back into the current. As she neared her climax, she suddenly felt a lurch as the boat tipped over the edge of the final drop, the three of them wrenched apart and falling through the air. Julia's orgasm hit and she managed a shuddering intake of breath before everything fragmented and many things happened at once: she saw a flash of fire rolling towards them as they crashed into the pool below; her head spun with the force of her orgasm; all three of them were showered with water, shaken apart and left gasping, stunned by their climaxes and disorientated.

The three looked around to see Viking longboats burning with gas flames and fire licking over the water around them. The boat was circling aimlessly, adrift at the end of the ride. Julia lay back against the seat, soaked and trembling, her clothes bunched up and her legs aching from the exertion.

John grinned at her, his face wet and shining.

'Welcome to paradise, babe.'

In the darkness, Julia tried to catch her breath, and saw in John's twinkling, devilish eyes the reflection of Robert's perversity. It seemed his presence followed her everywhere, no matter how hard she tried to escape.

11

Her hair was still dripping wet, her clothes splashed with water from the ride and creased from being roughly pushed aside by Mark and John. The cold night air was a refreshing blast and Julia could taste the salt spray on her lips as she walked to Robert's waiting car, the two of them silently digesting the night's adventures. As she sank into the leather seat beside Robert Julia felt again the strange sense of being intimately connected to a man she'd never slept with. Sitting next to him in the passenger seat she had a sudden feeling that they were joined together by her erotic explorations. Robert set up these situations as challenges, and not once had Julia backed out. Together they had shared Julia's first encounter with a woman, and her first threesome. Always Robert had been there, inspiring the action and watching, if not actually getting involved. It was as though he was fucking her through other people – playing out his fantasies with Julia while he tormented her with his untouchable distance.

'The more you push me to fuck other people, the more I want to fuck you.'

Julia spoke without thinking, realising as soon as she uttered the words that she had never explicitly told Robert she wanted him. She'd stripped for him, danced with him, taken part in his sex games – but she'd never before admitted that it was him she wanted most of all. Now, in the luxurious comfort of his dark car, driving in the small hours of the morning, she had let down her guard for a second. As the silence continued and Robert still failed to answer, Julia felt her anxiety growing.

'Did you hear what I said?' she asked, half hoping he hadn't.

'Yes.'

Robert was driving with one hand guiding the wheel and the other resting lightly on the gearstick. His face was lit up by the strobing streetlights of the motorway, and betrayed no expression.

'Don't you want to?' Julia knew there was a hint of desperation creeping into her voice, but couldn't help herself from asking.

'I would have thought you'd be sated after those two.' Robert was obviously joking. His voice was the wry languorous drawl that drove Julia to distraction, turning her on with his warm tone, yet frustrating her with his casual delivery. The more agitated she got and the more she pushed herself to turn Robert on, the more he seemed to lean back and enjoy her struggle.

'Wasn't that enough for you, Julia?'

Julia thought of him watching in the shadows, taking photographs of her and Sylvie. She'd had sex she'd never have imagined in her wildest fantasies, and it had been incredible. New worlds of dark and outrageous sexual possibilities were opening up in her mind, and Robert was the one who'd instigated this strange journey. Yet the hands she'd felt on her, the mouths and tongues and bodies that had explored her intimately, were not the ones she wanted most of all. She wouldn't be satisfied, truly satisfied, until she could do what she'd set out to do right at the start of this tour. She wanted Robert.

'No,' she said quietly, shaking her head in the dark. 'It's not enough. Not nearly.'

'Really? You're more of a challenge than I expected. I'll have to come up with something more imaginative next time, I suppose. What do you think, a full-blown orgy? Some bondage, perhaps? What are your taboos, Julia?'

'It's not my taboos that I'm talking about, Robert. It's yours.'

Robert laughed, an easy generous laugh that irritated Julia even further. He sounded genuinely amused.

'What, you think you don't have any?' she shot at him.

'Oh, sure, I've got taboos, Julia. I presume you've worked them out already?'

'You can't fuck.'

'Is that what you think?' There was still amusement in his voice.

'It's blindingly obvious. You can only watch, only get off on other people's pleasure. I don't know why, though. Perhaps it's a complex.' Now Julia was going too far. She was bitter and angry, and knew it showed. Robert didn't answer for a long while.

As they approached the lit-up tents of the field where the circus lay, he slowed the car to a stop and turned to look at Julia. Their faces were obscured by the darkness, the sparkle of lights caught in their eyes and the faint outlines of their bodies slightly paler shadows in the black interior of the car.

'Julia,' he said softly, his voice serious now. 'Do you think you've changed since you joined the circus?'

She was startled by the simple question, in a way the most intimate thing Robert had ever asked her.

'I've ... I've changed so much I can't recognise myself,' she admitted, knowing this was true. Robert nodded.

'What's different?'

Julia swallowed. She was used to sparring with Robert as part of their sexual adventures. She wasn't used to having conversations with him that involved real, deep feelings. Yet she wanted to tell him the truth, feeling the question was as much a challenge as his daring her to fuck two strange men at once.

'I feel like I've found a whole new world. Sex – sex used to be straightforward fucking.' Julia kept her voice controlled. 'And now there's so much more.'

'Julia, I can't explain everything because you need to find things out for yourself. But imagine what's out there, the experiences to be had, the excitement and the feelings. You've only just started to discover the circus.' He looked at her again. 'I don't mean Circus Excite.'

'You think sex is a circus, don't you?'

Robert laughed again.

'Yes, I do. Life, love, sex, work. It's all a circus, Julia.' He seemed to lose himself in thoughts for a moment, looking at the tents and lights of the circus in front of them. Julia wondered where his thoughts went, this man who seemed to control everything with such a light touch.

'Such stuff as dreams are made on,' he murmured finally, as he put the car in gear and drove them through the open gate and into the sleeping site.

It had been two weeks since the company had had a night off, and the atmosphere was jubilant. Around twenty of the crew decided to hit the centre of town, with Joe and Sarah drawing the short straws and declared drivers for the night. Crammed into the back of Joe's truck among ropes and toolboxes, wedged tightly between a couple of the roustabouts, Julia found herself looking forward to her first work's night out with the circus. She could only imagine what the reaction would be to the outlandish loud characters spilling onto the streets of Manchester.

She'd dressed down for tonight, feeling relaxed in a denim skirt and a sheer top that felt like a delicious refreshing change after a fortnight in stage make-up and glittering, extreme costumes. With just a slick of mascara and some blusher on her cheekbones, Julia felt ready for a night of exploration in a strange city. As the truck shuddered over the cobbles and swung round sharp corners, the laughter and shouts of her fellow performers put Julia in a very good mood. She'd worked damn hard on the new routine, and since her late-night drive with Robert she'd sensed a change between them. There had been no seduction, just the unbearable ache of sexual tension; his dares and teases were unrelenting, but Julia thought she had a glimmer of insight into the man. Julia suspected he might even be developing a certain respect for her and her dancing skills. It made her job easier, and she sensed that the other members of the circus were also warming to her presence, with even the prickly Rachel refraining from her bitchy put-downs. For the moment, at least. Rachel was out with the crowd tonight, travelling in Sarah's battered old Saab, and Julia felt uneasy knowing she'd be around.

'Here, get some fizz down you.' David, one of the sound techs, passed Julia a can of 'fizz' – cold lager. It seemed to be the drink of choice among the circus folk. Except for Robert, Julia thought, remembering the taste of the red wine he'd given her and Sylvie the night of the rainstorm. He was a solitary man, she'd noticed, politely declining to join the crowd going out in town, driving by himself. Though she supposed he needed to keep a distance between himself and his employees, Julia wondered if he ever got lonely, watching the crowds, directing the action, never joining in. For a moment she almost felt sorry for him, and then she quickly moved on as the lorry shuddered to a halt and the back doors were thrown open.

They'd parked in a narrow street of brick buildings right in the centre of town, the truck pulling in behind Sarah's car and the revellers making a noisy crowd that filled the street as they headed down towards Canal Street. Julia fell into step beside Sylvie, who wore a little white tutu and her ballet pumps, combined with a fake fur gilet and bikini top. This was a woman who wouldn't know the meaning of 'dressing down', Julia thought as she walked alongside her, listening to her descriptions of the cities of Hungary and Poland that she'd travelled to, and the shows she'd seen and performed in.

As the crowd moved along the streets they drew startled glances from passers-by, some people sniggering at the sight of them and some sneering. Julia noticed the vague sense of hostility they seemed to cause, and drew closer to the centre of the crowd. Some of the party did look outlandish, she knew: David's heavy black eyeliner and the tattoos that snaked delicately across Henri's temple and down his throat. Rachel was dressed in red, as ever, wearing a shockingly revealing lace basque and hot pants, combined with heavy black cowboy boots that were caked in mud from the site. Altogether, the crowd moved with a grace and dynamism that were bound to stand out on the street of a city, particularly when some of them were singing loudly and laughing with the throaty abandon of people who don't give a damn what anyone thinks.

A month ago, she would have been treading gingerly alongside this bunch, Julia thought. But tonight, she was marvelling at them. As Rachel responded to the leers of a crowd of guys in football tops with a swift V-sign, Julia suddenly felt a rush of wonderful freedom. She knew the skill and utter dedication the performers put into their shows, knew that they believed utterly in what they did. It was a hard gruelling lifestyle, and far from glamorous when you lived in a tiny caravan in a sea of mud for weeks on end. But it was also thrilling, exhilarating, rich and fascinating. With a toss of her hair, Julia grinned and turned to wink at Joe, close behind her and still looking nonplussed at the thought of an alcohol-free night ahead of him.

'Don't worry, Joe,' she called to him. 'There's other ways to have fun. We'll make it up to you.'

'How d'you mean, Julia?' Dave the sound tech chipped in, raising his eyebrows in a filthily suggestive way. 'You got a suggestion for tonight's entertainment?' The conversation dissolved into good-natured elbowing and laughter as the party found a pub with a beer garden by the water, where they instantly swarmed over three tables and started shouting loud drinks orders at the beleaguered Joe.

Above them the sky slowly grew dark as the drinks flowed and the night got rowdier. It was strange, for Julia, to see these people outside the circus setting. In contrast to the rest of the crowds they seemed more vivid, somehow larger than life. Henri was sitting next to her, and Julia was glad to listen to him talk about his great passions, art and film, with his strange long melancholy face expressing every thought. Tattoos like the stems and tendrils of plants curled round his temple, a subtle but exotic design that made Julia think of Maori warriors. As she listened, Julia watched the full moon rise, huge and white above the rooftops. Under its eerie glow, the face of her companion was lit with a faint unsettling light. Looking at the face of the moon, Henri's conversation once again strayed to Rachel.

'Am I just a fool, Julia?' he asked sadly, looking surreptitiously at Rachel as she threw back her head laughing, arm-wrestling the guys at the next table. She was cheating, Julia noticed, digging in her nails till the men surrendered.

'Henri, it's not foolish to love someone,' she said gently, wondering if she really had the right to suggest advice to a man with years more experience than her. And what of her unrequited feelings for Robert? She pushed the man out of her mind, for tonight determined not to even think of him.

'Maybe you need to change the way you're playing the game?' she said tentatively, reminding Henri of the advice he'd given her. 'Try to find what Rachel likes...' She stopped mid-sentence, noticing the expression of pain that crossed Henri's face. He closed his eyes for a minute, and then looked up to smile at Julia. The moonlight caught his teeth and the whites of his eyes, and Julia was struck again by the strange craggy beauty of the man. Something about him touched her.

'Julia, I don't even know if I really want her. I think I enjoy the desire more than I'd enjoy the thing itself.'

'Did you ever try?' Julia asked, curious despite herself. 'You seem to have a connection, you two. I think she feels more for you than you know.' She looked over to where Rachel was watching them, casting one of her toe-curling looks at Julia. She winked back cockily, feeling as though she could take Rachel's threats in her stride tonight.

'In fact, Henri, I think she might even be jealous.' Julia leant into his shoulder, letting Rachel see as she put her hand on Henri's arm and stroked it slowly. 'Don't move,' she whispered to him, 'don't look at her.' She moved closer, sure that Rachel was still watching, and lifted her mouth to Henri's. As her lips met his she felt the smooth cold flesh of his cheek against her mouth and tasted the sweet bitterness of beer. Closing her eyes, she sank into the kiss, letting her body fill with warmth as she experienced the strangeness of kissing him, allowing the arousal to spread through her although she wasn't sure why it turned her on. Perhaps the fact that she knew Rachel was watching, or maybe that she enjoyed playing the part of the tricky young upstart, stirring the waters between these two. Julia knew that the fact she was younger than Rachel was both an advantage and a weakness – Rachel could pull rank on her with her experience and worldly-wise attitude. But although she was well preserved and shone with glamour, Julia knew Rachel would envy her fresh young skin, her delicious toned curves. Julia was well aware of her attractions and how to display them. She let her breasts rise under the sheer fabric of her top, pressing them against Henri's chest and enjoying the feel of his hard gently muscular chest against her skin. When she first kissed him he'd almost jumped with surprise, but now he was responding to her mouth with a skill that Julia appreciated. It was a performance, but that didn't mean she couldn't have fun.

'What the fuck are you doing?'

Julia allowed herself a smile as she heard Rachel's question. She was standing next to them now and spitting with rage. Pulling away from Henri with a reluctance that was only half feigned, she looked up innocently at the woman who stood over her, a vision of fury in her sharp red outfit.

'Is there a problem, Rachel?' she asked innocently.

'Only that you seem unable to stop yourself from fucking anyone who crosses your path.'

Julia wasn't even slightly offended. She had heard so much criticism of her sensuality during her years at college that she was now totally immune to it – in fact it tickled her to think she was once again causing a stir by flaunting her voluptuous charms. And making a woman like Rachel jealous was a serious coup.

'I'm sorry, Rachel,' she said sweetly. 'Would you like a go?' Julia stood and motioned Rachel to the bench beside Henri. Now the two women faced each other, tension crackling in the air between them. The whole group was now throwing sidelong glances at them, curious to see if a fight was going to break out.

'Let's go for a walk,' Rachel said, looking from Henri

to Julia and back again. 'I think we've got some talking to do.'

It was a Friday night and the streets were full of rowdy clubbers, spritzed with aftershave, faces shining with excitement. The three circus people wove through them, making a strange picture – the strong wiry frame of Rachel in her hotpants, long brown hair falling in wild curls past her shoulders, fully made-up and with a face like thunder; Henri, dressed simply in black shirt and trousers but with his tall lean figure, shaved head, beard and tattoos hinting at exotic mystery. He walked with grace, loping through the cobbled streets, his face haunted and intense. Walking slightly behind them, taking her time, was Julia. Despite her light floaty outfit and hair pulled back in a simple pony-tail, she managed to exude an air of knowing sexuality. When the three reached a bridge next to the canal, where a bench lay in the shadows of a tall hotel building, they stopped as if by mutual consent. Julia and Rachel sat on the bench uneasily side by side, while Henri leant against the wall and waited. Rachel lit a cigarette, and Julia watched the smoke drift out over the black water of the canal, where the shattered reflection of the moon floated among the weeds. At last, she broke the silence.

'Julia, you can fuck Joe and Sylvie to your heart's content. I can even live with you drooling over Robert, though trust me, you won't get very far. But Henri and I have – an understanding.'

'Oh really? What if it wasn't my choice?'

Rachel gave a hard brittle little laugh, and looked over to Henri's long figure by the wall.

'Henri, you couldn't possibly tell me you found this cheap little slut attractive, could you?'

Henri spoke from the shadows with his usual deep slow tone.

'Rachel, you know how I feel about you. Have always felt. But you have to admit, she's alluring.' Julia couldn't see Henri's face, but she could hear the pleasure in his voice. Whether that was at the thought of fucking her or just the knowledge that for the first time he had the edge over Rachel, Julia didn't know.

'I have to say, I'm sorely tempted. Particularly as I know you wouldn't let me get close.'

'So despite all your whining about the spiritual love you have for me, despite mooning after me for all these years, as soon as some twenty-year-old with big tits comes by you'd toss all that away for a quick shag?'

'Maybe I'm just tired of it being so fucking painful all the time. Watching you and Robert...'

There was anger in Henri's voice now, and Julia felt the accumulated frustration of his feelings were threatening to spill over. She cleared her throat, not wanting to sit like a gooseberry while the two thwarted lovers had a slanging match. Particularly, she didn't want to hear about Rachel's history with Robert.

'I have an idea.'

'Oh please let us hear it,' Rachel snapped at her waspishly.

'Rachel, I don't want to fuck Henri.'

'Are you quite sure of that?'

'Yes,' Julia said firmly. 'I want to see you fuck him.' She looked at Henri, still leaning in the shadows, motionless. 'To be exact, I want to see Henri fuck you. I want to see you held down and given a thorough screw. Right here.' She laid her arm along the back of the bench, feeling her heart pound as she waited to hear the reaction. She knew this was a dangerous game to be playing, but she was developing a taste for the adrenaline of these uncertain sexual adventures.

It was Henri who moved first, walking slowly to stand behind the bench, putting his hands on Rachel's shoulders. She seemed to have been rendered speechless. Her eyes were flaming with anger, but Julia noticed that she didn't move away from Henri's touch. She didn't flinch when he ran his hands over her breasts, rubbing slowly and hard over the round curves under her basque. As Julia leant forward to unlace the garment and let Henri in to feel the flesh beneath, her lips parted and she started breathing hard. But she didn't say a word. She watched Julia with an expression that was a mixture of hatred, fury and arousal that Julia recognised well. It was just how she looked, she thought, when Robert played his games with her.

As Julia gently turned Rachel around and positioned her on all fours on the bench, she had a sense that this was how Robert would feel, directing the action of one of their voyeuristic scenes. Firmly, she yanked down Rachel's hotpants, exposing the woman's perfectly toned ass, which she noticed Rachel was raising slightly, rocking her hips back as though asking Henri to fuck her. The only sound she was making was a hard panting, an animal noise that Julia found darkly sexual. She was drawn to join in a little, and the satisfaction she felt as she gave Rachel a sharp slap on the bottom was deliciously rewarding. She gave a couple more slaps, relishing the jerks that Rachel couldn't help making under the sting of her hand. It was as though she were toying with a wild animal. Julia even dared to dip her finger in the warm crevice of Rachel's cunt and felt the wet of her arousal, knowing she wanted to be fucked as much as she resented the loss of control.

'Go for it, Henri,' she said, stepping back and letting him take over. She watched with fascinated excitement as Henri approached, grabbing hold of Rachel's hips with a surprising firmness. He didn't touch or caress her, just held her steady with one hand while he unzipped himself with the other. After years of submitting to her cruelty, Julia sensed a kind of sadistic pleasure from Henri as he held Rachel's thighs apart and sunk his cock deep into her, forcing a moan out of her that sounded like the gasp of relief she'd waited for for a very long time. As the two of them rocked slowly back and forth, their lithe bodies an angular jerking silhouette in the grey moonlight, Julia felt a strange new kind of arousal. She could imagine the way it felt for Rachel, and see how much they enjoyed this charged union at last. But more than that, she felt that she was living some erotic lucid dream, able to will the desire of the two people fucking in front of her. She knew they hadn't been able to break out of the old, practised roles they'd been playing until she gave them permission. She wasn't involved, yet was intimately essential to their pleasure. As long as she was there watching, Henri and Rachel were her willing acolytes. Julia felt a surge of unfamiliar power, and for the first time understood Robert's pleasure as he manipulated her sexual awakening.

It was a turning point, and she felt the strength of this new insight gather as Henri's movements became more urgent, as he pushed harder into Rachel till the woman stiffened to let him grind as deep as he could. Julia watched, entranced, as Henri started hissing through his teeth, on the brink of coming and struggling to hold himself back. Suddenly Julia knew what she had failed to do all along. What Robert wanted, and what he had been subtly trying to make happen for the past month.

As the realisation dawned on her, Julia thought of the intensity of their relationship, the balance of power and strength. What it was that made her want him, and the reason he wouldn't touch her. In front of her Rachel and Henri were reaching their climax, struggling against each other to attain that sweet moment of oblivion, calling out like birds, their voices breaking. Julia, without touching herself, felt the warm satisfaction of communion spread through her body.

She knew with total conviction what she had to do next.

12

Edinburgh was a gothic fantasy that captivated Julia: crenellated towers sticking out above the cobbled streets; the blackened stone walls of the castle high above; gardens spilling over with flowers and fountains and everywhere swarming with people. Bewildered foreigners bumped up against street artists and ticket touts, traffic fought its way along Princes Street, and the roiling harsh cry of pipes sounded from buskers on the street corners. Julia loved the buzz and the chaos, the mix of stylish opera buffs and barefoot shabby fringe performers. She had visited a couple of times before, once on a boozy college trip, once with friends to see a couple of dance shows. Never, though, had she arrived in the city in Festival time as a performer.

As the trucks rolled slowly up the bridge that led to the south of the city and the Meadows, where they'd set up for the last fortnight of their summer tour, Julia leant forward in her seat. Passers-by turned to watch as the convoy of dark six-wheelers moved slowly towards the site, twelve black lorries with 'Circus Excite' emblazoned across their sides. While there were many strange sights all over the city during the Festival, few were quite as imposing as the cavalcade of vehicles bringing the circus to town. The performers, stuffed into cabs and peering back at the onlookers, were also a source of great curiosity. As they neared the large rolling park which would be their showground, Julia felt the surge of excitement that she always got when she was the centre of attention, waving back at the gawping pedestrians and blowing kisses, to the amusement of Joe who sat calmly in the driver's seat ignoring the fuss.

'You just love causing a sensation, don't you, babe?' he teased Julia as she gave a wink to a group of lads standing watching the troupe's arrival.

'It's my inner diva coming out for the big show.'

'Biggest yet,' Joe agreed, blowing out his cheeks as he considered the work he had ahead of him. The circus was playing for two weeks, two shows a night. New programmes had been printed, and thousands of glossy flyers and posters would flood the city. Julia had secret fantasies of five-star reviews and packed houses shouting for more, along with a thrilling fear that it could all go terribly wrong.

She'd performed the new routine with Robert for the past week in Manchester, and had a taste of being the star of the show. Somehow, though, Edinburgh seemed different. It felt to her like the summer had been one long rehearsal in preparation for this – a chance to perform in front of the most discerning and difficult audiences in the world, outspoken art snobs half drunk and looking for a chance to heckle. The thought made Julia's toes curl.

'Still,' she mused, half to herself, 'five days to opening night. Time to check out the other shows.' Silently she wondered if any of her classmates were around. The Festival was a magnet for everyone in the theatre and there was a strong chance she'd bump into someone she knew. The thought gave her an uncomfortable flutter in the pit of her stomach – how would her peers react to the circus? Pushing her uneasiness aside, she turned her attention back to the site. The lorries ahead were already parked in a ring, forming the circular enclosure that would be Julia's home for the next three weeks. Joe rolled his truck in behind the others and they jumped out, shaking out tired muscles and nodding to the other crew as they surveyed the ground. Julia was used to the loud rough attitudes of the roustabouts now, had even come to enjoy the banter as they set up. For just over two months the circus had been her entire world: the gruelling manual labour and the dazzling adrenaline of the shows had formed her days and nights. The experiences along with the intense episodes of sexual discovery had woken an exhilarating sense of freedom in her.

As she circled the site in her scruffy work clothes, waiting for construction to start, Julia found herself almost dancing over the grass. She was brimming with nervous excitement and jittering like a schoolgirl.

'Look who's getting over-excited,' Henri called, giving her a lop-sided grin as he pulled a box from the back of his lorry. Since the night in Manchester, Julia had found a subtle shift in the atmosphere between her, Henri and Rachel. The other woman seemed to have retracted her claws and gave Julia a nod when she passed her. Occasionally she even flashed her a dangerous little smile, as though to remind her the ceasefire was temporary. There was an uneasy balance between them now, although Julia was well aware of the volatile nature of relationships in the circus enclosure. She was working her way into this strange new world, but every step seemed to bring new dangers as well as new possibilities. Still, as Julia looked around the green, tree-lined park she felt part of something bigger than herself – as though she were at last finding a place where she could dare to fulfil her dreams, even her darkest fantasies. It would never be an easy place to live, but Julia wasn't interested in a quiet life. Part of her was starting to enjoy even the highly charged spats with Rachel, as though they were indeed playing a game and she was starting to understand the rules.

Only Robert remained untouchable, closed off in his bubble of cool disciplined authority. No matter how Julia talked to him, no matter what she did, he never lost his poise. Although she still wanted him so badly it sometimes made her ache, Julia kept her fantasies to herself, treating him with calm respect and trying not to let him ruffle her when they performed. Before a show, when they waited backstage for their cues, Robert would try to provoke her. He'd tease her, let his gaze wander slowly over her body and remind her of what he'd seen. Slowly, Julia had learnt to harden her reactions to him. He may turn her on, he may make her so weak with desire it was hard to concentrate on the act, but she wouldn't let him know. Gritting her teeth, Julia would flaunt herself on the stage, dance so close she could smell his aftershave. She moved as though she were fucking him, using her body to turn on the audience. But when his eyes met hers, their dancing brown glitter inviting her to go further, Julia would return his gaze with a blank, cold stare. She refused to be drawn into any more of his games. She made do with silent fantasies of Robert – in her head she tied him to the scaffolds with ropes and tormented him in front of the whole crew, teasing him till he begged her to bring him off.

Today, he walked round the site frowning, looking as though he'd slept badly, Julia thought. His shirt was crumpled and there were dark circles round his eyes, which were still as intense as ever, but seemed to have lost the playful spark that both maddened and excited her. Curious, she approached him.

'Robert?'

His head snapped up at the sound of her voice, and for a moment he looked at her blankly.

'Julia,' he said, recovering himself and focusing on her. 'There's a box of flyers in Henri's cab, get yourself in costume and take a thousand.' His voice was rough, as though he'd chain-smoked forty cigarettes, but had the same note of authority that made Julia respond immediately.

'Where am I going?' she asked hesitantly. 'Which costume should I wear?'

Robert considered briefly before answering. He pointed at her.

'Noir suit. Full make-up and heels. Just walk round till you find an audience; you'd probably best head for The Mound.'

Before she had a chance to ask any more, Robert had moved towards the roustabouts and was deep in discussion. It was clear she was expected to work the rest of it out for herself, and she didn't waste any time. The chance to escape the grind of setting up and get a glimpse of Edinburgh was a welcome relief.

She approached Henri as he was unloading the crates from his van.

'Got some flyers for me, Henri?'

'Ah, damage control, is it?' Henri nodded knowingly at her.

'What do you mean?'

'Haven't you seen the review?'

Julia shook her head. Henri's face darkened.

'Robert's nemesis, venting spleen in *The Stage*. There's a copy in the cab if you want to see it. I warn you though, it won't make for happy reading.'

Julia climbed into the cab, wondering if she was about to find the reason for Robert's haggard appearance. Lying on the floor, with a bootprint on the page as though someone had stamped on it in disgust, was a newspaper. She skimmed the headline: 'PERVERT'S PROGRESS'

As she read on, Julia felt a cold nausea rise in her chest. The reviewer used the most vicious language he could to slate the Circus, and phrases stuck in her head with their brutal disdain: 'vile parade of freaks and tarts

... twisted brainchild of Robert York ... filthy and rotten to the core'. There was no mention of her act other than to acknowledge the 'misused' talents of the performers, but the attack on the circus and Robert himself was enough to leave her deeply shaken. It was a poisonous piece of writing, and Julia realised that in the flighty gossip-ridden world of theatre, it could be enough to wreck the show forever.

Julia had never realised just how many steep hills there were in Edinburgh, but after walking for half an hour in her stilettos up the Royal Mile and over the bridge to the chaotic centre of the city, she knew she'd never forget. In the strong August sunshine, her pancake make-up and ritzy costume were outlandishly uncomfortable. The 'noir' suit was tightly tailored, pinched in at her waist and stretching tautly over her ass to accentuate her curves. Her cleavage was shoved upwards and jiggled dangerously close to spilling over as she struggled towards Princes Street, drawing incredulous glances from passing tourists. She pulled a small suitcase behind her, stuffed with flyers for the show, and swore as her heels caught in the cobble stones. Stopping every so often to ask directions, she was keenly aware of the reactions to her garb – from shocked distaste to amused delight or, in the case of several males, blatant leering.

As she stalked along the street, dodging bus queues and scanning crowds of foreign tourists trying to single out likely audience members, Julia felt like she had been plunged into a particularly surreal performance. Anywhere else her outrageous appearance would cause a riot, but in Festival Edinburgh she was one freak among many. Mimes in extravagant stage costumes stood on every street corner; a clown with bleached dreadlocks tottered in stilts down the street; ticket touts shouted raucous banter as she passed. The whole city had turned into one riotous circus, she thought as she headed to The Mound.

Here, in the shadow of the castle, Julia found what seemed to be the heart of the Festival. The art galleries sat like Greek temples in a stone plaza above the gardens, their steps and colonnades swarming with tourists and performers. A unicyclist juggled fire in the centre of a crowd of noisy onlookers, while a band of East European musicians sang a plaintive tune a few feet away. Other acts milled around, posing for photographs and pressing leaflets into the hands of bewildered tourists. Market stalls sold cheap jewellery and trinkets, while hot dog vans wheeled their way across the square.

In the midst of the bustle, Julia stood and opened her suitcase, pulling out a handful of flyers. As she straightened, she put on her dazzling stage smile and started looking for possible punters. She knew the circus would only appeal to a certain type of patron, and scanned the crowd for those she thought had the verve-filled, offbeat appearance that Robert liked to see in the seats. Quietly, she wondered how many of these people would find the show so shocking they would call for it to be banned, as the review had. Would they even be allowed to perform? Complaints were still enough to scare the councillors who dished out public entertainment licences, and it didn't take much to cause a scandal.

Shaking herself, Julia tried to concentrate on the job in hand. She looked around for possible punters, but found they made a beeline for her anyway. The fact that she was dressed with a salacious mix of exposed flesh and extreme glamour helped to attract the attention of the more liberally minded in the crowd, and she soon got into the rhythm of banter with passing people. She found putting on an attitude of irreverent burlesque was the easiest way to catch a punter's interest, whistling or winking as the person approached and fluttering her diamante false eyelashes coquettishly. It was a performance all of itself, and after half an hour Julia realised she was working just as hard as she would have been on site, bumping her hips, bowing and dipping to the stream of people who passed her and flirting hard with anyone who stopped to listen. It was a task just to compete with the noise of traffic, street musicians and the chatter of many languages that filled the air.

She found herself suddenly surrounded by a gaggle of burly tanned men who seemed very taken with her costume, some of the bolder ones reaching out to try to finger the lace on her corset or pat her ass. They laughed uproariously and cajoled each other as they cracked jokes in incomprehensible Italian, disorientating Julia and starting to intimidate her. The group stood very close around her, smiling greasy smiles and sucking their teeth as though examining an animal at auction.

'Okay,' she said, smiling grimly and trying to keep her cool. 'Nice to meet you boys, but I really must get on . . .' She tried to move aside to escape, but found her way blocked by the largest of the men, who threw up his hands beseechingly, as though begging her to stay. It was a delicate situation, and Julia thought wildly of how to extricate herself, especially difficult when the men seemed not to understand a word of English.

'Just tell them *VAFFANCULO!*'

A voice behind her suddenly rang out, a young woman's voice that was blessedly familiar. Julia turned astonished to find Karin standing, arms folded, next to a tall and well-muscled man. Her strident shouting seemed to work, as the crowd of Italian men immediately started moving away, presumably to look for easier targets. Julia was overjoyed to be rescued, and particularly tickled by Karin's jaw-dropping outrage at the sight of her outfit.

'I seem to have a gift for international diplomacy,' Karin said, raising her eyebrow as she took in Julia's vertiginous heels and dangerous cleavage. 'Although, may I suggest that your get-up could be translated as the universal outfit of sluts everywhere. What the hell are you wearing, darling?'

Julia could only laugh as she gave her friend a bear hug, realising she hadn't even spoken to her on the phone in the months she'd been travelling with the circus. The intensity of everything had meant that she'd all but forgotten her old friends, and she felt a pang of guilt as she embraced Karin.

'This is Martin Woods.' Karin introduced the well-built man standing next to her with a hint of smugness. 'We shouldn't even be seen in public together,' she added in a stage whisper, winking at Julia. 'He's directing the show I'm in.'

'You're in a show! That's fantastic.' Julia was genuinely pleased for her friend, but noticed at the same time Karin's sleek elegant appearance, her linen suit and glossy understated haircut. Next to her she suddenly felt ridiculous, dressed in a pantomime whore's costume with her make-up melting in the hot sunshine and her feet aching from the high heels. How would she explain what she was doing?

'So what are you here for, Julia? What have you been doing all summer?' Karin seemed to read her thoughts, and Julia took a deep breath as she wondered where to start. Thankfully, Karin was already insisting that Julia must come for a drink, immediately, and the thought of a glass of chilled wine in a shaded bar was so appealing that she scarcely gave a thought to abandoning her work for the afternoon.

As they fought their way through the crowds and climbed the hundred steep steps to the Royal Mile, Julia listened distractedly to Karin's chatter about her summer holiday in Greece, her new flat in London and who she'd been hanging out with since Julia left. It was comforting to hear someone familiar; after the tense, fraught personalities of the circus Julia found it deliciously easy to listen to Karin's banal chitchat. At the same time, though, Julia was aware that something had changed. She was no longer able to join in enthusiastically with their usual bitch-and-gossip session. As they entered a large busy bar with a Deco interior, Julia found she had hardly anything to say to Karin. Everything she'd experienced in the past couple of months seemed so outrageous and unlikely she didn't know how to explain it. The bad review was weighing on her mind, too.

Karin sent Martin to the bar to buy a round, and took the opportunity to fill Julia in on the details.

'So he's a shit-hot director, made it big in New York and is the very latest new signing at the Rep,' she hissed, eyeing Martin's broad shoulders as he stood at the bar. 'Luckily he also happens to be straight, which was a phenomenally nice surprise, and he's "discovered" me just as I was about to give up and start selling crack to pay the rent.'

'So you're sleeping with him?' Julia asked, wondering whether Karin had fallen into bed with the man in a shrewd career move, or whether she was genuinely attracted to him.

'No, darling. I'm fucking him in hotels when his wife's at work. We don't sleep together.' She shrugged. 'It's one way to get a job as principal. *La Sylphide*. A modern interpretation, five stars in the *Guardian* review.' Karin gave Julia the news with a faux-casual shrug that hinted just how proud she was to be dancing for the Rep. It was a humbling moment for Julia, who realised she hadn't even seen a Festival programme and had obviously fallen out of the world she'd worked so hard to break into. Erotic circus wasn't on the same level.

The latest new signing for the London Rep chose that moment to rejoin them, setting down a large glass of wine in front of Julia and giving her the kind of smile that hovered somewhere between indulgent and suggestive.

'That should cool you down, sweetie,' he said pointedly, eyeing Julia's cleavage with a raised eyebrow. As he sat next to her he pressed the length of his thigh closely against Julia's fishnet-clad leg, while smiling unctuously at Karin. 'So tell me,' he said smoothly, 'what brings Karin's little friend to the Festival?'

Julia felt herself bristle. Martin had a certain kind of oily charm and he obviously was quite convinced of his own importance. Julia had met plenty of men like this at dance school; men who treated female dancers with contempt while simultaneously trying to get them into bed.

'I'm performing at the Meadows,' she said, determined not to let the man's credentials intimidate her.

'Oh really?' His voice was dripping with fake sincerity. 'I would love to see you perform, sweetie. Is this what you wear?' Julia was well aware that he was ogling her blatantly. Even in front of Karin he seemed to be unselfconsciously coming on to her.

'Yes,' Julia answered abruptly, and turned to Karin. She knew pointedly ignoring a man as well connected as Martin could be professional suicide, but she refused to join in his slimy act of gratuitous arse kissing.

The afternoon turned into evening, the uncomfortable situation seemed to ease as the drinks flowed, and by the time the sky outside was darkening Julia was laughing loudly at Martin's stories of New York dilettantes and allowing him to put his hand on her knee. Karin didn't seem to mind; in fact she was smiling brightly at Martin as though she was entirely unaware of her lover's overtures. Around them the bar filled with young, Bohemian-looking locals and the occasional stray performer, and Julia felt jubilantly as though she'd been released from a very long, strange dream. It had been too long, she thought, since she hung out with people who understood her love of dance, who knew the theatre. Despite herself, she found Martin's ideas about dance fascinating. He might be an odious lech, she found herself thinking in the foggy recesses of her mind, but he is a formidable choreographer. He name-dropped ferociously, mentioning Nureyev as though he'd been an intimate friend. He'd lectured in Paris, Moscow, the states. As Julia finished her fourth glass, she found herself listening, dazzled, as Martin described the Sydney Opera House and how he'd demanded a new stage with exactly the right amount of 'spring' he needed to make the show perfect. As she listened, Julia had thought nervously of the circus, and how different the people there were from the stage folk she used to work with. No one there seemed to have the breathtaking ambition of Martin Woods, and an erotic show was unlikely to win any major awards. The performers were skilled and worked like dogs to get the show perfect, but in the rarefied theatre world her role would be seen as little more than that of a cabaret dancer, a cheap titillation for the plebs. That is, of course, if it ran at all.

'Don't you fancy a whirl with us, sweetie?' Martin had suggested, eyes watering with innuendo as he looked Julia over. She was under no doubt that his suggestion would include giving extra favours if she wanted to dance for the Rep. His hot, sweaty hand had stayed clamped to her thigh for the whole evening, and he occasionally brushed against her breasts by accident as he gestured.

By the time she stumbled back onto the street and made her way slowly back to the Meadows, Julia's head was spinning. She'd drunk too much, she knew, but mixed in her addled thoughts were images of Karin, dancing her elegant sculptural role in the ballet and winning plaudits in the reviews. For the first time, Julia felt that she'd made a terrible mistake. When she'd explained her role to Karin she'd reacted with loud guffaws, finding the whole idea of an erotic circus ludicrous. She'd offered congratulations, of course, but Julia could tell that she was only being polite. Next to a role in an acclaimed sensational new ballet by one of the country's leading directors, Julia's achievements paled. Eventually, Karin had expressed a little concern for Julia's career, asking her if this show wasn't going too far.

'Isn't it all a bit louche, darling? I mean, you're not some cheap stripper, are you?'

Now, her words buzzed unpleasantly in Julia's head, leaving a sense of doubt and confusion that left her feeling on the verge of tears. She staggered down past the pubs of the Grassmarket, ignoring the whistles and cat-calls of drunken men sitting outside. Julia swore again as her heels nearly tripped her up, wishing fervently that she was wearing her civvies, and that she'd never even answered the advert for the circus. She was starting to feel sick as she thought of all the chances she was missing, the ballet roles that might have turned up had she not taken the job. It seemed to her that she was always missing the boat, from college productions to the present mess. She was starring in a show that had been ferociously, mercilessly panned.

The Meadows were a mass of inky black ahead of her, the trees forming a sheltered nook from where the tent poles of the circus were just visible. Julia thought of the struggles with Rachel and the humiliations Robert had subjected her to, of her narrow cot in the leaky caravan and the five-star hotel Karin was staying in. Why the hell had she got involved with these people? She looked at the cluster of caravans and lorries with angry drunken confusion. She'd worked her ass off all summer only to realise it was a dead-end. She was going on stage in five days, to perform with a man who watched her fuck other people, who wouldn't ever even touch her himself. And the show was turning into a no-star disaster.

13

From the inky black space under the trees came low voices, speaking as though they did not want their conversation overheard. Julia stood in her heels and costume, listening. She couldn't see who was there – the circus floodlights had not yet been rigged up – but she recognised the warm tones of Joe's Romany, and the dry reedy voice of Henri replying. Julia wondered if she could intrude on them. She wished someone could reassure her, tell her what to do. It was a hard decision to make, but Julia was certain she couldn't stay here. Martin's offer of a place on the corps de ballet had only deepened her confusion – from his hints she understood that the role would be available as long as she complied with his desires. He had spun her a line about how he needed to 'know' his dancers, and Julia was in no doubt that he would expect very intimate knowledge of her body. The thought repulsed her – but the alternative was a dangerous one.

The thought of going onstage after such damning and vicious criticism gave her a queasy feel in the pit of her stomach. What if the audience reacted as the reviewer had done? Could she bear to be ridiculed in the press, could she even take the risk? Julia swayed towards Robert's caravan, wondering if she could find some reassurance from him. Or should she tell him about Martin's offer? How could she leave five days before the show started? Julia's fuddled thoughts were only more confused from all the wine, and she suddenly hit upon the idea of pushing a note under the door. It would be the easiest way to break the news without a confrontation, and in her shaken state the last thing she wanted was to face Robert. Fumbling with her suitcase, she managed to extricate a flyer and her pen, and leant against the side of his van to scrawl a note on the back:

Robert,
I have to leave, I'm sorry.
Julia

After slipping the letter under Robert's door, Julia turned back to the site, wondering if she really could run off in secret without telling anyone. She could stay with Karin tonight, and send someone back to get her things later. Make a dash for it now, part of her urged, although the thought of leaving without saying goodbye made her heart ache. She'd grown attached to the circus crew and knew she was taking the cowardly option. Joe and Henri were by the trees; she could at least wish them luck before she cut loose.

On site, the usual chatter and bustle was absent. A strange unease seemed to hang in the air, with the performers staying in their caravans and Joe and Henri talking clandestinely under the trees. Julia stumbled towards them, her heels becoming even more of a hindrance on the soft grassy field. The haze of wine in her head made her sway slightly and as she reached the two men in the shadows she almost fell into Joe's arms. He steadied her wordlessly, noting immediately the state she was in.

'You've been gone a while, Julia.'

'I bumped into some friends. Ballet dancer and her shit-hot director man. *Sylphide* – five stars.' Julia knew she was rambling incoherently, but was past caring. She hardly noticed that her cleavage had at last spilt free of her top and a nipple peeked from the corset, adding to her dishevelled appearance and giving her the look of a ravaged libertine. Quietly, Joe took off his overcoat and wrapped her in it. Henri remained silent, pulling on a cigarette and blowing long blue streamers of smoke into the dark.

'He offered me a part. I could be in the *corps de ballet*. Ballet...' Julia tried to turn a pirouette, and practically collapsed. Joe gripped her arm tightly and sighed again.

'You know, most people don't run away from the circus, darlin'. Though I don't blame you for wanting to, tonight.'

'We're fucked, Joe. Aren't we?' The edge of despair in Julia's voice was blurred by alcohol, and she leant close in to him, wanting to feel a warm man's body, the comfort of his arms around her. 'I have to go.'

At last, Henri spoke.

'The last time I was here, we had a beautiful walk up the Calton Hill. It's a nice night for a ramble. Joe?'

'Might sober up this one.' Joe nodded at Julia, slumped against his shoulder. 'Come on babe, you need to get some proper shoes on. We're going to take you for an adventure.' He considered for a minute, before adding: 'And I think we should bring Sylvie. It may be a good time for Julia to hear her story, even if it is her last night with us.'

The group of four walked slowly through the dark streets of Edinburgh, still littered with drunken Festival goers loudly discussing the shows they'd seen earlier. The pubs would be open till the small hours, and hard-core revellers were taking full advantage of the city's generous licensing laws, filling the beer gardens and squares and trailing into late-night takeaways. Now dressed in her rough clothes, flanked by Joe, Henri and a recalcitrant Sylvie, Julia was subdued. She walked as though in a dream, absorbing the sights of the partying metropolis, letting her thoughts wander as they moved towards the black dome of Calton Hill.

The climb started at a small square steepled church, rising to a peak that overlooked the city. They moved up steep sloped steps towards where a Grecian folly stood in black silhouette against the orange night sky, forbidding and strange at the same time. As Julia climbed, she listened to the traffic noise receding, and found she was longing for a chance to sit somewhere quiet to calm her confused thoughts. The others seemed to share her desire, as they walked in silence towards the top of the hill. There was no noise apart from their breathing, growing heavier as they pulled themselves upwards over the grassy slope.

Reaching the ruined, half-built monument with its tall stone pillars, all four of them came to a halt to take in the view of the glittering lights of Edinburgh below. Joe crouched beside the wall and rummaged in his rucksack, eventually pulling out a flask and a bottle of whisky.

'Tea for you, Julia. Hot and sweet.' He winked at her as he poured a cupful into the lid of the flask and passed it to her. '*Uisge beatha* for the rest of us.' He produced a blanket from the rucksack and spread it over the ground, sitting back with a sigh of relief.

'Some climb,' Henri remarked, accepting the bottle of whisky and unscrewing the lid. 'Worth it when you get there.' He tipped his head back and took an elegant swig from the bottle, smacking his lips at the taste.

'Take a seat down here now, ladies,' Joe said, patting the ground beside him. 'It's time for a little history lesson, I think. Sylvie, you'll be shocked to hear your slave-girl is considering running off with the ballet.'

'Is that true?' Sylvie turned her round, cat-like eyes on Julia, who sipped her tea and shrugged awkwardly. She hadn't anticipated Sylvie's reaction.

'Is it something to do with the poison-pen rubbish in *The Stage*?' Sylvie demanded, obviously growing angry. She was wearing a long mackintosh over her jeans, and she buried her hands deep in the pockets now, leaning her head back against the stone and sighing noisily.

'That small-minded little prick. I should never have let him get involved.'

'Involved with what? You know this man?' Now it was Julia's turn to react incredulously.

'An old tutor of mine, a ballet director. And a vicious, jealous man with more ambition than talent.'

'You studied ballet?'

'At the Rep. Four years of sheer hell, and the worst part was fending off that dirty bastard.' Sylvie was almost spitting. 'He had an ego the size of Europe, and promised the best parts to any girl who'd let him in her bed. I never agreed, but it only spurred him on. He pursued me even after I'd left.'

Julia recognised the story from her earlier encounter with Martin Woods, and the correlation made her uncomfortable.

'What happened?'

'I met Robert, fell in love with the circus. I went to a show one night in Fitzrovia, a tiny dark little basement. You were there, remember, Henri?'

Henri nodded, smiling quietly.

'It was a revelation. Just a few acts, no stage, nothing in the way of a budget. But I felt like I'd discovered some strange heaven. There was a burlesque act, Rachel stripping. Henri, knife throwing. Rachel was about your age, then, Julia. Robert did the most amazing magic, disappeared a girl in front of the whole room, and the way he did it . . .'

Sylvie trailed off into a reverie, taking a sip of whisky and laughing softly to herself.

'I'd never been so turned on in my life. After the show, I had to meet them all. I wanted to be part of it.'

'You were gasping for a shag, if I remember right,' Joe broke in, the humour in his voice apparent. 'Practically panting. We were very happy to have you begging us to let you get involved.'

Sylvie gave him a wicked smile and blew him a kiss.

'My tutor was furious, though. I dropped out of the Rep the next day. Spent it in bed with Joe, in fact, discovering ways to practise contortion.'

Julia was pleasantly surprised to find she wasn't even slightly jealous of Sylvie's admission. Her relationship with Joe was warm and fun, but she didn't harbour any deep longing for him. She couldn't, while she was so fixated on Robert. Besides, she had also had the pleasure of exploring Sylvie's charms; she wasn't in any position to get possessive.

'He found out what I was doing, turned up one night at the club and caused a scene.'

'Called us all perverts. Even used the word "satanic" if I'm remembering it right,' Henri mused.

'I didn't object to being called a pervert. Just when the bastard started threatening to close us down, it really turned ugly,' Joe said.

Sylvie nodded. 'He's a powerful man, unfortunately. Friends with the local councillors, the arts board. He was in a position to threaten us, no bluffing. But Robert stepped in.'

Joe and Henri were both laughing now; it was obviously a favourite shared story. Sylvie turned to Julia with a twinkle in her eye.

'You know when Robert gets that idea in his head, he seems to turn into some kind of mesmerist. The whole place was watching, and he just walked up to the man and plucked a pair of lady's knickers from his breast pocket, as though they'd been there all the time. Asked if that was what he'd been looking for, only the young lady would prefer it if she could have them back.' Sylvie was laughing too now. 'He humiliated the old bastard in front of everyone, including a local journalist. It was a classic moment, and I loved him for it. Only since then, the man's taken every chance he can to sabotage Robert's work.'

Julia listened, transfixed. She felt a mix of relief and anger at the man who'd set out to ruin the circus because of some ancient vendetta. Robert believed in his principles, she realised, and would stand up for one of his performers rather than stay in the safety of the shadows, even if it jeopardised his career. She considered him with new respect. The more she found out about Robert the more curious she felt, and the more she wanted him, to explore his body and mind.

The four fell silent now, each lost in their own thoughts, watching the lights below them sparkle like a box of jewels spilled over the night. They sipped at the whisky and listened to the wind blowing around the top of the hill, noticing the sky was starting to lighten slightly in the East, over the grey sea that lay in the distance.

Julia had not slept in many hours and her head ached from the afternoon's drinking spree, but she felt a sense of lightness, as though the hours on the hill had refreshed her somehow.

'It's strange, but I'm feeling a hell of a lot better than I ought to,' she remarked sleepily to her companions.

'Must be the powers of Calton,' Henri replied. 'There's ancient festivals staged up here in the spring, pagan rituals and torchlight processions.'

'Beltane,' Joe nodded. 'A celebration of sex, the union of the goddess and the god. They go a little wild, I'm told.'

The image of a pagan carnival delighted Julia, as she pictured people fornicating under the shadow of such an imposing monument. She imagined the rituals intertwined with sex: a fascinating, explosive and beautiful pageant acted out on the hillside. A celebration of sex. Like the circus.

Fuck the hypocrites, Julia thought suddenly. Fuck the sleazy directors and bitter theatre critics. In Circus Excite, she could explore her own fantasies and desires. She didn't have to submit to the furtive lechery of the director to win a starring role. The circus revolved around sex with honest and open fascination. Nobody's desires were taboo, and nothing was reviled. They lived according to their own beliefs, not a hidden mess of snobbery and twisted transactions. It seemed suddenly as though she had made exactly the right choice, and Julia felt herself abuzz with a new optimism.

'Will the review do us any damage, do you think?' she asked, a note of anxiety still lingering in her mind.

Joe shrugged.

'It's a risky business, babe. No telling what might happen. All you can do is put on the best show possible and ignore the bad press.' He looked at Julia, his tanned face indistinct in the early morning gloom. 'You'll need to find that inner diva again, Julia, and give her a chance to shine. Unless, of course, you're still running off to be a ballerina?'

Julia sipped at the whisky and felt it warming her inside. A growing, dizzying sense of anticipation was building within her. She felt reckless, as though she could leap off the crest of the hill and soar over the city.

'Sylvie, come here and show me that back flip again,' she said, struggling to her feet.

She shrugged off Joe's jacket and let the chill of the air turn her skin to goosebumps, slapping her arms to warm up. She still wore her basque underneath, and the tight lacing and the cold stimulated her to move fast. She held out her hand to Sylvie, cajoling her to join her.

Together they started practising the acrobatics she had been learning. Julia felt her muscles start to warm up as they played around, balancing carefully on each other's backs and leaning forward into sideways splits. She hadn't realised Sylvie's flexibility had come from a childhood of studying ballet, but it all made sense as she watched Sylvie move gracefully from one position to the next. Admiring the petite, sleek figure of the other girl, Julia remembered with a warm flush their amorous encounter, and the feel of Sylvie's small firm breasts in her hands. Since then, she'd found Sylvie even more stimulating to work with, and the moments in their routine where she wound her body round the other girl's or leant to kiss her had become a pleasure. As they moved through a little routine of acrobatic poses and moves, Julia felt again the playful attraction between them, and realised that Sylvie was enjoying the rough and tumble as much as she was.

Behind them, Joe and Henri were calling out encouragement, and Julia realised their audience was not entirely oblivious to the girls' flirtation.

'Come on and join in, you couple of voyeurs,' she called out teasingly, as she let Sylvie's arms wrap gently around her waist and hold her as she leant into a deep back stretch, Julia bending backwards till her fingertips brushed against the dew-soaked grass.

In a moment, Henri and Joe were standing beside them, and they started to dance. Waltzing playfully over the grass in a swaying parody of a foxtrot, Julia gave in to the excitement that she felt running through her veins. As she was passed from Joe to Henri, brushing against Sylvie as they swapped partners, Julia noticed a russet flash in the corner of her eye. She turned to see a red setter running eagerly through the grass, followed by a bleary-eyed man in his forties, yawning in the dawn light.

Seized by a mischievous idea, she pulled away from Henri and motioned for the others to look downhill.

'How about we put on a little show for the early bird?' she called, eyes bright and face flushed from the exertion of dancing. The others turned to see the lone dog-walker wandering slowly uphill towards them, hands stuffed in pockets and eyes to the ground. A silent idea passed between them and immediately Sylvie started wriggling out of her warm clothes. Within a minute she was stripped to her underwear, so that her appearance matched Julia's – both girls displaying a shocking amount of flesh, their bodies glowing white in the half-light of dawn. Fighting to suppress wild fits of laughter, the girls whispered a few ideas to each other, quickly agreeing a sequence of steps. The thought of treating some unsuspecting man to a display of Circus Excite was so daringly reckless that Julia felt dizzy. She could feel the cold pinching her nipples into stiff peaks that stood proudly against the wired fabric of the corset, and seeing Sylvie in her see-through bra and French knickers, she felt herself thrill with the desire to shock, along with an undeniable arousal at the thought of dancing with Sylvie for pleasure, not work.

Behind her, Joe and Henri were grinning, both complicit in the act that Julia and Sylvie were planning. They removed their jackets and stood bare-chested, Joe rubbing his hands together for warmth.

'Come here and let me warm my hands on you, babe,' he growled to Julia, who moved close to him so she could drape herself over him. Sylvie and Henri adopted the same position, and the four of them waited as the unsuspecting man approached slowly along the path.

'Now, girls, if he should suffer a heart attack you're to be held responsible,' murmured Joe, as they watched the man reach the brow of the hill and look vaguely around him for the dog. When his eyes alighted on the motionless tableau under the folly, he froze. Exactly what he thought as he stared at the four half-naked sprites was a mystery, but it was certain that they had his full attention.

Without a word, Julia started to move. Using Joe's stock-still body as a prop to work against, she started winding around him, bucking her hips in time to a silent rhythm, noting Sylvie as she mirrored the same movements around Henri.

The man watched, entranced, as the two girls climbed over the bodies of their male partners. His dog lead hung, forgotten, from his hand, the red setter abandoned to roam over the hill. Julia felt with pleasure the bulge in Joe's trousers as he stood, arms folded, and let Julia rub herself against him, letting the friction warm her cold flesh as she shivered and worked her way down towards his ankles.

It was an improvised routine, the girls using every trick they knew and dancing with a fresh playful attitude that might have delighted their one-man audience. Julia couldn't tell, she was concentrating on synchronising her movements with Sylvie and trying to anticipate what Joe might prompt her to do. It was hard to concentrate, too, while she was in a state of half-arousal, distracted by Joe's unyielding flesh and the swelling of his erection as she brushed against him, aware at the same time that Sylvie was eliciting a similar response from Henri, teasing him by pressing her breasts against his arms, standing in front of him and spreading her legs wide before folding serenely in half, face down.

Julia imitated the movement, and noticed gleefully as Joe's gaze fixed hungrily on the crotch of her knickers, raking over the curves of her ass as it tilted upwards at an absurd and lewd angle towards him.

She knew the man was still watching, and delighted in the thought of surprising him with this surreal and exotic performance first thing in the morning. As ever, she moved with the silent rhythm that came easily to her, matching it to Sylvie's undulating movements and approaching the other girl to dance slowly with her, waiting for Joe and Henri to move in closer.

The show was building to a silent subtle climax, brimming with sparks of sexual tension passing between the four, Sylvie bobbing against Julia's chest and letting her tongue roll over Julia's neck, winding her hands into her hair as if she was knitting the two of them together. As she drew Julia closer to give her a lingering deep kiss, Julia felt Joe's hands wrap around her waist and lift her up till she was held aloft with her crotch pressing tightly against his shoulder, while Sylvie rose towards her in Henri's arms. The four of them moved to a huddle, forming a tight knot of limbs that linked with each other and balanced smoothly into a tower of flesh and taut muscle. Julia reached forward to hold Sylvie while she ground herself against Joe's collarbone, before freezing in the position that left her aching to move more, to bring herself pleasure against the bodies of her companions. Simultaneously, the others brought their movements to stillness and held the position, freezing once again as a motionless tableau as the sun suddenly broke from the horizon and spilt yellow daylight over the hillside.

The sound of one man clapping shyly, before hurrying away, was enough to make them collapse with laughter, four of them trembling with the effort of holding a difficult pose and the delight of getting turned on in public, while entertaining the passing walker. They moved apart reluctantly, each acknowledging slyly that the routine had got them all aroused.

It was a beautiful sunrise, and Julia watched it

wrapped in an exhausted but horny tangle of her friends and fellow workers, lazily stroking each other under the blanket as though continuing the performance. She let a hand wander inside her corset and squeeze gently at her aching nipple, while she pressed her cheek against Joe's taut warm belly and closed her eyes to the dream-like quality of their sex play. Occasionally she'd think of the show to come, while Sylvie gave her a nip on the ear or kissed her sweetly, and the pictures that flowed through her mind were a sumptuous wonderland; beautifully erotic.

While the four friends explored each other Julia let herself fall in love with the whole circus; the strange dangerous dream of it. The feel of Joe's tongue gently licking at her earlobe and circling lazily down towards her mouth was even more thrilling with the others watching, and the lovemaking felt increasingly like a complex dance. Henri wrapped his spidery limbs around her, pushing his long thin erection into the small of her back, while Julia twisted to reach down to play with Joe. He gradually hardened in her hand, and Julia felt the wonder of two pricks gently butting against her, the stiff monstrous size of Joe filling her palm, the point of Henri's cock rubbing against her ass. She was overcome by a desire to feel every inch of her skin against another body, the weight of bodies pin her down and smother her.

Trapped in the delicious pincers of the men, she let her mouth fall open and found Sylvie's hot, eager mouth suddenly against hers, the other girl's tongue tripping quickly between her lips, and she kissed back as though she was no longer in possession of her senses – only aware of the multiple movements, the increasing rhythm of the caresses passed between them.

Under the hazed damp light of the blanket the four

peeled back clothes to reveal each other's most intimate places: Julia allowing Sylvie's mouth to dance over her body; nipping at her breasts with sharp pearly teeth; feeling Joe pull her scant G-string aside as Sylvie worked closer to her pussy; letting Henri grind himself between the cheeks of her ass. It was as though they were lost in a strange subliminal place where only their pleasure mattered. The sequence of movements blurred into an overwhelming mix of sensations as Julia felt Sylvie's tongue slipping over her clit, Joe's fingers digging into her inner thigh, and Henri holding her tightly. She was held firmly while the other three explored her, while she strained to feel yet more of their bodies against her, trying to rub her face into Sylvie's crotch, wanting suddenly to taste the salty dew of her friend's excitement even as her cunt was assaulted by the others. She was like an animal caught in a trap, willingly tortured by the three hungry creatures, each pushing her against the other. A chorus of fingers, tongue and cock tried to find their way inside her, hands roving over her skin and agitating her to a point of frantic want. She felt, from behind, Henri holding her tits, squeezing her nipples between his delicate fingers as if he was playing an instrument, pinching her till he coaxed a note that was a mix of pain and intense pleasure from her mouth.

Julia cried louder, an unearthly sound coming from her mouth as he pushed the head of his cock against the tight hole of her ass, and she felt herself licked and sucked at the same time.

She let waves of furious arousal shimmer over her and through her, giving her a sensation as white-hot and dangerous as the feeling she had when she performed – knowing her entire body was being worked to fever pitch, that she was moving into a space that was not entirely sane any more. It was the moment when her body took over and became something outwith her control, a conductor of heat and energy that was no more than movement, sensation and eroticism.

As she felt the intent of the other three working her towards an orgasm she knew would blow her apart, Julia moaned and gave in. She felt Henri's dark intense movements, and the jubilant flicking of Sylvie's tongue against her clit, Joe's strong hands holding her as she came, holding her hips and bearing down on her to let the climax of this sequence crash through her and overpower her, the darkness explode in her head. She lost control, then, of her mind and body: bucking, writhing and half sobbing. Yet even as she convulsed with the orgasm, she knew somewhere within herself that this abandon was what drove her, what she had always been chasing, as she danced and flirted and listened for the roar of the crowd out beyond the stage. The sensation of being fucked beyond reason was the same as that of dancing herself to a frenzy, surrendering to the desires of the audience, of her lovers, her own body.

14

It was early morning when they walked back across the quiet empty city, the only other souls awake a few workmen clearing last night's litter and debris from the streets. Julia felt as though she were floating through a silvery grey dream, the lack of sleep and after-effects of love-play combining to give her a feeling of altered reality. Bumping gently against Joe's side, wrapped in the soft blanket, she let herself be led through the sleeping city to the quiet green expanse of the Meadows. Her eyes were half closed with fatigue and her skin felt sticky from her own sweat and that of the others, from their shared small playful intimacies on the side of the hill that left Julia turned on and blissful.

Since she'd joined the circus it seemed she'd been in a perpetual state of arousal; hyper aware of every nuance of her body's responses from the touches of others or from the vivid provocative spectacle of the show itself. It had been an intense, confusing experience, and she felt the exhaustion of days overwhelming her. Yet as the morning slowly brightened she was flooded with a new energy. Her desire to perform was stronger than ever, and it was with a fresh confidence that she arrived at the tree-shaded site where the rest of the circus still slept.

The circle of caravans was quiet and dark, with curtains drawn and the generator lying idle and silent. As the others said goodbye and headed to their caravans, Julia remembered the note. The light was on in Robert's van, and she realised with a lurch that he would have read the letter last night, no doubt ensuring his night was as sleepless as hers. With a whispered explanation to Sylvie, she crept towards the silver trailer, half hoping that Robert would be asleep.

She knocked tentatively, and heard the scrape of a chair inside. Robert opened the door and stood looking at her, his face distracted and unshaven, the puffiness under his eyes betraying his exhaustion. He nodded at her.

'Still here? I thought you'd abandoned the sinking ship.' His voice was rough and scratchy, as though he'd spent all night smoking. Julia noticed the accusation, but tried to ignore it.

'Can I come in?'

'Be my guest.'

He stood aside to let her pass, and Julia slipped into the caravan to be greeted by a chaotic mess of papers strewn over the table, floor and sofas, an ashtray and dirty wineglass abandoned on the desk. Gingerly, she moved aside a pile of folders and sat on the sofa. It was a very different scene to her last visit – obviously Robert had been up all night.

'So, is this a goodbye call?' he asked, folding his arms.

'I'm not going, Robert. I just got scared. Like you said, the circus isn't an easy way to live.'

He studied her with a hard gaze.

'Julia, the whole show runs according to exact planning. You're well aware of that. We put you in an important position and would expect you to honour your commitment.'

His tone was sharp, but Julia was prepared for it. She nodded.

'I just needed reminding of something.'

'Which was?'

'More important, even, than being obliged to perform. I'd forgotten what it is I love, the whole reason I'm here.'

'The spotlight? The glory? Might not be much of that to go around,' Robert spat bitterly, and Julia realised how much the review had shaken him. She shook her head, watching him carefully.

'No, Robert, it's not important. It's the dance I love, the movement and the playfulness of it. I love the freedom, and the Circus Excite is the first place I've felt like I could show – everything of myself.'

Robert gave a short bark of laughter.

'I thought you objected to being called a stripper.'

'So did I, to begin with. But I've learnt a lot since then.'

'Yeah, well I'm glad the show's helped you find your inner slut, or whatever it is you think you've got a hold of. But I wouldn't hang your hopes on the circus.'

Julia was stunned. She'd never heard Robert talk with bitterness, and despite the fact neither of them had slept last night, she gathered his anger was more than just exhaustion. The circus was Robert's whole life and she couldn't believe he would doubt himself. He had dropped abruptly into a chair, hanging forward as though he was utterly drained, rubbing his eyes. His usual easy languor had evaporated, and for the first time Julia thought she saw a human weakness about him.

'I saw the review,' she said softly.

'You and the whole of the theatre world,' he said, shoving his hands into his hair. 'We've been written off as a cheap sex show. The bastard might be a hypocrite, but he's got power. It's not just the article. He'll make sure the guys at the licensing department are aware of the "perversity". He'll spread the word round his cronies in the press, the theatre critics. He'd do anything he could to shut us down. As it is, we're running on a loss . . .' Robert trailed off, letting the note of despair hang in the air between them.

It was almost heartbreaking, Julia thought, to see this man who'd worked tirelessly to create the circus destroyed by a vindictive piece of criticism. Robert was a wreck, and in contrast to Julia's new surge of optimism, he was obviously on the edge of a dark chasm. She sat for a minute watching him. The change had not diminished his attractiveness, she thought; in fact a part of her wanted more than ever to approach this strange lonely man and press her body against his. He lived in a world that was distant and unknowable, but in that moment she thought she glimpsed a little of his true self, and the feeling excited her. Although she was dizzy with lack of sleep, Julia sensed the chance to touch Robert now, to move closer to him in a way she hadn't imagined before.

'Do you remember the first time I came to your caravan?' she asked, feeling her way tentatively.

When Robert made no response, she continued, determined to reach him.

'You made me undress and held a mirror in front of me. I was terrified, and when I got turned on I was ... ashamed.'

Robert lifted his head and looked at her. Though his eyes were still shadowed with tiredness, Julia saw a cold spark in them that made her catch her breath.

'I sat like this,' Julia continued, leaning back in the seat and slowly spreading her legs apart. 'I was at my most vulnerable, Robert. I could never have imagined ... touching myself in front of a stranger.' As she spoke, Julia let her hand drift over her body, reaching to her breast and resting gently there, cupping the soft swell. She started rubbing at herself, scuffing her nipple and letting it harden under the insistent pressure of her hand.

'I wasn't sure if I was doing something very wrong, something that could end with humiliation and misery.'

Now, she unzipped her jacket and pulled it off. Underneath, the corset was still on but unlaced, dishevelled from the mauling of the night. It was easy to pull her breasts free and let them rest on the top of the bustier, and she let her head fall back, still kneading at her nipples, leaving herself naked and open in full view of Robert.

'Part of me wanted to cry, I was so scared of what might happen. But at the same time, I was burning up, I was so turned on.'

Now Julia moved her hands down, slid one down the front of her knickers. She felt the heat between her thighs, the swell and the wetness as she slid her fingers between her legs, rubbing with the same slow rhythmic pressure she'd applied to her breasts. As she lost herself in the pleasure of fingering herself she continued to talk to Robert in the same low voice.

'I was shaking when I left, as horny as an animal. I could hardly walk.' Julia knew she was doing to herself what Robert had made her do that night, but this time she was the one in control. She stopped herself from looking at him, though she was dying to see his face and the expression of intense fascination and amusement that he had when he watched her. Struggling to stay present, she moved her fingers inside herself, twisting into the mouth of her pussy and tugging a little at her lips, letting the excruciating tenseness of the situation build. She wanted to involve him, this time, to elicit a response from him, good or bad. Nuzzling at the cushions with her head, she let her mouth fall open a little, a moan escape. Under her hand, her hips bucked and she knew Robert was watching as she fucked herself.

The early morning light lent a cold dream-like atmosphere to the scene as Julia slowly let her arousal build while Robert watched. She was half performing for him, showing him her stiffened nipples and the glistening of the moisture that wet her thighs, knowing her face was twisted in concentration as she explored herself. As she moved around, splaying her thighs and writhing, grinding herself into the fabric of the chair and the soft cushions, she let herself drift in a state of such arousal that she was almost unconscious, every moment drawn out in a long blissful buzzing of tension, every flicker of her fingers sending crazy thrills through her whole body. The pressure of the very air on her nipples seemed enough to make them tingle, as though Robert's gaze, his rapt attention, was a physical sensation stroking over her, compelling her to prolong the act though she yearned to feel the shock of orgasm.

'It's like since that night I've become someone else,' she said, her voice shaky with desire. 'I found my pleasure, all the ways of exploring it.' Julia felt her pulse quicken, and held herself back in case she should come. All night she'd been hovering on the edge of orgasm, and the tension was becoming a deliciously drawn out torment. Her thoughts were spinning through her head as though she were on drugs.

'You're the one who helped me find what I love.'

As she heard herself say the word love, Julia opened her eyes, looking directly at Robert with eyes that were suddenly bright with urgency. She'd almost said something she hadn't even imagined she felt, that she might feel for Robert something greater than lust and anger. She lay sprawled in her seat, undone with the intensity of the silent room, feeling as though she'd opened herself more fully to him than she ever had before.

He was sitting straight in the chair, as though poised to move, with a shine to his eyes that Julia recognised as his familiar engaged self. The two of them locked eyes, and a moment of understanding passed between them that was as close as Julia had ever come to being at ease with him. A smile spread over her face, unbidden, and she realised her small intimate performance had shifted something within Robert.

'I do love watching you, Julia,' he said, warmth and guile mixed in his voice. 'You're truly fascinating. Enough to make me forget the world.'

He stood to leave the room, throwing a comment over his shoulder as he did so: 'You know, I think it's time I showed you something too.'

Julia took a deep breath to calm her racing pulse and rearranged herself. She didn't cover her nakedness entirely – it hardly seemed worth affecting modesty with Robert any more. When he reappeared she was sitting with her corset casually pulled straight, her hair tangled and dishevelled. She felt strangely as if she'd spent the night with a new lover and was just waking up with him.

Robert knelt in front of the low table, his arms full of battered books, which he laid in front of them as though spreading out gifts for her.

'This is how I fell in love with the circus, Julia.' He pulled a brown suede-bound album open and motioned for her to look. Inside was a small poster, written in Cyrillic script and unintelligible to her. The paper was yellowed, cheap and wrinkled, but the image that caught Julia's eye immediately was a delicate detailed drawing of a woman, frozen in a lewd arabesque. Her legs were scissored apart as though she was opening them for a lover, and her body leant backwards in a posture of abandon.

'St Petersburg, in the winter of 1989. The woman is Elena Matrovka, the one who introduced me to sexual theatre. It was an underground show, by invite only.' Robert smiled as he leafed through the album, showing Julia brief glimpses of performers, naked and adorned with feathers, beads, body paint. The people were Slavic,

Indian, Eastern; exotic and intriguing. Julia felt a shiver of curious excitement as she perused the photographs, saw the expressions of mischievous daring and the lascivious poses of the performers. It was a gallery of theatrical erotica – faded photographs and drawings, pages cut from books in languages Julia didn't recognise, all Robert's history revealed in scraps of images. Robert showed her other books – Indian paintings of round-breasted women and men with huge erections, Chinese lithographs showing Emperors with their concubines, twisted, perverse images that were executed with beautiful skill and artistry. The two of them lost themselves in the books, moving further into the world of erotic visions and every so often stopping to look at a particularly arresting image.

Julia sat on the floor, half undressed and sharing Robert's fascination with the obsessively detailed pictures. Through all of the pictures she recognised a certain quality, an edge of dangerous and bold transgression that aroused her as much as the graphic depictions of sex acts. She realised slowly that the thing which she found exciting was the way the subjects displayed themselves or appreciated each other, the way a Victorian girl with shy eyes looked timidly from behind her hair at the photographer, her ghost-white body a soft blur of flesh, the dark hair of her pubis shrinking neatly to a point between her legs which she kept demurely pressed together. An Indian miniature, rendered in deep inky blues and complex gold leaf, showed a prince rapt with attention as a woman danced before him, tilting her hips to show him the delicate pink flower of her sex, her nipples dotted with henna, full breasts proudly displayed.

'This is how I became a voyeur,' Robert said, smiling again, and it was then that Julia felt things settle into place – the way he watched her, how he loved the theatrical, the visual feast of bodies and sex.

'Is that all you are?' she asked, intrigued by this new perversion, wondering if Robert's mystique could be so easily explained.

But Robert only laughed, his old easy rough laugh, so that his eyes creased and he seemed once again self-possessed, coolly confident. When he looked at Julia she saw again the distance that stretched between them, her guileless naivety and his unexplained history: the confidence that has been earned through experience and effort and doesn't need to prove itself. She saw Robert's character reassert itself, and he became the languorous charming magician again.

Whatever they had shared in that quiet charged morning had dissipated and he was once again the ringmaster: wry; suggestive but untouchable. Julia realised that the moment of intimacy had passed and once again, she'd been left dissatisfied. Now, with her mind full of the lush images and vivid descriptions of his pornography, her body still aching from unfulfilled desire, she thought she had an idea of how to play his game. She knew he was aware of her barely concealed nakedness, and of how turned on she was. Before, she'd railed against his lack of physical touch, but this time she felt the shimmer of tension between them and relished the distance. Sitting beside him, so close she knew he could feel her breath on the side of his face, smell and feel the warmth of her eager young body. Without moving closer, she started to talk.

'I like this pose,' she said, pointing to one of the photographs. A couple were intertwined, the man's tongue curled between the buttocks of the woman, her figure prone on a hotel bed. Looking steadily at Robert, she continued.

'I'd like to feel you do that.'

'You want to act it out?' Robert's voice was low and even.

'I want to lie face down and hear you move around behind me. I want to feel your hands on me.'

Robert watched her closely, but made no move to touch her.

'Imagine your tongue pushing into me. Imagine how I'd taste.' Julia's heart was thudding in her chest, the words spilling from her mouth shocking her even as they did so. She hadn't ever told Robert explicitly what she wanted, and although she'd shown him how much he aroused her she had never spoken so boldly before.

'Is that all you want me to do?' he asked.

'I want you to do everything in these pictures. I want you to touch me, and lick me and fuck me.' As she spoke, Julia felt herself growing more heated, wanting so badly for Robert to respond to her suggestions she thought the lack of his touch was almost painful.

Closing her eyes, she let the feeling grow inside her, imagining Robert reaching out for her, pushing her onto the floor and leaning the weight of his body over her.

'I think I'm learning how it's beautiful not to touch. It's difficult, like walking a tightrope.' She smiled, opening her eyes again to look at him. 'But I think I understand. I want you to watch me, and every time you see me, I want you to ache for me.'

Inside the caravan was still and silent, only the sounds of birdsong filtering in from trees surrounding them, the shaded hush of the Meadows outside. Julia felt the sensation of longing stretching within her and growing in the silence, as though it was altering her from the inside. It was a curious feeling, to want something and not act on it, but instead allow the wanting to course through her veins till it was a physical presence in itself. She felt her lips tingling with the desire to press them against

Robert's skin: her fingers itched as though the need for his flesh were an irritation. Inside she felt as though she were being pulled in several directions at once, as though the memories of the summer's erotic encounters were imprinted on her body and were replaying now, echoes of desire flickering across her skin.

'You look so fucking good right now,' Robert murmured, bringing her back to the present with a jolt. 'I love watching you get turned on.'

'I want you to fuck me with your eyes.'

'Oh, I am Julia, I am. Your nipples are getting stiff. Sticking out like it's cold.'

'What else?' she murmured.

'Your cheeks are flushed. You're biting your lip. You look like a woman looks when she's being fucked. As though I'm inside you right now.'

'I'd like that.'

Robert laughed again, amused by Julia's entreaties.

'Not yet, darling, not yet. For now, just enjoy showing yourself to me.'

'And later?'

'Who can tell?' Robert was still teasing her, even though Julia knew he was turned on. 'Anything's possible.'

His voice was heavy with mystery, as playful as it had been the first time Julia had met him, when she'd auditioned for him. Only now she sensed more to it, a hint of promise that left her hanging on, waiting for more. She had the feeling she was edging ever closer to him, learning more about her own desires and simultaneously uncovering glimpses of Robert, suggestions of the games he liked to play, the games he wanted to play with her. If only she could find the secret, she thought, she could win the game and take Robert to her bed. The thought drifted through her mind like the lightest touch of a lover, stroking slowly, achingly slowly, over her.

15

'Sexy picture,' said Sylvie, as Julia hung the framed photo above her narrow cot. 'Who's the girl?'

Julia smiled as she looked at the joyous figure of Josephine Baker, cart-wheeling over the back of her dance partner.

'The most inspirational dancer that ever lived.'

After her trip to the hill and the hours with Robert, Julia had slept for a deep dreamless twelve hours and woken with a sense that her world had changed irrevocably. As she lay in bed, feeling the aching muscles of her legs and the stiffness of her body after the long strange night, she imagined her body itself had undergone some transformation. It was as though the hours on the hill and her voyage of erotic history with Robert had taken her to a new place, where her sexual life had fused with the circus and turned her into a new creature. She felt as though her sensuality shimmered over her skin; the sensation of being watched and admired had polished her body till every movement she made was part of a sexual display. As she rose and stretched, she remembered the difficult pleasures she'd found at dance school, the joy there was in pushing herself to new and harder disciplines. Her body hadn't forgotten the sweet feeling there was from working through pain, and for the first time in months she felt the urge to practise.

In the empty tent, in the quiet space with daylight filtering softly through the canvas and turning the stage into a half-lit platform, Julia gripped a bar of the scaffold and started stretching. Around her the roustabouts came and went. Julia barely nodded to them as she absorbed herself in a simple sequence of exercises, feeling with delight her body's remembered response to the movements. The old positions seemed infused now with a new sensuality, and even in a simple *plié* Julia felt her hips arching, her breasts swaying gently. It was a wonderful surprise to find her old routines fitting so beautifully with the sensuality of her body, as though she'd finally discovered the secret of how to dance her own way. She moved now with a new freedom, a mixture of the discipline of dance school and the daring of the circus, and as before she felt the silent rhythms pulse through her body, a beat that echoed the rocking motions of sex, the push and pull of forces moving through her. Slipping lithely over the stage, dropping suddenly to the floor, winding herself around the centre poles that surrounded the stage, Julia lost herself in the pure joy of sensual movement. The sweat beaded on her skin, and she tasted the salt of it as she worked, breathing hard and abandoning herself to her body's instinctive desire to move. As she danced, Julia felt herself still turned on, as though a switch had been flicked and she could no longer distinguish the act of dancing from the act of love. Every bump of her hips was like the thrust of a woman fucking, every time her hands trailed over her chest she felt the stiff points of her nipples, teased to an agonising hardness.

It was dancing with the discipline and grace of her training, but now she was so suffused with the pervasive movements of seduction, Julia knew her body lent a new sensuality to the actions. She was all curving leg muscles, rounded ass and softly swelling breasts, the lines of her drawn like one of Robert's lithographs, depicting a woman whose life revolved around the pleasure her own body brought her. Instead of trying to keep her movements straight-backed and cold, Julia found she was happy to give in to this new swaying sensuality. As she danced over the stage, her thighs rubbed gently together and excited her sex, and she felt her silky smooth skin tingle with arousal. She was using the movements of a stripper, bucking herself against the floor, rubbing slowly against the dusty canvas of the stage so that her body rocked upward, pushing her breasts out as though presenting them to be fondled.

While she felt her arousal grow, Julia let her thoughts drift back to Robert, his face as he surveyed her, as he flicked through his pornographic scrapbooks.

He was her audience, she realised; even in his absence she was aware of his intense horny gaze. And every movement she made was an effort to bring him closer to her, to show him a little more of her inner sexual life. Her dancing slowed as she let the images run through her mind – Robert watching her as Joe fucked her; as Sylvie licked her; taking photos; as she was passed between the two men he'd arranged for her; his collection of pictures; his voracious appetite for the spectacle of sex. She almost came to a standstill on the dark stage as she let the idea form slowly in her head. Standing with her arms hanging loosely by her sides, Julia suddenly realised what she had to do.

With a mixture of fear and excitement, she let the plan form, imagining a new dance, an act that centred on her summer's adventures, a mixture of voyeurism and provocation. Looking around at the rows of seats circling the stage, Julia imagined the audience, their reactions. She visualised a performance that they would be an integral part of – a show that they would never forget, that would turn them on and disturb them in equal measures. In her imagination, the seats filled with eager horny audience members, and the glint of the lights caught in their eyes, reflecting back the dazzling orgiastic display of the stage. She thought of the men in Blackpool, their hunger to touch her. She remembered Robert's camera, his desire to capture the image of her, the sight of her undone and splayed open.

Walking slowly back and forth across the stage, occasionally slipping into a loose dance move, Julia pondered. As she let the sweat cool on her skin, she allowed herself to fantasise. By the time she climbed down from the stage, wiping her neck with her shirt, she was biting her lip in concentration.

It was a new kind of arousal. The idea had turned her on, in a very real way: she felt the warmth spreading from her core to the tips of her nipples, like the familiar agitation she felt when she worked with Robert. Julia was horny, as she often was after her performances, but this time she wanted more than to relieve her frustration with mindless fucking. This time her arousal was making ideas well up in her, thoughts that tumbled into forms, into movement. She was dreaming of a new dance, a new act.

As she returned to the caravan, half entranced with the vision that was forming in her mind, Julia remembered her inspiration – the picture of Baker in the Dance of the Savages – and resolved to work for this new dream of hers with more dedication than ever before.

She had hung the photograph above her bed and let Sylvie admire the figure of the young Josephine with her. Beautiful as her nubile body was, there was another quality that drew Julia to the photograph. It was some spark of daring, of rebellious spirit, that made her shake her head in admiration when she imagined the teenaged Baker flinging herself onto the Paris stage and causing a scandalous reaction with her naked, sexual dance.

Sylvie drew her finger over the curves of the photograph, murmuring as she did so.

'The beautiful form, *n'est ce pas*? It gives me a buzz just looking at her.'

'Sylvie,' said Julia slowly, thinking as she spoke, 'you choreographed your own act, didn't you?'

'Of course I did.' Sylvie almost spat with fierce pride. 'From the very first conception to the last stitch of the costume.'

Julia nodded. She knew she wouldn't be able to pull off the new idea that was slowly forming without help from others. She could count on Sylvie, Joe and Henri, she was sure. But the visions she had in mind would need more than able performers. She would need lights, music, costumes.

Looking at the photo again, Julia studied the beads and feathers of the dancers, the minimal costumes that had caused such mayhem in 1920s European society. Josephine wore a curling plume of an ostrich feather between her legs, and smiled as though it tickled her deliciously. Her nakedness was enhanced by the shocking scant costume. Julia knew the value of dressing a nude figure just enough to provoke the audience's imagination.

'Eva has a stack of old costumes in the trailer, doesn't she? Left over stuff from old shows?' she asked.

'No doubt. She never throws anything away.' Sylvie shrugged. She eyed Julia curiously, aware that the new girl was acting in a manner that she hadn't seen before, with a confidence and mysterious determination that Sylvie thought she recognised.

'Julia,' she asked, 'what exactly went on last night in Robert's caravan? What are you planning?'

There were four days till the circus opened in Edinburgh, and the performers were making the most of the break, taking in the riotous buzz of the city in full Festival swing. It was as if, Julia thought, the whole city was a circus, a non-stop pageant of spectacle and theatre that engulfed the ancient streets and filled the town with colour. The performers left the site almost deserted, heading into town every afternoon and returning in the small hours of the morning. The circus fell quiet in these hours, when usually groups of the company chatted outside their caravans and practised acrobatics out on the grass. For a few days, Julia realised, she would have the time and space she needed to develop her idea. The tent was set up and lying empty, and she could practise onstage without interruption.

While the other members of the company indulged in all the pleasures of the swarming streets and bars, Julia worked. The germ of an idea that had come to her as she danced was now gathering momentum, and she found the people she asked for help were as intrigued by the plan as she was. Eva seemed more than willing to put together costumes, finding armfuls of ostrich feathers and sequins in crates in the costume van, advising Julia on how to fix the outfits so that they draped well and allowed the performer to move easily. Julia had little time, but found Eva's expert eye could put together an outfit with lightning speed, knowing just which parts of the body to emphasise, which to hide under tantalising strings of beads or scraps of silk. It took only a couple of hours to come to an agreement with the older woman, who was excited to be working on something more intriguing than mending hems. Julia left her with sketches of figures and costumes, and a promise that the costumes would be finished in time for the rehearsal.

She spent hours with Joe examining the lighting board, working out how to use coloured gels and spotlights to enhance the movement onstage, planning her spectacle in minute detail. It was a new aspect of performing that she hadn't considered before – thinking of the best ways to realise her initial vision and working out how to get the effects right onstage was something that had always been left to others. But she enjoyed working with Joe, their rough banter and hastily snatched fumbles under the shadow of the lighting box providing some moments of laughter even as Julia's anxiety grew. She flirted with him just enough to keep him interested in the project, promising later he could join her for a celebratory fuck if the show came off well. But despite her flippant promises, she was aware of the dangerous territory she was treading. The preparations would be the easiest part.

The hardest would be persuading Robert to watch it, and she thought with trepidation of the time when she'd have to confront him. He'd been withdrawn and virtually absent since the company arrived in Edinburgh, hardly leaving his quarters. Although she felt she'd lightened his mood that night in the caravan, Julia knew the threat of disaster was weighing on his mind. The review had subdued their arrival in Edinburgh, and the shadow of bad press still hung over the circus. She knew Robert bore the heaviest burden of the pressure, but she needed to find a way to get through to him. Leaving the problem to later, she concentrated on her frantic preparations, and confronted the other problem which had dogged her since she conceived the idea.

Her act included some complex tech gear, and Julia despaired of how she would find the money for the equipment she needed – until she explained to Henri exactly what she wanted to do. After a few hours, he turned up at the site in a van, the back of which was filled with sleek black suitcases and neatly coiled cables. With a smile he explained to Julia that he had contacts in a theatre in town, and he'd managed to borrow most of what she needed for a couple of weeks.

'Henri, this is amazing. You are amazing,' Julia said, overwhelmed, reaching up high to nuzzle into the older man's cheek. 'I owe you big time.'

She looked over the complicated machinery, the tiny buttons labelled with incomprehensible names and colour-coded wires. The thought of what she was trying to do suddenly overwhelmed her, and she felt panic rising in her.

'Henri, how do I work all this stuff? It's a nightmare.'

Henri just smiled his sorrowful enigmatic smile, and tapped the side of his nose.

'You leave the detail to your technical staff, Julia. If you're going to be a stage manager, you have to learn to delegate.'

He gave her an affectionate squeeze, before letting his long bony fingers trace a gentle line over her cleavage.

'You bring us the juicy ideas, my dear, and we'll help bring your dreams to life.'

As her plan became more detailed, and involved more people, Julia felt her energy levels rise to fever pitch. She was working harder than she ever had before, enlisting the help of the stage crew and her fellow performers, cajoling them to help with a mixture of pleading and flirtation, swearing all of them to secrecy for fear of Robert getting a whiff of what was going on. As the days passed horrifyingly swiftly, Julia was more and more keenly aware of how crucial it would be to take him by surprise. She knew he wasn't a man to be easily persuaded, and the danger was that she was straying into his territory by planning a new act, daring to compete with a man of vast experience and charisma. Yet her determination grew along with her anxieties, as though the project had become something larger than herself. As she rehearsed the moves of the piece by herself in the tent, Julia sensed she was creating something that went beyond a dazzling piece of showmanship. The central idea of the piece was so dangerous it gave her thrills to think of it. She had no idea of how the audience might react, and was mindful of stories of the chaos that ensued after Josephine Baker's debut – crowds leaving the theatre, shocked and bewildered.

But none of her misgivings seemed to dissuade her. She was intent on giving this idea her best, putting all of her feelings on sex and her body, on theatre and the audience, into a single ten-minute explosion of incredible sensory overload.

After three days, Julia knew she couldn't delay the moment any longer. Robert would have to see the show. There was a dress rehearsal that afternoon, a refresher after the company had rested for those few days, and now was the only time to show him. Robert would be in the tent, overseeing the final preparations.

Trembling with nerves, she entered the tent and waited for her eyes to adjust to the murky light inside. He was standing by the curtains, watching the boys adjust the lights, a morose look on his face. Julia was unnerved by the change in him – before, Robert had been a silent presence, but his being there was enough to drive the company to its utmost efforts. Today, he looked pale and worried, as though he was uncertain of his own decisions. Julia approached with a sense of foreboding, steeling herself to ask his permission for an unheard-of favour.

'No, Julia. Absolutely not.' He frowned at her. 'Why aren't you in costume? Get your ass into Eva's trailer and get ready. Now.'

'Robert, please. I haven't ever asked for a favour before . . .' Julia trailed off as he turned his back on her. He was looking over a lighting plot with the sparky and ignoring her already. Julia felt her determination rise up like steel in her spine.

'You owe me this much,' she said quietly, reminding him of his time alone with her in the caravan. 'Just let me show you what I've done.' She watched as Robert fell silent, letting his shoulders drop. When he turned back to her, it was with an expression that seemed so ashen and exhausted, she wanted to reach out and warm his cheek with the palm of her hand. When he spoke, however, his voice was as cold and deep as an empty well, and she knew he was as distant as ever.

'Ten minutes. I'll watch what you've got. No hold-ups, and no other chances. Understood?'

Julia nodded, a knot of anticipation and fear welling up in her.

'And Julia, just promise me – this act will turn me on, won't it?'

'I hope so, Robert. I truly hope so.'

News of Julia's act had spread round the site, and by the time three o'clock approached, the entire company was assembled in the tent, most in costume and ready for the rehearsal afterwards. Only Julia and her cohorts were absent from the seats, waiting tensely backstage, Sylvie restlessly pacing back and forth, Julia whispering last-minute instructions to the sound engineer. Outside, the company made a loud and animated audience, already calling for the show to start. It was unheard of for a young, green performer to press the ringmaster into auditioning a new act, and Julia heard Rachel's derisory shouts with a sinking heart.

She closed her eyes, wishing fervently that someone had persuaded her not to undertake such a foolish move.

Her heart hammered in her chest and she felt sick with nerves.

'Okay, Julia?' Henri's voice was tight, but Julia was grateful for his concern.

'I'm okay,' she nodded. 'Just feel like I'm about to throw up.'

'That's a good sign,' Joe said. 'It means you'll give an edgy show. Now come here and give me a good-luck kiss before you go on.'

Julia laughed with disbelief as Joe caught her wrist. She could feel the dampness of his palms and knew he was as unsure about performing this routine as she was – but even so, he was a pro. He knew the best way to deal with performance anxiety was to throw yourself completely into the act. He pulled Julia close to his chest, burying his head in her hair and letting her feel the long hard muscles of his body press against hers. With his mouth so close to her ear that his breath tickled her, he whispered: 'Remember what you dreamt of in the first place, Julia. Remember what it's all about.'

He let his hand travel down to her sex, slipping quickly under the silk folds of her dressing robe, to brush teasingly over her hairless pussy. Julia felt the thrill of his solid presence, his predatory desire for her. She let him stroke her until her juices started to flow, oiling her body in preparation for what she wanted, which was to put on the horniest and most daring show she had ever imagined. Her heart was racing with adrenaline, and Joe's insistent ministrations increased her pulse rate till she felt dizzy with excitement. Next to them, Sylvie looked on with amusement, licking her lips. Her eyes were fixed on the small movements of Joe's hand, and Julia knew she was joining in their preparations. In the cramped dark space behind the curtain, the three of them worked each other up, Sylvie coming close to the other two and pressing her small frame against Joe's body, also slipping her hand in between the folds of Julia's robe, where she joined Joe with her quick pointed fingers and manipulated Julia to fever point. With the two of them rubbing and caressing her, Julia started to worry she would be brought to orgasm and left shaking and weak before she even got on the stage. She tried to pull away, but found herself pinioned, held firmly under Joe's strong arm. Sylvie seemed to sense she was dangerously close to coming, though, and lessened the pressure of her fingertips, leaving Julia groaning with frustration, and distracted by the knowledge she was about to bare her soul onstage.

'What's going on back there?' Rachel's harsh whine rang out from the seats in the tent, jolting the three back to the present situation. Julia looked at the other two with terror-stricken eyes.

'We've got to go out there,' she said, voice trembling with hesitation and unrelieved tension.

'Don't worry, girl.' Sylvie's voice was as slow and heavy as syrup, and she loosened the tie at Julia's waist as she continued talking in a hushed sweet voice. 'Let them wait. It only increases the anticipation ...' She let Julia's naked body show under the flat glare of a lead light. The oil that she'd smeared over her earlier glistened in the white lamp, and Julia's full breasts heaved as she tried to take deep breaths to steady herself. 'You should know that by now. Joe and I are going to make sure you're half crazed before you go out there.'

With this, Sylvie bent her head to lick at the very tip of Julia's breast, letting the wet heat of her tongue lap gently around the aureole and tickle her nipple, a sensation that Julia found hard to bear.

'You've got to get in character, babe,' Joe said, his hand still reaching slowly inside her legs to where she burned with the desire to be fucked. 'No acting, remember. This performance is the real thing. We aren't going out there and pretending. You have to put your whole self into this one. Every inch of your body has to be burning up.' Joe slipped his other hand over her ass, between the crack of her cheeks to rub at her anus gently, a shockingly unexpected feeling for Julia. 'Every inch, baby,' he reminded her, working the tip inside her tight little hole, letting her buck forward and slip his fingers further into her pussy as she did so.

It was a slight, incredible assault on the most sensitive parts of her body, and Julia writhed with a mixture of pleasure and anxiety. Outside, the company were growing restless – she could hear them slow hand-clapping – but Sylvie and Joe showed no signs of concern. The more she struggled to free herself, the more the two of them held her firmly, Sylvie giving little bites to her breasts and suckling at them hard when Julia tried to move away. It was a delicious torment, but just as Julia felt sure she was about to dissolve with the most earth-shattering orgasm of her life, the two pulled away, leaving her gasping and shivering, bereft of their touches.

'I think you're good to go, babe,' Joe said, a delightedly wicked look on his face. Julia knew he wanted to fuck her, could see the swell of his cock straining at his shorts, but he stood back with his arms folded and a twisted smile.

'Let the show begin,' he said, patting Sylvie on the ass. Her lips were swollen from her suckling of Julia's tits, and she only smiled lazily, letting Julia know that this particular game was only just beginning.

16

The music that poured from the speakers was a low throbbing dance track with a bass line strong enough to make the hairs on the arms of the audience vibrate. Julia crept onstage in velvety darkness, her heart pounding. When the lights came up to reveal her, she was standing in front of a plain white screen. She felt the heat of the stage lights warm her skin, and the arousal of her body continued – the backstage groping had primed her to a point where she felt herself so full of the buzz of sex she was magnetic, as though she were drawn inexorably towards the audience like they were a room full of lovers.

On her own, in a single white spotlight, there was no way she could relieve the burning want in her body for fucking, other than by turning it into a dance, channelling her desires into movement. She was dizzy with heat, weighed down with her own sexuality, and as she stirred onstage the whole company in the seats watching could see her obvious lasciviousness. She dragged her head slowly upwards, letting the glossy plaits of her dark hair slide slowly over her back and spill across her shoulder, where they dangled suggestively just at the level of her nipples. Her breasts were bound loosely with a criss-cross string of beads that cut a little into the soft flesh and made it swell around the thin strips of brocade. The strings snaked around her body like the slightest suggestion of a dress, a skeleton of an outfit that barely covered her pubis and nipples, and wrapped several times round her thigh. In her hand she held a white ostrich feather, a curling plume with which she tickled the curves of her body, letting the waving tip of it dance lightly over her nearly naked skin. Julia kept all her movements slow, in sync with the ominously thudding bass beat, standing proudly onstage to let the audience appreciate her beautiful form.

Only after a minute of teasing herself with the feather did Julia start to dance. She moved with an aching sensuality, dragging her arms over her head to let her breasts swing slightly under the constraining bands of the costume, tilting her hips so that her rounded ass was sticking out prominently, and turning slowly to let everyone get a good view. She danced with her eyes closed, imagining herself alone with a huge invisible lover that surrounded her on all sides, watching intently as she displayed first one part, then the other of her body. Still, she kept her thighs pressed together to preserve the mystery of what lay between them, sliding them a little against each other to keep the frisson of horniness buzzing through her.

The music grew in complexity now, a woman's voice sighing over the beat, her low exhalations melting into the music like a strange instrument. Julia moved from her stretched position through a series of poses, parodies of erotic dancers, lifting her breasts upward, opening her mouth, swaying her hips, half trying to excite the crowd and half mocking them. It was a difficult balance, but she struck it perfectly, eliciting whistles from the watching performers. Their response gave her a tremor of relief, and she hoped fervently it meant that the company at least were supportive. What Robert thought, she could only guess at, and the thought of his critical judgement made her shiver a little. Besides, the act had only just started. The tricky bit was yet to come.

As she gyrated on her platform, weaving in and out of the beam of the spotlight, other figures started to filter in from the shadows. Sylvie crept on from back-stage, and Sarah climbed stealthily up from a seat hidden among the audience. Three other figures joined them, slowly approaching Julia as she danced by herself. These other performers were wearing black: tight cat suits buckled and zipped to cover every inch from their black work-boots to their chins, leather gloves and dark glasses giving them wasp-like black eyes. The suits were sheer enough to show the defined curves of the figures underneath, clinging tightly to well-formed muscles, stretching over breasts and asses so that the figures looked almost like their coverings were painted on. As the sinister creatures inched closer to Julia, their blank faces turned towards her and a sharp metallic element was introduced to the music. Backstage, Henri was controlling the sound, carefully mixing music according to Julia's instructions and watching the stage intently to ensure the synchronisation was perfect.

These figures carried equipment: sleek black objects, which they pointed towards Julia, taking aim. She continued to writhe and pose on the raised platform, apparently oblivious to the people moving in closer to her.

Then suddenly the stage was filled with a barrage of blinding white flashes, as though sheet lightning were ripping through the tent, accompanied by the noise of bulbs popping. The lights continued to flicker, and now images of Julia were being projected on the tall white screen behind the stage. From every angle, the audience could see flashes of her body close-up – a profile focusing on the line from her shoulder to her thigh, breast outlined against the black shadows of the tent; shots of her bare feet bound in strips of beaded brocade, her startled face with open mouth turning wildly to find the source of the attack; a shot of her from behind with the dip of her back and the moving target of her ass. It was clear the figures in black were carrying cameras, filming every angle of Julia, trapping her in a web of images which were being magnified and displayed so large that the sight was almost surreal – a visual explosion of Julia's intimate parts, exposed and broadcast for the whole tent to see. Lurid and vivid, the shots were a barrage of pornographic snaps, Julia licking her lips making a debauched picture when isolated and projected in a twelve-foot high image, the intrusion of the camera so voyeuristic it made every part of her body sexual.

While the images continued to flash across the screen, becoming ever more extreme close-ups of Julia's bound breasts, her shaved pubis and the writhing frame of her hips trying to shield herself from the intermittent bursts of hot white light, one of the figures started to turn towards the shadowed seats in the audience. It was Sylvie, tiny but formidable in her skin-tight suit, moving her camera towards the shadows. A spotlight panned through the figures in the seats, skimming over the audience and catching the glimmer of open mouths, eyes reflecting with points of light. On the screen the pornographic close-ups of Julia were interspersed with this roving view of the audience, the frame swinging wildly through the crowd and occasionally fixing on an individual, focusing on their face and sweeping over their body.

Joe had sneaked round the stage to sit among the other performers in the crowd, his costume a casual white T-shirt and jeans, as though he were any punter who'd wandered in for the spectacle. Now, though, Sylvie's camera fixed on him, meeting the point of the spotlight and zooming in to pick out his face among the other, bewildered audience members. With a shout, Sylvie summoned a couple of the burly roustabouts to where he sat, and Joe was roughly pulled to his feet. He played his role with shocking believability, protesting and struggling a little, trying to laugh off the surly advances of the bully boys who hustling him steadily towards the stage. Their faces were impassive, but the threat of their vast muscular arms was enough to compel Joe to the foot of the stage. Here, he was pulled upwards by a knot of black-clad camera operators, who tugged at his clothes as they did so, loosening his T-shirt and spreading hands over his crotch. He responded to their rough fondling with a dazed incredulity, and the audience were treated to more close-up shots of Joe's half-naked torso, glimpses of the hard muscular body that was being mauled by the camera operators even as they filmed it. Steadily, he was pushed towards Julia, and shoved to his knees.

Now the voyeur, the innocent watcher of Julia's earlier exposure, was sprawled at her feet. Julia moved one foot to place it on his shoulder, and the figures circled the two of them as they froze in tableau, Joe looking up with fear and lust at the view afforded by Julia's raised leg, the white feather held over her pussy to frustrate his furtive attempts to catch a glimpse of her secret cleft. Slowly, every movement filmed and projected onto the screen, Julia reached down to hold Joe's head steady. She stroked herself with long movements of the feather, letting the fronds stray over her clitoris and between her ass cheeks, tickling every inch of her most sensitive parts in front of his face. With her other hand she held onto his hair, fixing his what her display on her self-pleasuring, and Joe continued to gaze with awe-struck fascination.

Pulling his head close to her body, Julia allowed Joe to feel the feather stroke over his cheek, so that the fluffy white tendrils obstructed his view, even as her sex was only inches from his face. The cameras were filming every moment of this lewd exchange, focusing on the shadow between Julia's sex and Joe's sweating face. While the details were hidden, obscured by the blurred image of Julia's thigh and Joe's shoulder, there was no doubt that Joe was gazing at the most intimate part of Julia's body. In the audience, people shifted uncomfortably, either from arousal at this flagrant display and the palpable tension as Julia played with her voyeur, or perhaps from uncertainty that they may be singled out next to be victimised and exposed by the cameras.

Another camera was trained on Joe's crotch, and the image on the screen now showed a black-gloved hand move over the buttons of his jeans, tugging them open. The music increased in intensity, but wasn't enough to overwhelm a gasp from the crowd as Joe's fly was ripped open and Sylvie's small hand seemed to cradle his cock. Leaning down, she put her mouth to his lap and moved her head, apparently working him over with her mouth. The images were blurred and partly obscured by the limbs and moving hands of other performers, still interspersed with close-ups of Julia playing a game of hide-and-seek with the feather between her legs. Sometimes the images on the screen became amorphous ambiguous shapes, shifting shadows so out of focus one couldn't distinguish which flesh was Julia's and which Joe's.

The music grew louder and more intense, Henri bringing the beat to a pounding crescendo and increasing the sound of a woman sighing. Crackling and buzzing interrupted the melody now as the images became less and less distinct, Julia and Joe crouched so close together the audience could not see what was going on between them, only guess from the hazy and moving images which Sylvie continued to broadcast over the screen. Then a strobe speeded up, giving a disorientating jolt to the audience, showing bursts of sudden shocking images, the figures onstage captured in bizarre and orgiastic tableaux with every flash of light. Sylvie and the others began unzipping each other and emerging bit by bit as naked and oiled figures, still wielding their cameras but showing now only the vaguest blurs of flesh, teeth and mouths on the screen, and every so often the proud protrusion of a nipple or a pair of thighs spreading open to reveal the briefest glimpse of their sex.

It ended in a tumultuous tangle of strobing images, a crashing of electronic cymbals and banging drum beats, the half-clothed figures writhing over Julia's magnificent glistening nakedness, Joe thrusting his hips into hers, the entire stage strewn with abandoned clothes and the cameras dropped on their sides, filming skewed and unfocused footage of the orgy onstage.

The lights dropped with split-second precision, at the exact moment the music built to an almost unbearable level and then ceased, leaving the audience breathless and dazed, plunged suddenly into the dark and suffocating silence of the tent.

Onstage, Julia lay panting under Joe, sweat running in rivulets down her back, chest heaving with the effort of her exertions. She hardly dared to move, terrified of what the reaction might be. Had she pushed it too far? Mauling members of the audience might be enough to infuriate Robert. As she listened to the silence in the blacked-out tent, Julia felt her worst anxieties start to loom over her. There was no sound other than the ragged breathing of the performers onstage.

Then, just as Julia thought she would have to steel herself for the disgrace due to her, the house lights started to glow dimly. A shout rang out – Rachel's voice, Julia realised, incredulous:

'Bravo!'

The shout was brief, but strong and decisive, and it seemed enough to open the floodgates for the rest of the raggle-taggle audience to start. Gradually at first, and then with growing volume, a torrent of claps, whistles and shouts flowed over the stage. Feeling relief and delight surge through her, Julia pulled herself slowly to her feet and took in the sight of the entire circus applauding her. Their faces were stunned, but smiling delightedly, heads shaking as they saluted her outrageous spectacle. And Rachel stood at the back clapping loudly. Julia felt a particular rush of unexpected pleasure in noting her most formidable enemy applauding her.

It was far from a full house, nor even a true paying audience, but Julia was keenly aware of the high standards of her fellow performers and their long ovation was more than she could have dared to wish for. As she gave a brief buoyant bow and tripped off the stage, she felt almost on the verge of tears. It was her first show, choreographed, planned and executed according to her vision. She gave Sylvie a fierce hug backstage, whispering her thanks in the girl's ear.

'I couldn't have done it without you,' she said.

Sylvie laughed, and squeezed Julia back tightly, giving her a playful pat on the bottom. Sweating and breathing heavily, she was nevertheless smiling gamely at Julia, who was well aware of the risk the other girl had taken to perform without Robert's blessing.

'Always happy to help a fellow artist, girl. Especially when the act's as hot as that one.'

In the midst of the bustle backstage, even as she thanked all the others who'd given their time and effort to help her pull it off, Julia was mindful of the hovering presence of Robert. As usual he'd watched from the wings, from where he had an optimum view of both the stage and the audience, and now Julia caught sight of his tall figure standing by the curtain. His head was buried in a sheaf of papers, and Julia felt her heart lurch as she wondered for a moment if he'd even watched the act. Brow furrowed, he was leafing through the papers in his hand, giving no indication he was even aware of her standing a few feet from him.

Julia was still wearing her scant costume of beads and glitter, but somehow her near-nakedness seemed to give her confidence rather than make her feel vulnerable – as though she were draped in the success of the piece she'd devised. Walking towards Robert, she bit her lip nervously, hardly daring to imagine what his response might be. Her fellow performers had loved it, of that she was sure, and from the buzz of adrenaline now surging through her veins, Julia knew that there was something to the act that went beyond a simple spectacle. She'd created a work of art, from the things she felt most passionately about, from her experiences of the summer and her long training in dance. It was her finest achievement yet, and she was high from the feeling.

'Robert?' she asked, standing before him, her nudity defiantly on show. Around them the crew and performers were hustling around, now making ready for the dress rehearsal, and Julia stood her ground, trying not to let the jostling technicians get in between her and Robert. He looked up briefly.

'Julia.' He nodded, curtly. 'Nice act.'

It was his usual understated response, but Julia felt pride flood over her. He hadn't sneered at her, nor had he exploded with rage. And his carefully meted out praise meant more to Julia than the entire response of the rest of the company.

'Does that mean I can perform it for the run?' she asked, impatience overcoming her hesitation.

Now Robert did laugh; a short bitter chuckle.

'Julia, the production values were good, and there were some interesting ideas in there. But there is absolutely no way I'd let you toy with members of the audience, planted or not. We'd have mass walk-outs, refunds, chaos. I can't afford to take that kind of chance.'

Julia felt her heart swoop down with disappointment, and then crackle with anger. She wanted to lash out at Robert suddenly. Yet again, he was refusing her the one thing that she wanted most, and this time she felt sure that he was unjustified. Jealous, even.

'It's a risk, I know. I've never done this before, Robert,' she admitted. 'But you heard what the crowd thought. They loved it! Surely their opinion counts for something?'

Now Robert looked at her, a brisk businesslike stare.

'Julia, your audience are performers who work in this world day in, day out. They're pretty hard to shock. Do you really think your average Festival goer is used to seeing things like this? We're treading a thin line as it is, Julia. The licence is under threat, the show is on the verge of attack from that damn journalist, and I'll be happy to make it to the end of the run, let alone escape a scandal. There is no way we can get away with stripping audience members onstage.'

His tone was curt and Julia knew she should hold herself back, but she couldn't help herself. Her emotions were stretched to breaking point as she felt herself once again standing vulnerable before Robert and being cut down to size.

'Since when were you scared to take a risk, Robert? I thought that was the whole point of the show, of your work? In fact, I never imagined you'd back away from a challenge, or let some shoddy journalist scare you like this.'

Robert's eyes burned darkly with anger, and Julia realised with a start she'd hit a nerve. With terrifying self-control, he let his gaze drift down over Julia's sweat-soaked trembling body and brought his eyes back to meet hers.

'Julia, you're a talented dancer. And I told you the act was fair. Promising, even. But remember what you were hired for. Remember what I use you for.'

His words stung Julia even as they set off a chain reaction of pictures in her head: Robert's cool piercing stare as she lost herself in bizarre sexual encounters that he engineered; the feeling that she was tumbling further into a dangerous mysterious world of sexual adventure; the trembling that he seemed to cause every time he turned her on and kept her hovering at a distance, desperate for his touch and battling not to show her desperation. He used her, he was freely admitting it. She felt suddenly as though the ground had been swept from beneath her feet – she was nothing but a plaything for his twisted fantasies, an object to be enjoyed when he wanted a little live sex show, another curio in his harem.

She felt the tears prickle behind her eyes and a flush rise in her cheeks, and even though she struggled to keep herself calm, Julia knew she was about to say something she'd regret.

'I won't forget the people I've fucked for your pleasure. I enjoyed them. It's just a shame you don't have the guts to say what you really want, and you'll never know just how good it is to fuck me yourself.'

She knew she'd already stepped over the line. Even if she and Robert had shared the darkest intimacies, he remained her boss, and was more than capable of ending her career there and then. Recklessly, she blurted her parting shot:

'I know what you really are Robert: a coward hiding in the shadows. You're just forcing other people to indulge your perversions.'

Robert watched calmly, his face betraying no flicker of a response.

'Finished, Julia?' he asked. 'I think you'd better go and

change. Sort your face out as well please, I don't want you going onstage with eyes that puffy.'

He turned back to the rest of the company, apparently signalling the end of the conversation with Julia. She stood, spent, swaying slightly, as though she'd just fought six rounds and lost. Turning one last time, Robert motioned her brusquely to leave the tent.

'I told you. Cold water on your face, and back here in costume. Half an hour. *Move.*'

Numbly, Julia walked in the direction he indicated, feeling her dream fall in tatters around her. As she emerged into the afternoon sunlight, dazzling after the gloom of the tent, she felt the last of her energy drain from her and walked slowly towards her caravan. She barely noticed as Joe approached, grinning broadly and eager to hear how Robert had reacted.

'So, what happened?' he asked, searching Julia's face anxiously for her response, and quickly gathering that she'd been turned down flat. He heaved a sigh.

'No cigar, hey? Sod it, Julia, it was a long shot anyway, babe. Pretty good effort for a girl in her first professional job, don't you think?'

Julia shrugged, unable to find the words to agree with him. Trying to console her, he looped a heavy arm over her shoulder and squeezed.

'I bet Josephine Baker had to work at it before she got to shake her tush in Paris, too. Julia?'

Remembering the story of Josephine's earth-shattering appearance at the Folies Bergère, Julia felt a spark of her dream glow again deep inside her. The reaction to Josephine's magnificent nudity, her barbarous eroticism, had frightened the young starlet so much she ran into the wings – people rushing to the stage, roaring, half horrified, half entranced. She was described as a revolution, a tidal wave, and she'd won that acclaim because she'd dared to do what no one else had done before.

Despite some parts of her audience whistling with disapproval, Josephine had continued her dancing, moving with the confidence of a panther, throwing her sensuous gestures to her partner as though she were out of control.

Walking over the grass with Joe, Julia felt her resolve return. Robert had years of experience, it was true, but that wasn't the only thing that mattered. Julia had passion, and talent. Her act had been something new and exciting; she could feel it without a trace of doubt. It was risky, but that was the whole strength of the show, daring to transgress what people expected, shocking the audience into a new appreciation of the sensual, exposing their complicity, ultimately, enveloping them in an overwhelming experience of sex and spectacle.

She would still perform the act, Julia found herself certain of it then, as though there had never been any doubt. With or without Robert's approval, she would realise her dream, and she would show him, finally, how far she would go.

17

The Meadows were soaked in blackness, lit up with strings of streetlights that lined the path to the circus site. They dimmed next to the blaze of spotlights strung over the tent, the centre pole standing high among the trees, black pennants snapping in the wind. Fire-eaters circled the ground outside, weaving around the side-show tents and streaking flame through the night. The crowds that approached over the grass were buzzing already, reeling from nights in theatres and bars, curious to see the 'lurid fantasies' awaiting them.

The talk around town was that this circus was a tangled mess of filth and depravity, and bookings had been frantic. Julia heard the shrill laughter of women, the fierce whispers of the audience as they approached the tent, half desiring to be shocked, half scared. The atmosphere was tenser than usual, as though a storm was brewing. Backstage, Robert was pacing around in his costume, a deep frown shadowing his brow. The area between the curtains and the showmen's entrance was crowded with performers itching to take the stage. Julia was dressed in her slave costume, hair coiled into ringlets clogged with white paint, make-up so ghostly pale she seemed like a statue come to life. Sweat beaded over her pancake foundation and she bit her lip furiously, watching Robert from the corner of her eye. They would reveal all of the performers in turn in an opening parade that gave the audience a brief glimpse of the acts to come. Sylvie would be leading Julia onstage. As usual, Robert was looking them over, tweaking costumes every so often, leaning to whisper in the ears of certain performers.

The moments just before the show started were always agitated and restless, and Julia felt herself hovering on the brink of panic as she let herself get worked up by the stirrings and noises of the crowd outside. Normally she'd whisper to the other performers, sharing in the adrenaline rush. Tonight, though, she was silent, knowing that she was about to attempt something that was so reckless it could be called crazy. Looking nervously around, she caught the eye of Henri, his face frozen in grim determination. He too was aware of the dangers of what Julia had planned, but had agreed to give his assistance when the time came. As had Joe, Sylvie, Sarah, the girls, and a couple of the stagehands. Julia had been careful not to let word spread. Though she needed the help of a few people, she wanted to make sure nothing would endanger her plan. Standing in the wings now with Sylvie, she felt her stomach lurching with nerves, and tried to focus on the show. She would still be performing her usual acts, and needed to calm herself so she could concentrate.

'Good luck, girl,' Sylvie whispered before they took the stage. Julia merely nodded, too focused now on the show to respond. She felt the usual buzz as she stared at the stage, lit up now so that the audience were a dark mass of anonymous watchers in the shadows. Since she'd joined the circus, Julia had learnt how to turn her nerves into excitement, and the feeling of sickening anxiety that she'd felt the first time she performed was now almost enjoyable – like the moment when she undressed for a lover, she anticipated showing herself to the audience with a shiver of uncertain sexual delight.

Robert was walking forward now, his shoulders drawn back and his spine straight, ready to face the crowd. Julia could see from the set of his jaw that this was not going to be an easy gig for him. There was a beading of sweat on his brow and his usual laconic smile was absent. Turning to the line of performers he gave them one last instruction before striding onstage to start the show:

'Play your hearts out, ladies and gentlemen.'

Julia danced that night with her body at its most sensual and responsive – she couldn't stand to focus on what might happen after the show and so she concentrated on every beat, every rhythm and every movement of her limbs and torso. Even with the shadow of her plan looming over her she found the tension only sharpened her performance – she moved with such ferocious sexuality that she drew admiring whistles and applause from the audience even before her acts had finished. Dancing Pepper's Ghost with Robert was a fraught episode for her, knowing it may be the last time she could enjoy working with him. By the next morning, she could be out of a job. When the lights fell on the tableau created by her and Robert, the reflection of her body draped over his, Julia felt a keen sadness wash over her, as though the fading spotlight were the last time she would feel any warmth from Robert, or be able to dance for him in one of his private shows. It was an aching loss that seemed to pull her heart as much as her body, but at the same time she knew that she was prepared to sacrifice her nascent relationship with the ringmaster. At any cost, she wanted to perform the dance that meant so much to her.

By midnight, Julia's nerves had all but disappeared to be replaced by a strange calm. As the company assembled for the final 'blow-off' – the parade to close the end of the show – Julia checked round quickly for her accomplices. Receiving nods from Henri in the lighting booth and Sylvie backstage, she turned to the stage and took one last deep breath.

Just as Robert was about to step between the crack of the curtains and start the parade, Julia slipped recklessly in front of him, a black floor-length cloak wrapped over her shoulders and covering her costume. Behind her she heard him start to protest, before the noise of the audience and the stage lights took over and she ran to the centre of the platform aware only of the burning desire to perform.

It was a terrifying moment, standing alone on the stage with Robert and the rest of the circus watching from behind, frozen with confusion at Julia's unexpected appearance. It was unheard of for the show to deviate from its meticulously planned plot, and Julia knew how shocked her fellow performers would be.

For a full minute she stood in silence, waiting for Henri to start the music for her routine. Julia thought she might pass out or scream, as the audience started to shift in their seats and whisper loudly. Was it obvious something had gone wrong? What was happening in the sound booth? At any moment, Julia expected Robert to send on a couple of the roustabouts to tear her from the platform and carry her offstage. She had never felt so exposed, as though the entire audience and all her colleagues were watching her darkest, most intimate nightmare come to life. She started to wish that the earth would open and swallow her as the moments dragged by.

Then, at last, the deep beat of the music boomed from the speakers and Julia knew there was no going back. She was bound to perform this act now, even if it meant the end of her circus career. Trembling, she unfastened the catch at her throat and let the cloak fall to the ground, allowing the audience see her in her slight costume of chains and one white feather.

If Julia had dreamt of emulating Josephine Baker when she imagined her act, she couldn't have anticipated the strength of the audience's reaction. At first they watched with appreciative noises, enjoying the sight of Julia gyrating her nearly-bare body before them, believing they were being treated to another sensual display of eroticism.

But when the black-clad acolytes started combing the audience with spotlights and cameras, there was an uneasy shifting in the seats. Julia heard shrieks of nervous laughter as the audience saw themselves projected on the giant white screen behind the stage, saw people turning their heads in an effort not to be filmed. There was a general rumbling of nervous excitement and she knew the act was disturbing them in a totally unexpected manner. As Sylvie climbed down among the front rows, moving like a shadow through the rows of seats, the atmosphere started to change. Some people seemed eager to get close to the performer, leaning forward in their seats and licking their lips as she passed them. Others were standing to leave, hastily shoving their jackets on and making for the doors. There was the sense that the tent was on the point of anarchy and no one could tell what would happen next.

When the hapless Joe was plucked from the audience and dragged onstage the mood turned again – now a certain line had been crossed and the audience waited with trepidation to see how the act would develop. Rather than sitting passively and watching the show, they were now moving around, some standing to better see what would happen, some trying to make sure they had an easy escape route. There was a fierce noise of chatter and the entire tent was stirring, either with shock or delight. Julia couldn't tell but she knew she had to keep going. The cameras onstage were still filming close-up shots of her body, and now Joe's as he was slowly stripped and dragged towards her. The clicking of cameras surrounded her in a flurry as the audience tried to capture this unbelievable scene – the innocent bystander caught and forced to take part in some strange sexual performance. It was building to a crescendo, just as she'd hoped, and as she moved in closer to Joe and pressed herself against his face, Julia heard the noise of the crowd swell and mix with the music. It was bedlam – Julia and her accomplices onstage working their asses off while the audience gave in to their fearful delirium, their shouts and cat calls almost drowning the music as Joe was stripped and worked on by Sylvie.

As the show moved closer towards its climax Julia felt the pounding of her heart and the hot slick of sweat on her skin, tumbling over the bodies of the other performers and knowing the sight had the audience utterly captivated. She was working harder than she'd ever imagined, shaking with the effort and the fear, yet pushing her body to move with more vigour and passion. She felt strong jolts, shivers of desire that were amplified by the crowd's reaction, turned on like never before. This, wild reckless act was the closest she'd ever felt to the audience, their horrified pleasure so tangible she could almost taste it in the white-hot atmosphere of the tent. A hundred sensations were building around her: the sweating and gasping of her fellow performers; the hubbub of the crowd; the throb and wail of the music and the steadily increasing frequency of the strobe lights nearly overwhelming her as they all hammered closer to the final chaotic moments of her act.

* * *

The final parade passed in a blur. Julia was exhausted, her nerves shaken and her body aching with exertion. She couldn't bring herself to meet Robert's gaze, knowing the cold fury that would be emanating from him. She'd dared to interrupt his masterful performance to show her own crazy act – an act that had lost them a good few audience members and seemed to stir up a dangerous reaction in the crowd. The response was loud, the applause thunderous, but Julia knew she'd pushed her luck too far. It was going to be an unpleasant scene when she finally confronted Robert, and she wished she could disappear without having to face his anger.

As the performers finally left the stage, Julia slipped quickly to her caravan, avoiding the crew members who were eagerly trying to attract her attention, thrilled by her kamikaze actions. In the sanctuary of her narrow bunk, Julia collapsed and closed her eyes, burrowing her head into the pillow. Outside, she could hear shouts as the after-show party started, the performers still high on adrenaline and ready to cut loose. Her whole body was buzzing as though there was an electric current running through her, static crackling over her skin. For the first time, Julia had achieved something she'd never dreamt possible – found a way to express her exhibitionism and sexuality in a form that stirred an audience. In a moment she'd have to go and thank all the people who'd put themselves at risk to help her. She wanted to see Joe and Sylvie, and let them know how grateful she was, but at the same time the shadow of Robert darkened her thoughts.

Opening her eyes, Julia saw the picture of Josephine Baker hanging above her bed. The impish smile of the woman who'd dared to take Paris by storm seemed to wink at her and she felt a new stirring of joy. Even if she was now sacked, nobody could take away the buzz she'd felt when she heard the applause of the crowd.

'It was worth it, Josie,' she said out loud, quietly thanking the image of the woman who'd driven her to try and realise her dream.

She cleaned the greasepaint from her face as though preparing herself for a firing squad. She dressed slowly, half listening to the sound of the party outside. As she pulled on an old shirt and jeans, she heard Sylvie's laughter and gave a tired smile. It was going to be a late night, and she had every intention of enjoying herself. It may be the last party she ever got to share with the strange and fabulous creatures of the circus.

As she stepped out of the caravan, she was taken off guard by the sudden whoops and cheers of the party cavorting round Joe's truck. Most of the company were assembled there, half of them still in costume, make-up smeared. All of them were turning to greet her, bottles of beer in their hands and teeth shining in the darkness.

'A toast to the hottest ballerina I ever met!' Sylvie's voice rang out over the Meadows, jubilant and loud as she raised a bottle of beer to salute Julia. The others joined in a warm 'hear hear', and Julia felt herself start to grin as they clapped her. It was the most welcome ovation she'd ever heard, and she stood on the steps of the caravan and gave a humble deep bow in return.

'And a toast to all my accomplices,' she said, nodding back at Sylvie.

As she walked forward to join the party Julia noticed a tall figure standing apart from the group of happy performers, watching in silence. It was Robert, his face still pale with panstick, hands in pockets. Julia knew his gaze was fixed on her, and knew that she couldn't avoid him forever. Her heart did a flip as she thought of the anger she'd seen in him once before – a slow-burning and implacable anger that he expressed with a low even voice. The thought of confronting him made her feel lightheaded, as though he had mesmerised her. Julia was the adept who had turned on her teacher – the upstart girl who'd dared to wreck his show. What could he possibly do to her that scared her so much, she wondered. She was strong enough to withstand the harshest criticism, the most vicious insults from her strict ballet masters. Yet the thought of Robert's disapproval filled her with a vast and uncertain dread.

'Have a drink, Julia?' someone called to her, and she turned to see Joe's warm smiling face. 'I bet you could use one after that performance.'

Julia hesitated. Part of her wanted badly to join the others, stay in the shadowy circle around the truck and discuss the show. She felt like celebrating, and the exhaustion was starting to take its toll. Her body was limp, her eyelids heavy. But she knew she couldn't rest yet – not until she'd seen Robert.

'Thanks, Joe, I've got something to clear up first.' She gave him a wry smile and steeled herself to approach Robert. When she looked back, he'd disappeared.

Julia guessed where he'd be.

She ducked to enter through the gap in the canvas, and looked around. The house lights were still on, motes of dust dancing in the beams of white light. The air was still thick with the smell of dry ice, the stage abandoned and silent.

'Robert?' Her voice fell flat in the empty tent. It was a strange feeling, to find the place so quiet after the pounding music and furore of the audience. Julia thought she could almost hear echoes of the night's show, but there was no sign of Robert. She walked slowly to the stage and pulled herself up, standing under the soft house lights and looking out at the rows of empty seats.

'Can't get enough of the stage, can you?'

Robert's voice came from behind the curtain that

screened the backstage area, so low and velvety it was as though he'd run his hand over Julia's shoulders and stroked the back of her neck. She whirled round, searching for him.

He walked out across the stage till he was standing so close Julia could smell that faint cedarwood of his skin, the smell that made her think of dark shady theatres. The powerful musky undercurrent of his sweat made her dizzy. Julia couldn't bear to meet his eyes – were they burning with suppressed rage, or was he laughing at her? She kept her head down and breathed in the scent of his body.

'Were you looking for me?' he asked.

She was thrown again by Robert's unpredictable moods. She had expected her dressing down to start right away.

'I wanted to explain...' she started.

'Explain how you managed to pull off something like that without me getting wind of it? That I'd like to hear.'

'I meant to tell you the reason why.' Julia felt herself floundering, wishing that she didn't find herself struck speechless by Robert every time.

'Why you wanted to stage your act?'

'Yes.' She realised Robert was moving even closer to her. She found she was shaking – not since the audition when he'd reached up to draw a feather from her hair had he come this close.

'You think I wouldn't understand, Julia?'

He spoke softly, and Julia watched as though he were moving in slow motion. The warm dusty air of the tent seemed to stand still as he reached out to tuck her hair behind her ear. The gesture was so intimate, so gentle, that Julia felt as though the ground had been swept from under her feet. The thudding of her heart was sending urgent signals to her body, and she was flooded with that same aching tingling sensation that made her want to touch him so much. As her eyes rose to meet his she thought she sensed something there, a new glimmer of colour and warmth that she recognised. Did he share the same yearning desire to touch her? His faraway look had been replaced by the hungry intensity she'd seen when he'd watched her perform, onstage or in their private sessions.

Before, he'd been a catalyst, directing the action of their sexual encounters yet remaining on the periphery, untouchable. This time he placed his hand on her cheek and pulled her towards him.

'You understand?' she asked, hesitantly.

'Of course. I understand your hunger, Julia. The things that drive you. I'm a showman too.'

Julia felt his hands stretching across the great divide between them, reaching to her and the warm responsive body that had wanted him for so long. When he touched her it was a strangely soft and tender feeling, his hand working at her shoulder through the cloth of her shirt, kneading at the muscles as though he were trying to feel the very substance of her.

'What you said, about the audiences, about performing.' Julia felt the words rushing to her lips now, and the sudden need to explain everything to him that she'd experienced since she arrived at the circus. She wanted him to know all her thoughts, all her feelings. As he pulled her arms upwards to rest on his shoulders, she talked as though the words were spilling out of her.

'I was thinking about how I feel, on the stage. And how the audience feels, what they look for.'

'How you turn them on?' Robert seemed to be laughing at her, gently.

Julia nodded. She hesitated, unused to speaking so openly to Robert, but the situation between them was changing, even as she did so. He was holding her against him now, and the parts of their bodies that touched were buzzing as though currents of electricity were passing between them.

'I was – I was thinking of you,' she admitted finally, feeling her cheeks flush as she let her breasts brush against his chest and felt the swell of his cock bump gently against her belly. It was an unbearably erotic feeling – after wanting him so long, to finally feel his body was a deeply shocking epiphany. Julia was so acutely aware of the feel of his strong wiry muscles under her hands that she thought she was communicating with him solely by touch.

He leant in then to kiss her, and Julia felt the heat of his mouth as the hottest, sweetest touch of her life. Under the pale light from the lighting rig they pressed against each other. Julia felt herself falling into Robert as though she were finally coming home, her hands searching roughly under his shirt to find the smooth flesh she craved.

His body was warm and real. So real. She'd felt many men's bodies against hers, but never one that seemed to respond so swiftly to her movements. It was as though Robert had unleashed all the pent-up desire of the summer, running his hands over her, exploring her, licking and biting her neck and nuzzling his head down towards her breast without ever taking his lips away from her skin. Julia felt the roughness of his stubble and then, suddenly, a wave of disbelief. After so long teasing her, toying with her, why was Robert at last giving in? Was he taking advantage of her one last night before he sacked her? She struggled to pull away from him.

'Why, why now?' she asked, her breath ragged. Robert kept his hands clamped around her waist, and looked at her with that familiar flicker of amusement.

'Because we're equal now.'

'What do you mean?'

'Julia, you turn me on. Always have done. But I wasn't about to start screwing you.'

'What, you thought I was beneath you?' Julia laughed in disbelief.

Robert shook his head, reaching out to run a finger round the inside of Julia's collar.

'This circus revolves around sex. Just because I found you beautiful, and you made me horny, wasn't enough.'

'And now?'

'When you pulled off that little coup, you showed me just what you're capable of. Proved your mettle.'

Julia felt herself start to melt again as Robert traced the outline of her breasts with his fingertip, aware of her mind struggling to keep a hold on the conversation as he flicked gently at her nipples, coaxing them into stiff points. She felt her mouth curl in a smile.

'I won the game, then?'

Robert laughed. 'I could have killed you. But then again, Julia, subversion is what it's all about.'

Now he held both her breasts in his hands, squeezing gently. Julia tried not to close her eyes, tried to keep her head. As he started pulling her buttons open, one by one, she leaned back, curious to know his reaction.

'Did you like it?'

'Oh yes. I always enjoy watching you.'

'People walked out.'

'I know.' Robert shrugged. 'You should take it as a compliment.' He hesitated, concentrating now on removing her shirt and laying her body exposed to his gaze. Julia shivered as he looked her over, knowing that this time his enjoyment of her voluptuous nakedness would not be purely visual.

'Shocking an audience is hard these days. I admire your courage.'

'So you're not going to fire me?'

'On the contrary, Julia. I'm going to fuck you.'

The conversation ended there, and they sank to the floor.

He pressed her back so that she lay on the stage, surrendered under his slow hungry kisses. The feel of his mouth on her belly, his tongue rolling over her curves, was enough to make her drunk with arousal. She could feel the cold surface of the stage under her as he slid her jeans down, and the heat of the spotlight that shone on centrestage beat on her skin. The most intimate performance she'd ever given on this stage. Sinking back to lose herself in the sensation of his kisses, Julia felt a heady joy wash over her, as though she were tasting the rewards of the summer. Her hips bucked against Robert's face as he gripped her by the haunches, the better to probe inside her with his tongue.

When at last he eased his cock into her, his eyes were still closed, and Julia knew that they were connected in the most beautiful act possible. The simple glorious act of fucking. There were no barriers between them now, and she felt his cock fill her as though he was reaching as far as her heart. They were silent as they moved against each other, communicating in a language of skin and touch, of warmth and hunger. Julia raised herself on her hips to take him in further. They were no longer looking at each other, hardly aware of the empty tent around them or the sounds of the party outside, lost in the worlds of each other's bodies. Robert fucked with the languor that Julia might have expected – letting his whole cock slide into her with a slowness that let them both appreciate the exquisite shock of their bodies joining, letting his pleasure build slowly. Julia felt her own slow-burning climax start to shiver from the root of her body.

All the pent-up wanting of the summer finally fell away, and she bathed in the sensation of being so close to Robert that there was no space between their bodies. With every rocking motion they seemed to be trying to move further inside each other, using the hard stage floor to push against, feeling the dust and dirt stick to their skin as they fucked. It was by turns so tender and so urgent that Julia felt almost on the verge of tears, as though the emotion and the physical forces inside her were more than she could bear. Finally, she felt the hardness of his cock start tensing, pulsing inside her, and felt the friction of the tangle of hair at his groin rub against her, agitating her clit till it threatened to tip her over the edge. Holding onto his hair, biting at his mouth, Julia held her breath and let the universe swim up towards her, the warm black surge of her orgasm crashing and spreading through her whole body just as Robert started bucking and pounding at her, unable to hold back any longer, letting himself explode deep inside her.

They rocked together, floating in oblivion, Julia feeling the aftershocks shudder through her as she relaxed and fell back against the floor. They lay sprawled, limbs entangled and slick with sweat, both half undressed and breathing hard.

Julia managed a smile as she realised it was the first time she'd ever seen Robert lose his cool. After a summer of playing cat and mouse, she'd finally hooked him.

He leant back on his elbows, gasping for breath and regarding her with those lazy brown eyes that seemed to be always amused, always curious. A look passed between them, and Julia knew that everything had changed. She was a different person from the girl who'd turned up in Brighton with a suitcase and high heels. After the most intense summer of her life, after playing the game of the circus and discovering her own desires and dreams – she'd never be the same.

Robert had been her tormentor, her guide, her boss. Now he had the most fascinating role of all – her lover.

She reached out and touched his face, stroking a line down his cheekbone to the point of his tapering sideburn, dragging her fingers over his lips.

'I've been wanting to do that for a very, very long time,' she said.

Epilogue

The dressing room was a riot of dancers and props, everyone thrown into the panic of pre-performance. Julia ducked as a screaming half-dressed girl ran past, false eyelashes glittering hysterically. She grinned, recognising some filthy swear words among the torrent of loud French that the girl chattered as she scrabbled in the clothes rail for her costume. Backstage in Paris was no different than anywhere else – there were the same tantrums, the same crises. The same flirtations.

Julia sat calmly in front of her mirror, applying the pancake for the first act. Her hair had grown longer since the summer, was now long enough to brush against her nipples as she leant forward to apply mascara. Her body was still as supple and curvy as ever, but she carried herself with a new confidence now: even when walking she seemed to shake her hips with a slow luscious shiver – as though her sexuality was woven into her being and infused her every movement.

The door opened slowly and Robert's face appeared, looking for Julia among the chaos of the dancers dressing. When he saw her he nodded approvingly, taking in the chain mail costume and the heels she wore for the act.

'Ready to set the stage on fire?' he asked, moving forward so he could touch her hair and weigh the long curled tresses in his hands. Since their first night together in Edinburgh, he hadn't held back from touching her, making it quite clear that she was his. Julia responded with a wink, knowing that after the show he'd be as fired up as always, cock straining inside his trousers, hands itching to touch the body that had teased a full house for the past two hours. Their sex was warm, urgent, passionate, as though the long summer spent watching each other had kindled an inexhaustible eroticism.

Even as they worked, watching the other performers gyrate onstage, twisting their bodies to ever greater heights of abandon, Julia and Robert knew that their shared intimacy was deeper, more deliciously wild and arousing than the spectacle of the circus could ever be.

Still, they enjoyed teasing each other, and now Robert leant down to whisper in Julia's ear.

'You're sure you can measure up to these French girls?'

She laughed, sure of her own power whether onstage or in bed. The act she'd devised was now a permanent part of the show, and drew the most reaction from the audience wherever they performed. Reviews had been mixed, some declaiming in horror the idea of audience participation, many analysing Julia's ideas, and calling it 'post-modern erotic'. Her name was now recognised among the small world of contemporary circus, and she knew it was just the start. She'd come to love the circus with the same passion as Robert, the whole strange sexy affair.

'Five minutes, Julia,' Robert said as he left, and Julia started her breathing exercises. She remembered the way Joe and Sylvie had prepared her for the show, their enthusiastic games of sex and flirtation, and felt the familiar pulse of heat between her legs. She was open now to so many things, knowing that her sexuality was a thing that changed as she did, feeding both her art and her life. Her body was her whole world, the pleasure of movement and the manipulation of her own arousal. The gift of turning people on was her most precious attribute.

Looking up, she blew a kiss at the photo pinned above her mirror: the dancing figure of Josephine Baker, cartwheeling through the air, frozen forever in the act of causing a scandal.

Visit the Black Lace website at
www.blacklace-books.co.uk

LOOK OUT FOR THE ALL-NEW BLACK LACE BOOKS – AVAILABLE NOW!

All books priced £7.99 in the UK. Please note publication dates apply to the UK only. For other territories, please contact your retailer.

ELENA'S DESTINY
Lisette Allen
ISBN 0 352 33218 2

The year is 1073. The gentle convent-bred Elena, awakened to the joys of forbidden passion by the masterful knight Aimery le Sabrenn, has been forcibly separated from her lover by war. She is haunted by the memory of him. Then fate brings her to William the Conqueror's dark stronghold of Rouen, and a reunion with Aimery. Although he still captivates Elena with his powerful masculinity, Aimery is no longer hers. As the King's formidable knights prepare for war, Elena discovers that she must fight a desperate battle for him against her two rivals: the scheming sensual Isobel and a wanton young heiress called Henriette, who has set her heart on becoming Aimery's bride. The backdrop of war tightens around them and dangerous games of love and lust are played out amidst the increasing tension of a merciless siege.

Coming in June

WILD CARD
Madeline Moore
ISBN O 352 34038 X

When Victoria Ashe lures an ex-lover to her London hotel room, their passion is reignited with startling intensity. She's out to prove to Ray that intimacy can be just as exciting as the thrill of the chase. Ray Torrington might actually agree if it weren't for Kinky Bai Lon, a Hong Kong bombshell who doles herself out one delicate morsel at a time, always in public. And Penny, a champion poker player known as 'The Flame of London', also has her sights on the saucy jackpot. The scene is set for a high stakes game of sexual exploration. When the wild card keeps changing it's difficult for even the most accomplished player to know who's bluffing and who is telling the truth. In this lusty tournament of champions, the winner takes all.

SAUCE FOR THE GOOSE
Mary Rose Maxwell
ISBN O 352 33492 4

Sauce for the goose is a riotous and sometimes humorous celebration of the rich variety of human sexuality. Imaginative and colourful, each story explores a different theme or fantasy, and the result is a fabulously bawdy mélange of cheeky sensuality and hot thrills. A lively array of characters display an uninhibited and lusty energy for boundary breaking pleasure. This is a decidedly x-rated collection of stories designed to be enjoyed and indulged in.

Coming in July

THE ANGELS' SHARE
Maya Hess
ISBN 0 352 34043 6

A derelict cottage on the rugged Manx coast is no place for a young
woman to hide out in the middle of winter. But Ailey Callister is on a
mission – to find and overthrow the man who has stolen her inheritance.
Battling against the elements and her own desire for sexual freedom,
she fights ghosts from her past to discover the true identity of Ethan
Kinrade, the elusive new owner of the vast, whiskey-producing estate
that by rights should be hers.

THE DEVIL INSIDE
Portia Da Costa
ISBN 0 352 32993 9

This is exactly what happens to the usually conventional Alexa Lavelle
after a minor head injury whilst holidaying in the Caribbean. And in
order to satisfy her strange and voluptuous new appetites, she is
compelled to seek the enigmatic and sophisticated doctors at an
exclusive medical practice in London.

Their specialist knowledge of psycho-sexual medicine takes Alexa
into a world of bizarre fetishism and erotic indulgence. And one
particularly attractive doctor has concocted a plan which will prove to be
the ultimate test of her senses, and to unleash the devil inside.

Black Lace Booklist

Information is correct at time of printing. To avoid disappointment, check availability before ordering. Go to www.blacklace-books.co.uk. All books are priced £6.99 unless another price is given.

BLACK LACE BOOKS WITH A CONTEMPORARY SETTING

☐ ON THE EDGE Laura Hamilton	ISBN 0 352 33534 3	£5.99
☐ THE TRANSFORMATION Natasha Rostova	ISBN 0 352 33311 1	
☐ SIN.NET Helena Ravenscroft	ISBN 0 352 33598 X	
☐ TWO WEEKS IN TANGIER Annabel Lee	ISBN 0 352 33599 8	
☐ SYMPHONY X Jasmine Stone	ISBN 0 352 33629 3	
☐ A SECRET PLACE Ella Broussard	ISBN 0 352 33307 3	
☐ GOING TOO FAR Laura Hamilton	ISBN 0 352 33657 9	
☐ RELEASE ME Suki Cunningham	ISBN 0 352 33671 4	
☐ SLAVE TO SUCCESS Kimberley Raines	ISBN 0 352 33687 0	
☐ SHADOWPLAY Portia Da Costa	ISBN 0 352 33313 8	
☐ ARIA APASSIONATA Julie Hastings	ISBN 0 352 33056 2	
☐ A MULTITUDE OF SINS Kit Mason	ISBN 0 352 33737 0	
☐ COMING ROUND THE MOUNTAIN Tabitha Flyte	ISBN 0 352 33873 3	
☐ FEMININE WILES Karina Moore	ISBN 0 352 33235 2	
☐ MIXED SIGNALS Anna Clare	ISBN 0 352 33889 X	
☐ BLACK LIPSTICK KISSES Monica Belle	ISBN 0 352 33885 7	
☐ GOING DEEP Kimberly Dean	ISBN 0 352 33876 8	
☐ PACKING HEAT Karina Moore	ISBN 0 352 33356 1	
☐ MIXED DOUBLES Zoe le Verdier	ISBN 0 352 33312 X	
☐ UP TO NO GOOD Karen S. Smith	ISBN 0 352 33589 0	
☐ CLUB CRÈME Primula Bond	ISBN 0 352 33907 1	
☐ BONDED Fleur Reynolds	ISBN 0 352 33192 5	
☐ SWITCHING HANDS Alaine Hood	ISBN 0 352 33896 2	
☐ EDEN'S FLESH Robyn Russell	ISBN 0 352 33923 3	
☐ PEEP SHOW Mathilde Madden	ISBN 0 352 33924 1	£7.99
☐ RISKY BUSINESS Lisette Allen	ISBN 0 352 33280 8	£7.99
☐ CAMPAIGN HEAT Gabrielle Marcola	ISBN 0 352 33941 1	£7.99
☐ MS BEHAVIOUR Mini Lee	ISBN 0 352 33962 4	£7.99

☐ FIRE AND ICE Laura Hamilton	ISBN 0 352 33486 X	£7.99
☐ UNNATURAL SELECTION Alaine Hood	ISBN 0 352 33963 2	£7.99
☐ SLEAZY RIDER Karen S. Smith	ISBN 0 352 33964 0	£7.99
☐ VILLAGE OF SECRETS Mercedes Kelly	ISBN 0 352 33344 8	£7.99
☐ PAGAN HEAT Monica Belle	ISBN 0 352 33974 8	£7.99
☐ THE POWER GAME Carrera Devonshire	ISBN 0 352 33990 X	£7.99
☐ PASSION OF ISIS Madelynne Ellis	ISBN 0 352 33993 4	£7.99
☐ CONFESSIONAL Judith Roycroft	ISBN 0 352 33421 5	£7.99
☐ THE PRIDE Edie Bingham	ISBN 0 352 33997 7	£7.99
☐ GONE WILD Maria Eppie	ISBN 0 352 33670 6	£7.99
☐ MAKE YOU A MAN Anna Clare	ISBN 0 352 34006 1	£7.99
☐ TONGUE IN CHEEK Tabitha Flyte	ISBN 0 352 33484 3	£7.99
☐ MAD ABOUT THE BOY Mathilde Madden	ISBN 0 352 34001 0	£7.99
☐ CRUEL ENCHANTMENT Janine Ashbless	ISBN 0 352 33483 5	£7.99
☐ BOUND IN BLUE Monica Belle	ISBN 0 352 34012 6	£7.99
☐ MANHUNT Cathleen Ross	ISBN 0 352 33583 1	£7.99
☐ THE STRANGER Portia Da Costa	ISBN 0 352 33211 5	£7.99
☐ ENTERTAINING MR STONE Portia Da Costa	ISBN 0 352 34029 0	£7.99
☐ RUDE AWAKENING Pamela Kyle	ISBN 0 352 33036 8	£7.99
☐ CAT SCRATCH FEVER Sophie Mouette	ISBN 0 352 34021 5	£7.99
☐ DANGEROUS CONSEQUENCES Pamela Rochford	ISBN 0 352 33185 2	£7.99

BLACK LACE BOOKS WITH AN HISTORICAL SETTING

☐ MINX Megan Blythe	ISBN 0 352 33638 2	
☐ THE AMULET Lisette Allen	ISBN 0 352 33019 8	
☐ WHITE ROSE ENSNARED Juliet Hastings	ISBN 0 352 33052 X	
☐ THE HAND OF AMUN Juliet Hastings	ISBN 0 352 33144 5	
☐ THE SENSES BEJEWELLED Cleo Cordell	ISBN 0 352 32904 1	
☐ UNDRESSING THE DEVIL Angel Strand	ISBN 0 352 33938 1	£7.99
☐ FRENCH MANNERS Olivia Christie	ISBN 0 352 33214 X	£7.99
☐ LORD WRAXALL'S FANCY Anna Lieff Saxby	ISBN 0 352 33080 5	£7.99
☐ NICOLE'S REVENGE Lisette Allen	ISBN 0 352 32984 X	£7.99
☐ BARBARIAN PRIZE Deanna Ashford	ISBN 0 352 34017 7	£7.99
☐ THE BARBARIAN GEISHA Charlotte Royal	ISBN 0 352 33267 0	£7.99
☐ ELENA'S DESTINY Lisette Allen	ISBN 0 352 33218 2	£7.99

BLACK LACE ANTHOLOGIES

☐ WICKED WORDS Various	ISBN 0 352 33363 4
☐ MORE WICKED WORDS Various	ISBN 0 352 33487 8
☐ WICKED WORDS 3 Various	ISBN 0 352 33522 X
☐ WICKED WORDS 4 Various	ISBN 0 352 33603 X
☐ WICKED WORDS 5 Various	ISBN 0 352 33642 0
☐ WICKED WORDS 6 Various	ISBN 0 352 33690 0
☐ WICKED WORDS 7 Various	ISBN 0 352 33743 5
☐ WICKED WORDS 8 Various	ISBN 0 352 33787 7
☐ WICKED WORDS 9 Various	ISBN 0 352 33860 1
☐ WICKED WORDS 10 Various	ISBN 0 352 33893 8
☐ THE BEST OF BLACK LACE 2 Various	ISBN 0 352 33718 4
☐ WICKED WORDS: SEX IN THE OFFICE Various	ISBN 0 352 33944 6 £7.99
☐ WICKED WORDS: SEX AT THE SPORTS CLUB Various	ISBN 0 352 33991 8 £7.99
☐ WICKED WORDS: SEX ON HOLIDAY Various	ISBN 0 352 33961 6 £7.99
☐ WICKED WORDS: SEX IN UNIFORM Various	ISBN 0 352 34002 9 £7.99
☐ WICKED WORDS: SEX IN THE KITCHEN Various	ISBN 0 352 34018 5 £7.99

BLACK LACE NON-FICTION

☐ THE BLACK LACE BOOK OF WOMEN'S SEXUAL FANTASIES Ed. Kerri Sharp	ISBN 0 352 33793 1
☐ THE BLACK LACE SEXY QUIZ BOOK Maddie Saxon	ISBN 0 352 33884 9

To find out the latest information about Black Lace titles, check out the
website: www.blacklace-books.co.uk or send for a booklist with
complete synopses by writing to:

Black Lace Booklist, Virgin Books Ltd
Thames Wharf Studios
Rainville Road
London W6 9HA

Please include an SAE of decent size. Please note only British stamps
are valid.

Our privacy policy

We will not disclose information you supply us to any other parties.
We will not disclose any information which identifies you personally to
any person without your express consent.

From time to time we may send out information about Black Lace
books and special offers. Please tick here if you do <u>not</u> wish to
receive Black Lace information.   ❏

Please send me the books I have ticked above.

Name ....

Address ....

....

....

....

Post Code ....

Send to: Virgin Books Cash Sales, Thames Wharf Studios, Rainville Road, London W6 9HA.

US customers: for prices and details of how to order books for delivery by mail, call 1-888-330-8477.

Please enclose a cheque or postal order, made payable to Virgin Books Ltd, to the value of the books you have ordered plus postage and packing costs as follows:

UK and BFPO – £1.00 for the first book, 50p for each subsequent book.

Overseas (including Republic of Ireland) – £2.00 for the first book, £1.00 for each subsequent book.

If you would prefer to pay by VISA, ACCESS/MASTERCARD, DINERS CLUB, AMEX or SWITCH, please write your card number and expiry date here:

....

Signature ....

Please allow up to 28 days for delivery.